Saving Poppy

Jennifer Froh

Jennifer Froh

Wilted Wallflower Books
Mustang, Oklahoma

Hello,

My name is Poppy Fae Monroe. I want to bring you along with me on my senior year of high school. I should warn you that my life is filled with darkness. My journey is going to be difficult to be a part of since I'm surrounded by, but not limited to, graphic violence, abuse, child abuse, stalking and harassment from my father, who is an alcoholic from grief. But just like the flower my mom named me after, I try to withstand the obstacles life presents to me by always trying to find the light of the world.

Sincerely,

Poppy

CHAPTER ONE

A loud crash wakes me up, and my father vehemently cursing at me, "POPPY, GET YOUR ASS OUT OF BED!"

I sit up and look at the clock that is on my nightstand. I sigh in relief when I realize that I didn't sleep past my alarm, my father is up early, and he's demanding breakfast. I hear my father's expensive loafers tapping on the hardwood floor in the hallway outside of my bedroom door. I hastily jump out of bed, nearly tripping over my comforter, and I practically run to the kitchen still wearing my pajamas. Not taking the time to change might not be the best idea, but I don't want to keep him waiting any longer, because that could only make him angrier.

My father looks up from his phone when he hears me enter the kitchen, "Poppy, since you want to sleep in this morning and take your sweet time, you can do without breakfast this morning."

I pause for a moment and mentally scold myself for not changing, because my dad is already planning on how he wants to punish me. This must have been one of his tests. Maybe if I tread carefully, he'll let me have lunch money. My father likes to keep me guessing, and I won't know if I get any lunch money until I leave for school and look in my center console to see if he left me any money. My father is a smart man, I mean, he works in the law field, and he makes sure that we look like we have a good life for a widower and a motherless child. He uses his knowledge and control issues to gain more power over me. For example, he will have these little tests, because he likes to see if I slip on his rules. There are times I can get away with something, and then there are times that even the smallest mistake will lead to a greater punishment. My punishments vary depending on what his end goal is, but he tends to use food as punishment, because that leads me to feeling dissatisfied and hungry.

I gather everything I need to make a simple and fast breakfast of bacon, eggs, and toast. I would make him oatmeal or pancake, but he seems to enjoy what I'm making now the best, because he will eat everything that I'm making now versus anything else he'll only eat about half of his food.

"Are you ready for school today?" I hear the rustling of my father's newspaper over the sound of bacon I'm putting in the heated pan. He'll read until he eats.

I make the mistake of glancing in his direction, because our eyes meet for a short moment, and from the looks of them, I can see that he is excited about something which only makes me nervous. He must still be testing me, and I get this one wrong. My next punishment may be worse than a missed meal.

I flip the bacon waiting long enough for it to cook to the perfect chewiness my father likes. I better not make any part of his bacon crispy, or he will get angry, and that leads to plates being thrown in my direction. I make him four over medium eggs and toast with butter and strawberry jam for his plate.

I set his breakfast in front of him, "Yes sir," I wait until I am in my chair to answer him.

My father finishes the last of his toast before dropping his fork noisily on his plate.

"DO NOT make a fool of yourself, because that will only get you into more trouble than you are already in. Do I make myself clear?" He narrows his eyes at me, and his thin lips pull into a smug smile, almost like he is wanting me to smart off to him.

My father pushes away from the table. I want to cover my ears from the sound of the chair scraping against the tile floor, but I know better than to do that. I'm not allowed to move until he is gone. If I do, that'll just lead to a punishment from my father that would make us both late, and that's not how I want to start my senior year.

I wait until I hear the purr of my father's expensive black BMW before I get up from the table. I go to the window by the front door and watch until I can't see his taillights anymore. I need to get ready for school, but I should have time since my father woke me up an hour before I normally need to get up. I turn around and see the piano by the stairs, and I would love nothing more than to play right now, but I should probably get ahead on my chores, so I don't risk running out of

2

time to get them completed before my father gets home from work.

After I do the breakfast dishes, clean the kitchen, and put them away, I look at the clock on the stove. I have just enough time to get ready before I leave for school. Thankfully, I don't have to rush through my morning routine, and I can enjoy some quiet.

I walk into my closet and look around before trying to decide on what to wear. I don't really like my clothes mainly because my dad picks out what I can get. I pull a soft red basic tee free from a black velvet hanger, then I go to my dresser and grab a black denim skirt. Once I'm dressed, I slip on some black high-top Converse and a lightweight black cardigan.

I run a brush through my straight pale blonde hair. I also apply a couple swipes of mascara before I run out to my car. As soon as I close the door, I feel a little lighter even if I still feel tension in my shoulders. I always feel like I can breathe a little better when I'm out of my father's house.

I know what you're probably thinking. How can I have a car if I can't even pick out my own clothes? Well, my dad needs me to have a car so I can go to school and run errands for him like going to the grocery store or the pharmacy, but I can't use my car for anything else unless I get permission. I don't have any friends, so according to my dad, there's nowhere else I should be going. However, there are places that I would love to be able to go to. I think my father knows that if I'm allowed to do what I want after school, I wouldn't be home until curfew and if I'm not home, my father cannot control me.

I start my shiny red mini convertible and my father's gravelly voice taunts me, "If you want to go anywhere outside of school, you better ask. This is still my car, and if I find out you're not doing as I say, then I will punish you more than just taking your car."

I used to wonder if I just stopped somewhere on my way home how would my dad really know. Well, I tested that theory one day and went and got an ice cream after school. I had my car for almost four months, and when I got home with the most delectable cup filled with vanilla ice cream with peanut butter cups mixed in, my father was in the driveway waiting for me.

He grabbed me out of my car as soon as I parked. The burn from his grip left an angry handprint shaped bruise. "Do you think I'm stupid?" he asked, spitting at me. "I don't just track your phone, so if you turn it off, I can still find you."

My father sat in my driver's seat and felt under my steering wheel once he found what he was looking for, my father stood back up and showed me a small silver disk. The look on my face must have been priceless. He hid the tracking thing in a different spot since then, and I haven't been able to find the silver disk since.

A shiver runs down my spine, and I open my favorite songs playlist. I hit shuffle and smile as one of my new favorite songs plays through my speakers. I turn the volume up and reverse out of my garage. The drive through my neighborhood is beautiful, even though I hate living here because of my home life.

The houses don't look the same and they are more upscale than most of the houses in our town, except for the Taylor family. Their house is practically a mansion and the oldest house here. The owners got to completely design their own house, or I guess the architect they hired did. No one had to pick between a certain model type or floor plan. The further you travel into our neighborhood, the bigger the houses get.

Before I can turn onto the main road, one of the buses stops at the entrance to pick up some of the spoiled rich kids that think they can run our town. The stop sign on the bus folds in, and I don't even have a chance to see if the road is clear to merge into traffic, when some jerk honks their horn at me. I look in my rearview mirror and see a shiny red Jeep.

"Of course, he's such an asshole," I mutter looking both ways, and before I turn, I throw a quick wave over my shoulder, but I really want to flip him off.

The Jeep behind me goes around me, laying heavily on his horn. He merges back into our lane and speeds off down the road. I drive the rest of the three miles to school, trying to distract myself from my annoyance with music.

I pull into the mostly full parking lot and see a spot free that is on the opposite side from the popular crowd. I turn down the lane, and a car speeds in, cutting me off just to get the damn spot. There is no other option for me to park in the place that will force me to walk past the football team.

I reverse into the parking space and sit in my car as three songs play through my car, feeling my ears and calming my nerves. I get out of my car and walk as fast as I can through the parking lot with my head down, hoping that no one will notice me.

"HEY, POPPY!" I hear a deep mocking voice yell at me over the rumbling from cars and the other students hanging around as I pass a big blue pickup.

This can't be happening; he is the last person I want to talk to right now. I need to just get inside the building and find my class. I need to get through this day without any issues, and I can't do that with an interaction with him.

I move past the front doors where the cheerleaders are squealing about some guy one of them hooked up with at the unofficial back to school bash that is at the river every year. I keep walking until I get to the hallway where my first class is, but I get stopped by the music teacher Mr. Menders.

"Poppy, I was disappointed when I didn't see your name on the list for my new music composing and writing elective. I developed this over the last year and got it approved. I specifically pushed for approval, so I could have your talent in there." He moves his glasses to the tip of his nose looking down at some papers he has on a clipboard.

"I asked, but my dad wouldn't sign off on the consent form." I shrug, trying to appear like I'm not upset that I can't take his new class.

"I have one last spot for you, if you would like I could talk to your dad and explain that I think this class would be a wonderful opportunity for you."

"Oh, um, if you want to go to all that trouble."

"I'll see what I can do and get back to you about the class." He looks down at his watch, then leaves me standing in the hallway stunned.

"So, you'll talk to that old man, but not me?" I stupidly glance over to the same person who was just yelling at me in the parking lot.

He is leaning against a locker on the opposite side of the hallway from me. His arms are crossed over his wide chest, but the teasing smile on his handsome face has my heart sputtering. I don't understand how someone so rude could be as popular and good looking as he is.

"Lewis, what do you want?" I cross my arms, mimicking him.

Lewis's best friend roars with laughter. Jax is a good guy that likes to joke around, although he is very inappropriate most of the times, I've been around him, but he is never rude or teases me like Lewis does. Jax is the co-captain of the football team and just as much of a ladies' man as Lewis is, if not more, because girls love his carefree personality and the fact that he is super-hot is a bonus.

"Lewis, stop trying to get into Poppy's skirt and let's go." Jax laughs at his own joke like he does most of the time.

Lewis looks over his shoulder at his best friend. "Only in her dreams." Lewis turns his attention back to me.

"What makes you think I want any part of you touching me, if I'm unconscious or not?" I resist the urge to poke him in his chest.

"Poppy, you have jokes! That's it. You're my new best friend. Lewis, you have been replaced!" Jax walks over and puts his heavy arm around my small shoulders. I try to shrug him off, but my attempt to break free of his arm useless against his weight.

"Shut up, Jax!" Lewis snaps.

I look over Lewis' shoulder as a crowd is forming around us, and most of them are his football buddies. Lewis is about to embarrass me first thing this morning. I should be used to this, since Lewis is like this all the time. I just hate when the whole school is watching.

A few people see me struggling under his weird embrace, and they laugh. All I want to do is get through the day without any problems. I want nothing more than to be left alone. I honestly don't think that's too much to ask for. I shouldn't have to worry about if I'll be picked on at school. However, with Lewis here, that isn't the case. I'm not saying he picks on me every day or anything like that. Most of the time we hardly ever see each other, and if we do, Lewis mostly gives me a dirty look unless he is bored; then, he will tease me.

Jax's arm feels like it weighs 100 pounds, so I try to shake him off again. A few others see my struggle, and they laugh at my lame attempt, but they are quick to shut up when Lewis opens his big mouth to spout off something.

"What's your schedule this year?" he asks, holding his hand out in my direction.

I pull one arm through the strap of my backpack which only causes Jax to move his arm long enough for me to remove my backpack. I unzip the front pocket, and I pull out a folded piece of paper. Instead of handing the paper to Lewis, I flash the sweetest smile I can before I raise my other hand and flip him off.

Lewis returns an amused crooked smile and snatches my schedule from me. "Hmm, looks like we have science together."

He balls my schedule in his hands, making my schedule a wrinkled mess. My blood begins to boil. Who the hell does this guy think he is? That was so rude and uncalled for!

"Make sure we're science partners." He throws the ball of paper at my feet and walks away with Jax who is laughing so hard, he can barely breathe.

"Only in your dreams," I mutter to myself, mimicking what Lewis said to Jax a little bit ago.

There is nothing I would love more than to go up and teach him a lesson in manners. I can't believe that he is the guy all the girls want and that I had a crush on him when I was a little girl. He used to be the boy next door and my best friend, but now he is anything but those things. I guess I can say this has been one of the more pleasant interactions I've had with Lewis, though, in the past couple of school years.

The walk to class gives me a headache. The other students are loud as they reunite with their friends. Walking in these hallways feels lonely, knowing that you have no one your age; well, really anyone in your life that cares enough to ask how your summer was, or even a friend to hang out with after school. Somedays, having someone to eat lunch with would be nice.

I've always hated the first day of school run down in each class. If I'm lucky enough to have a class with windows, that's always where I choose to sit, so I can stare out of them and daydream. My first four classes seem easy and from the syllabi, this looks like there is not going to be too much extra work, considering I'm in all accelerated classes.

The lunch bell rings, and I make my way to the cafeteria, as most of the senior class goes in the opposite direction to their cars. Seniors can have off-campus lunch, but my father doesn't allow that, so I go to the lunch line.

Lunch will be good today, because this morning, I got enough cash in my car so that I can buy a tray for two days and get a snack for study hall that I have for seventh hour, too.

I choose the pizza over the teriyaki chicken that is being served today and grab a bag of chips to put in my bag for later. I pay the lady quickly. None of the tables are empty, so I find one that has some girls that are in my third hour and sit down. They glance at me, but they go back to whatever they were talking about before I sit down.

"Did you see how hot Lewis looked today?" the girl with dark brown curls gushes.

"Yes, we are going to go watch practice-" I put my headphones on and tune them out with music, but thoughts of Lewis creep their way in.

I can't help but get the little boy that Lewis used to be in my mind. I don't like feeling sentimental about things in life, because in my experience, looking back on memories, whether they are good or bad, just brings me pain.

Lewis and I were childhood best friends. We did almost everything together, back when my life was simple. Our moms became friends in college, and they remained close. When they were able to, they built houses right next door to each other. I haven't seen much of his family since my mom passed away ten years ago, but in my defense my whole world came crashing down.

Do I think I made a mistake by pushing Lewis away? Yes, I do. I hurt him and I lost my best friend, but I didn't know what I was doing back then. If I knew what I know now that pushing him away would be a huge mistake when I told him that I no longer wanted to be his friend, I wouldn't have, or I would have tried harder to figure out a way for us to still be friends.

Jewel taps me on my shoulder to get my attention.

"Lunch is over." She gives me a small smile and walks away.

I toss my tray and slowly walk to the only class that I should have with Lewis.

My science class is on the second floor, and the stairs are packed with people kissing, talking, laughing, and even two students yelling at each other. I shoulder my way through, trying to get to class. This is freaking annoying. My body hurts, and my ribs burn in protest at my jerky movements. I push hard one last time past one of the cheerleaders that plasters herself onto Lewis's lap on a regular occurrence, even though they aren't dating.

"Watch out, loser!" Lana flips her overly bleached hair in my face and shoves me back.

I stumble at the force she puts into the push. I almost fall onto the hard tile floor that I'm sure hasn't been properly waxed in a decade or two. This day just keeps getting better and better. I can't wait to get out of here. I walk around Lana to my class.

I walk in with my chest burning from either the anger that is fixing to explode out of me or from holding my breath so I don't say anything that would cause me to get a call made to my father. I look around for Lewis, and I relax just a fraction because he isn't sitting in any of the stools. I look around and take one of the two empty stools in the room. I put my backpack on the floor next to my chair. I nervously rub my hands on my skirt as I wait for Lewis to get to class. Maybe I'll be lucky for once today, and the teacher will assign partners and give me anyone but him. He has not come to class yet, but knowing him, he will most likely be late. There are only two seats open and thankfully, they are not next to each other. I take the one in the back and leave the one closest to the door free. The girl at the table to my right gives me the side eye like she is pissed that I'll be her lab partner. I'd be happy with a lab partner like me, because I would make her do all the work, but she doesn't know that.

The tardy bell rings as the cocky football player stops in the doorway of the classroom. He looks at every table with his brows furrowed and his pouty lips pursed. When Lewis's eyes finally stop bouncing around, I know that he found me. He grins for just a split second, like he just won the winning touchdown at Friday night's game before scowling at the poor girl sitting in the stool next to me. I bite my lip trying to hide my delighted smile for him being irritated that he didn't get his way. A laugh is tickling my throat, threatening to explode as I watch Lewis Walk over here with heavy footsteps. I push my fingernails into my palms needing to distract myself from the glee that I'm feeling right now since I didn't follow his instructions.

Lewis looks down at the girl with a playful but mischievous smile, "Thanks for saving my seat."

The girl looks around the room, probably to see if anyone else is witnessing Lewis flirting with her. The only thing she doesn't realize is he is not wanting to ruin his reputation as a ladies' man by being an asshole. I do think she will search him out later and ask for a proper thank you.

She smiles at him and caresses his arm. "Anytime." She gets her stuff and sits next to the girl at the door, and they immediately begin talking, and a few giggles erupt from them.

Oh gross! I think I'm going to vomit.

"Tiny Flower," he uses the nickname my mom gave me, and that hurts to hear him call me that, "I thought we talked about being lab partners this morning?"

My eyes widen, and I sit up a little straighter. I want to give him a piece of my mind, but the fact that he is watching me is nerve wracking. I know I can argue back to Lewis, and he seems to enjoy when I do. My stomach begins to warm as frustration begins to boil in my blood. I'm so annoyed that I can't get the courage to stand up to my father like I can with Lewis.

I look up into Lewis's eyes while fixing my face to convey confidence, even though I'm anything but confident. "All the chairs were full but two. I took this one, and you charmed that other girl into the other. How you managed that with very few words is beyond me."

"Good afternoon, class," the teacher finally arrives at class, five minutes after the tardy bell, and he thankfully interrupts any chance of Lewis replying now. "No need for introductions right now. Collect all your belongings and come to the front. I will be the one to assign your seats and lab partners. That will be your introduction to your peers in this class. So, pay close attention, I'm only going to call your name once, and you will sit in your designated seat. The person at your side table will be your partner in all labs and assignments. If we do a bigger group project or assignment, then you will be with all your whole station. Do not bother asking me to switch. The answer will be no."

I hope that this isn't a trend with Mr. Franks, because Lewis would have time to taunt me every day.

He starts calling names at the first table along the wall with windows for four people at each station. Mr. Franks is moving fast from table to table. Once he gets to the fourth and last table, he calls my name which is the third one to be called, and the girl that thinks Lewis was flirting with her is across from me. I guess the good thing about my seat is that I won't have anyone sitting behind me. I walk to my new spot, and before I can even get to the table, Mr. Franks calls, "Lewis Jacobs," at the spot right next to mine.

Of course, Lewis is going to be assigned with me.

I sit and look down at the black tabletop as spots begin to appear in my vision, and I try to blink them away, but tears begin to fall the harder I try to stop. This is literally one of my worst nightmares. I take a shaky shallow breath, and I can feel my heartbeat in my chest harder and harder, as I hear Lewis's footsteps approach my side of the station. I don't look up as he pauses then walks around me. When the stool next to me scrapes the tile floor, my stomach turns as vomit tries to come up.

I count to ten before I look up at Lewis. The shit eating grin and the spark of joy in his eyes at my clear disappointment from us being partnered up together makes my face heat and my fists ball in anger. I look away from him and give him a "humph," indicating that I don't want to talk to him. This school year is looking just as shitty as the rest of them. I guess not everyone gets the senior year that is full of fun, but mine will is going to be one that I remember, even if I don't want to.

"This is going to be a fun year, for sure," I shoot daggers at Lewis from his hushed teasing, but he only winks at me in reply.

I look down at the tabletop again as defeat surrenders me. I try to focus on the sounds around me, like the teacher who is still assigning the other students the seats in the last row, but all I can focus on is the sound of Lewis's foot tapping on the hard tile floor over and over. I unclench the fists I've had since I sat down, just to ball them up again. I keep repeating that movement, slowly calming me down. Lewis elbows me hard in my ribs. I try not to cry out from the jab. Lewis has no idea that my ribs are already tender, because I think if he did, he wouldn't have done it to begin with.

Once the throbbing in my side becomes bearable, I'm annoyed when I look up at Lewis.

"Don't give me that look. Do you what other girls would do, to be in your spot right now." Lewis winks at me with a Cheshire-like grin. However, his joking only gets on my nerves more. He could use a few shots to the ego and come back down to earth.

"Do you always have to be so cocky and inappropriate? I don't care what those other girls would do to be anywhere near you. I don't want to be your partner in the damn class, but can we at least use manners?" My face is turning red, and my shoulders tense as my anger builds with each word I practically spit through my teeth at Lewis. I'm trying so hard to keep my voice low and not yell at him. Maybe if I just scream at him, I will feel better, but I can't afford to get in trouble and have the teacher call my father.

"All right class. you will be doing a lab safety poster. This should be a review, since you have done the same thing every year since middle school. I will use this as a test grade. Tomorrow, you will have the lab safety contracts sent home for your parents to sign before Tuesday of next week. That is when we will have our first lab day. You can use the last fifteen minutes of class going over how you would like to do this project due tomorrow. The posters and supplies are on the back wall," the teacher waves a lazy hand to the back of the class before sitting in front of his computer.

I turn around and almost run into a lanky guy with ginger hair and thick tortoise shell framed glasses, going to get supplies too. I flip through the bright colors and find one of the last white posters and go back to my seat.

"Meet me in my driveway at 11:00-"

"I can't go out that late-" I interrupt Lewis.

"Sneak out if you have to." He cuts me off.

"Fine, but you get to carry the poster and the supplies we'll need for this project." The last thing I need to worry about when I sneak out is the things we need for this project.

Lewis moves his attention to the girl across from me. "Are you free after I'm done with football practice?" The girl, I don't care to learn her name, laughs, and I know that's my cue to tune them out and work on the project.

I have two more classes left, and I'm even more excited since I have study hall last in my schedule. I try not to focus on the fact that Lewis is still flirting when the bell rings. I rudely push the stuff he needs to take home with him and practically run to my next class. I hate that I am jealous. I want a guy to see me as beautiful and worth flirting with.

When I walk into my next class, there are only a couple of people in here. I sit in the back row on the side of the room that is furthest away from the door. The teacher is outside the door, chatting with Mr. Menders. This is one of my elective classes, and the other is study hall. When the bell rings, my new teacher walks in, and she looks nervous as she starts taking attendance. She gives a brief breakdown of her class, and then I tune her out with heavy thoughts.

My life feels like a double-edged sword slicing through my heart at any chance it can. I don't want to be at school, because I'm lonely here, I have no friends, and then there's the teasing I get from Lewis. I guess school wouldn't be so bad if he wouldn't cross the line most of the time. Fear is a constant feeling that surfaces, no matter where I am or what I'm doing. The need to always look over my shoulder for danger is why I don't like people to be behind me. No matter what dread is constantly clawing at me, school is nothing compared to how intense it is at home.

If I had a choice of which monster I would rather face in my life, I'd pick anything over the one I live with. At least, with Lewis I can smart off and attempt to stand up for myself without any actual consequences. My father explodes if I talk to him like I do with Lewis. A shiver runs down my spine at the eerie thought of what my dad would do if I had that courage.

The bell rings, and I try to wait in class for as long as I can, before going to the library for study hall, but after the third or fourth glance from the teacher, I go hide in the bathroom down the hall from the library until the late bell rings.

Study hall is typically the best elective to have, and you need to get a slip signed off by the librarian and the principal to get enrolled in this class. I have had study hall every year since I was a sophomore.

The rules are simple: check in with the librarian, and if you need to go do anything else, let her know where you'll be, but we can't leave campus unless we have a school activity or we get checked out. Most students stay here and hang out or do homework, but some of the others will go help teachers make copies, and the jocks typically go to the gym or weight room. I'm happy that I can get my homework done before school lets out, because it will give me one last thing to worry about.

I walk to the two steps that lead to the study section and go to the back where the windows are. A few rectangular tables are full, but the one right next to the window is free. The layout on the small, raised platform is nice. The tables are partitioned off from a more casual seating area with couches, accent chair, and some oversized bean bags with large bookshelves, full of all the research style books you may need for an assignment.

I should have brought the poster with me, so I could have something to do, but I don't think I want to track down Lewis, just to get the poster, even though that would be a better option than risk getting caught trying to sneak out.

I grab my journal from my bag and a pen. I love when I get the time to write. I love composing music, creative writing like lyrics, poetry, and short stories. Writing helps me escape the nightmare I'm living in, because I feel free, and I also have a lot to say, since I can't say what I want out loud. I can put everything I'm feeling and thinking into my notebook, and I don't have to hold back or sugar coat anything. I can just be me and for those rare moments I finally feel free.

I would love the chance to play the piano or one of my guitars, but I can't use the school's instruments, since I'm no longer in the music program and my father took away my guitars. He punishes me anytime I try to play the piano we have at home. I think music reminds my father of my mom, since she taught me how to play.

The final bell rings, slicing through my heavy thoughts, and I gather my stuff to leave the library, and that's when I hear a boisterous laugh. I look between the shelf to the side of the library where the couches are, and I'm stunned to see Lewis. I'm pissed because I could have done that damn poster. The air around me warms up, and I begin to sweat. I need to get out of here without being seen because I'm pretty sure a panic attack is fixing to take over all my senses.

I rush through the library door and towards the parking lot. I just need a minute alone in my car to calm my erratic breathing and my pounding heart. I grab my keys and phone out of my backpack when I'm on the front steps of the school, and I walk slowly to my car, trying to inhale and exhale slowly. I unlock my door, and I can hear some of the girls surrounding the car next to mine talk about what they want to do before they go home.

I turn my car on as soon as I'm in my seat and the door is shut. I hit shuffle on the same playlist from this morning. Once the chorus starts, I lean my head against the headrest and sing softly to myself until the song comes to an end. I open my eyes, and I see that the parking lot is still full of people chatting with their friends around me. I put my seatbelt on and put my car into drive. I carefully maneuver my car around Lana and the rest of the cheerleaders. Lana doesn't look pleased about something, and I have a feeling that she found out that Lewis is going to hook up with someone else after he is done with practice.

Part of me is glad that I don't have that kind of drama in my life, but maybe having boy problems is better than the issues I face at home.

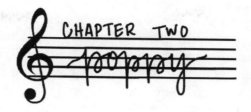

CHAPTER TWO

Being in science class everyday with Lewis is a cake walk, compared to sting at my father's dining room table watching the clock as the second hand slowly ticks. The clock reads 6:30, and I'm waiting with my knees bouncing up and down with anticipation on what kind of mood Dad will be in when, or if, he comes home. I've been sitting in my normal spot for 30 minutes and he still hasn't come home yet. This could mean that he isn't coming home for dinner, and he is going to drown his demons at the bar, or he is testing me, like he did this morning.

My father spends most of his nights at one of the two bars we have in town, but on bad days, he'll go right after work. When my father is gone, those are sometimes the best nights I have at home. I know I'm safe, only because my father isn't here. I don't have to worry so much about the rules or what kind of mood he is going to be in until he comes home. That can depend on if he is exhausted and comes home just to pass out or if he is irate about something then that usually ends with him in a raging fit that he takes out on me.

My father likes to have dinner ready at 6:00, whether he is home or not. I can clean up at 7:00, if he is not home, or if he is, then I'm ordered to wait until my dad is done eating and has left the table. I get to have a small portion of dinner that I cook every night and if I don't break any rules, then I can get seconds or whatever is left after I make his lunch for the next day. Sometimes, he will come home in a bad mood and say something is wrong with the food, and he will begin by banging his fists on the table, followed by throwing the dishes at the wall or me. Once he is done with that, he feels that I still need to be punished for ruining good food that he paid for. These events usually end with me being ordered to clean up the mess he made and him going to medicate his temper with amber liquor.

I'm never sure what is next with him. My father enjoys the games he plays with me, because he never loses. For example, he likes to come home at random times to see what I'm doing, and if I'm not following my schedule, he has posted on the fridge at the times he specified for me to do them, he gets to reward himself with a punishment of his choosing for me. He could be home at 5:30 every day, but if he did that, then that gives up some of his fun. I can't wait until I can leave for college after I graduate high school.

I sigh when the grandfather clock in the foyer chimes, telling me that 7:00 is here, and my father is not home yet. I wait fifteen more minutes before I begin clearing the table. I put cling wrap of my dad's plate to heat up later tonight and his lunch. I make a small plate for myself and eat the room temperature dinner, since the food has sat on the table for over an hour. I'm a decent cook, considering I taught myself. My meager dinner did nothing to satisfy my hunger pains. I do the dishes and clean the kitchen with my stomach growling, begging for something more to eat.

I turn the lights off and go through the house to my room, looking over anything I might have missed when I was cleaning after school. I go up the stairs and to my room that I need to straighten up.

My stomach rumbles again in an almost desperate attempt to plead with me to eat more, but I know better to give in. I sit for a moment on the edge of my bed, exhaustion clouding my brain. I sway a little as my eyelids get heavy with sleep. This is a bad idea; I go to my bathroom and splash cold water on my face. I just need to be able to get through the rest of the night without something happening, or if tonight ends in disaster.

I don't even know how to sneak out. I've always been afraid of what would happen to me if I got caught. Do I just need to stuff something in my blankets and then mess up my bed enough to make it look like someone is sleeping in here? I need to figure something out because I need to leave now, while I know my father is still not here.

I decide to grab three pillows off my window seat and hope that if he comes in while I'm gone, he won't check on me or if he does, he will be too drunk to notice they aren't there, and this looks like me through glassy eyes.

I stop at the top of the stairs and listen for any sounds that could be coming from outside. The house is so eerily quiet, goosebumps prickle my scalp. I creep along the stairs on my daunting quest to the front door, even though I could just walk normally to the door and get out faster. I still don't hear anything other than my hushed movements around the house. I finally tiptoe through the house and to the front door. The sound of the lock unlatching breaks the silence, and I curse at myself. Get a grip, Poppy; no one else is here. I open the door and see that the driveway is still empty. I slam the door and as I'm locking the door from the outside, headlights flash over me.

I turn around with horror clenching my heart in a painful grip. I quickly duck into the bushes that are planted along the wall close to the front door. I can see my father's car from here and from the way my father is angry with his arms flailing around as he is trying to fight the seatbelt off him. Once he is free, he pushes the door open and falls to the ground hard. I cover my mouth to stifle my laugh, he is so stupid for not only drinking but even more for driving home drunk. He finally manages to get on his feet, and he closes the door with a wimpy push. He begins stumbling up the walkway, and the way he struggles to raise his foot high enough to take the step up to the porch is comical. My father stops in front of the door patting his jacket in pants. I think he is trying to find his keys.

I watch as he finally finds them and struggles to get them free of his pocket. He drops them and once he picks them back up, he shoves a key in the door. He stands there swaying, muttering to himself. My stomach rolls as the pungent scent of stale cigarettes, whiskey, and body odor radiates from his pores. My father finally unlocks the door and shoves it open; he takes four large steps inside, then kicks the door closed.

I peek around to see if there is any movement on the other side of the decorative window on our front door. Once I'm sure I'm safe, I scramble out from my hiding place and make a mad dash toward Lewis's house. I can barely keep my feet under me as I run around my father's car. I fall several times in the grass that separates my driveway from my neighbor's. Each time I fall I get back up and start running again, just to fall as I reach the pavement. I barely register the pain, because all I can think about is getting away from my father's house without him seeing me. I bet if someone was watching me right now, they would laugh or think I'm being chased by zombies. I stop in front of Lewis's Jeep. I hunch over and put my hands on my legs above my knees as I gasp for air.

A chuckle to my left gives me the chills. Lewis's laugh isn't creepy like my father's, but rather one filled with humor. The chills are from who the laugh is coming from. Lewis sometimes gives me butterflies in my stomach and the chills. I can't stand my traitorous body right now. I was just running for my life, and I can't get distracted by my crush on Lewis.

"Poppy-" I hold my hand up, cutting him off. I can't process what he is about to say, with my heart pounding and my ears ringing.

I stay like that with my hand raised until my breathing mellows out, and I can see clearly that I'm safe right now. My heart is still beating erratically, but at least I can hear whatever Lewis has to say. I slowly straighten my body into a mostly relaxed stance and turn to look at Lewis. I awkwardly wave as the thoughts of how good Lewis looks in the moonlight scream in my head,

"Poppy, you're late. Let's go," At least he didn't comment on my clumsiness or the fact that my father was drunk out of his mind when he came home tonight.

Lewis begins to walk into his garage, and I only have two options. I can either go back home and attempt to sneak back in, or I can do what I came here to do, because I know no matter what I decide, the risk of my father catching me now is significantly greater since he came home.

Lewis is at the door in the garage that leads to a mud room. Just as I jog pass under the garage door, a hum above sounds as the metal slowly closes trapping me in here like a damn prisoner. My palms begin to sweat as I step into their mud room. I haven't been here in over ten years, and one thing I will always remember is the smell and let me tell you that hasn't changed. Lewis's mom's kitchen always has had this delectable aroma of fresh baked treats, and tonight there is a hint of tartness. I wonder if his mom made cherry pie. My stomach grumbles, and I instinctively put my hand on my belly trying to conceal the sound.

Lewis doesn't talk to me as I follow him. Almost everything in the house is upgraded to look more modern with a rustic feel to the homey feel surrounding me. I see pictures of the family at all different ages, but there is the photo of Lewis and me after a scrimmage when we were about eight. Sadness takes over as tears pool in my eyes. Why would they want to have me on their walls after all this time of Lewis and me not being friends? Being here still feels like home to me, and for the first time I finally feel safe.

Lewis stops halfway up the stairs, waiting for me as I look around the house. He still hasn't said anything to me, but I walk up the stairs to the second floor. He shakes his head at me when I look in the direction of his sister's room. She is off at college, so I know I won't run into her while I'm here. Lewis goes into his room, but I hesitate.

"I am not going to bite, unless you ask me politely." He waves me in, and when I still don't make a move, he comes over to me and grabs my hand.

I think he is going to help guide me in, but instead he yanks me into his room. I trip over my feet and fall into his warm chest. I breathe deeply, filling my lungs with the woodsy smell of his cologne. Damn, he smells good. Lewis laughs, and I know I've been caught smelling him. I turn away from him, so I can hide my embarrassment. I take a couple of more steps into his room, and he follows closely behind me. I feel Lewis's chest brush against my back.

I freeze from the brief contact, but he doesn't notice and bumps right into me. I fall forward, but before my face can hit the hardwood flooring, Lewis's hand painfully grips my upper arm and pulls me back to my feet. When he lets go of me, I lightly rub my arm trying to soothe the ache. I look around the room, and I like the way that Macey decorated Lewi's room with dark wood furniture, red bedding, and a small leather couch in front of an entertainment center. The last time I was in here, Lewis had a cool red race car bed with superhero sheets.

"Everything you need is on my desk." He sits on the couch and turns on his TV.

I sit down and begin working on the poster. I should only be here for 15 to 30 minutes, if I don't let anything distract me. I move some papers out of my way, and I get the markers out of the package as shooting sounds makes me jump. I turn around and see that Lewis is playing some army game.

After I'm more than halfway done, my stomach growls so loud I'm sure the whole house could hear how hungry I am. I'm mortified as Lewis laughs. I will not look at him. I'm just going to keep working so I can go home.

"Do you want a sandwich or something?" I continue to work rather than answer him.

Lewis is being polite right now, and I know not saying anything to him is rude, but I can't say yes; I'm starving.

Lewis gets up and leaves. He doesn't look bothered that I never answered him. Even though we don't have the best interactions and are no longer friends, I doubt Lewis would be rude and not take care of someone that is a guest in his parents' house. His mom raised him with better manners than that. I turn back to the project and begin to color the last section.

Lewis is still not back by the time I'm done, and instead of sitting here awkwardly, I grab a pen out of a cup on his desk and I write a couple of examples under each titled rule.

There is nothing else I can add to the poster, so I will just clean up my mess. I don't know where Lewis went or what is taking so long, but if he isn't back soon, I'm going to have to leave. I'm putting the last pen back in the cup when I hear Lewis clear his throat behind me.

"Take a break and eat. Your stomach growling every two seconds is getting annoying." He smiles, and the lightness of his voice is humorous as he holds out a plate for me.

I slip my shoes off before I sit on the couch, tucking my legs under me making myself comfortable. Lewis hands me the plate and sits next to me. I look down at the massive pile of chips that is almost covering a sandwich. My mouth waters as my eyes dance over the yummy looking meal I'm about to devour.

I pop a chip into my mouth and try not to crunch too loudly on the salty goodness of a fried crispy potato. Is there any way you can cook a potato badly? I think not.

"Do you need a blanket?" I looked up at Lewis, confused, only to see that he's eyeing the cardigan I'm wearing.

I don't know what to say to him. I don't think there is really a good answer to his question, because I'm not cold; his room is warm for August. Lewis adjusts the way his is sitting, so now he is facing me. I just give him a shrug and eat another chip.

I eat two more chips in silence, hoping that Lewis will just leave me alone about my sweater. I don't think he means anything by what he asked, but he just doesn't know anything about my life now.

"You don't talk very much anymore. Well not unless I make you mad or you're answering a teacher."

Why does that sound like he has been watching me, and why does that not creep me out as much as it should?

"Thanks for making me something to eat. I didn't have a chance to eat dinner," I pause briefly. I need to figure out what to say, without saying too much. "Lewis, can I ask you a question?" I look down at my plate and move the chips that are on top of my sandwich to the side.

"Fine, but I get to ask you questions too," he quips.

"Fine, but I'm going first." I stick my tongue out at him.

He takes a huge bite out of his sandwich, watching me, "I want to go first. Why did you stop talking to me after your mom died?"

We sit on Lewis's couch not talking. The only sound filling the room is the sound of our chewing, which I find oddly comforting.

"Well, there was a lot going on after the funeral, but my dad told me to stop." I speak so fast, I'm not sure how much Lewis understood.

"Well, shit, I wasn't expecting that, but that makes sense."

"Why do you tease me now?" I don't quite know the best way to phrase this, but I think he'll understand.

"I was angry with you. I remember when you told me you didn't want to be friends with me." I eat the last of my food while Lewis answers. He takes my empty plate from my lap and leaves me alone again.

I sit there on the couch, even though I know I need to go home. I want to know more about Lewis, and I want him to keep asking me things, so he can get to know me again, too. After ten minutes, I slip my shoes, on because I really need to be going home, and Lewis is still not back. I turn to the door and jump when I see that Lewis is leaning against the door frame. I noticed he does that a lot. We stand there staring at each other. I'm held captive under his gaze, but for him, I think he is starting to tease me again.

Lewis pushes away from the door and walks to me. He doesn't stop until he is dangerously close to my ear. A shiver betrays me, and my arms begin to tingle as goosebumps appear under my cardigan. Lewis's hot breath tickles my ear, making me gasp. What is wrong with me right now? This can't be happening right now. I need to get out of here before something happens and I leave here heartbroken, or with more fuel for Lewis to tease me.

"Are you trying to leave me?" Lewis's raspy whisper sends chills down my spine.

"Oh um, I was just-" I trail off from the lies I was going to tell him.

Lewis has yet to move away from my ear, and the closeness is just making me dizzy and my mind fogs up with desire that I'm not used to feeling. I try to put some space between us by taking a step back, but Lewis has other ideas. He straightens back up to his full height and takes a step and presses me against him. What is he doing? This is not what we do! Lewis raises his hand, and I flinch away from him. I watch as that hand continues to move up until his hands run through his hair. How can guys still be hot after messing up their hair like that? I would crazy if I ran my fingers through his hair like that.

"I just have two more questions tonight. You need to get home before your dad finds out you're gone, or I decide to keep you," Lewis winks at me, and any other girl would flirt back, but he isn't flirting with me.

What he doesn't know is that I would willingly let him keep me, because that would mean I wouldn't have to go home. I go back and sit on the couch like I did before, but this time, when Lewis sits next to me, he turns until he is facing me, and he sits close enough that his knee is touching mine.

"Do you think you would have stopped talking if your dad didn't tell you to?"

I look at him for a few short seconds before answering. I think part of me thinks that if I drag out answering him, he will know how serious I am when I answer, even though I think I'm just trying to delay going back home.

"No."

He nods his head, but his expression is unreadable. I can tell he is trying to hide whatever he's feeling from me.

"Sometimes, you call me the nickname my mom gave me. Why?" I don't see the point in elaborating; I think he'll understand what I mean.

My mom called me Tiny Flower growing up, and there's really not many other people that call me that. Occasionally, my father will call me Pops, but only on a good day, and I can't remember the last time we had one.

"I call you that because sometimes you will smile. I don't see you smile anymore, and I know that some of that is because of me," he says truthfully, but his tone almost sounds apologetic.

I give him a lopsided smile, but I brace myself because I know I'm not ready for his next question.

The smirk Lewis gives me before speaking makes my insides quiver. If only he knew what that smirk does to me. On second thought, I'm positive that he knows what that smile does to girls, because he always has one hanging all over him. "Have you ever kissed anyone?"

I blush. That's not the question I was expecting, and it embarrasses me that I haven't ever been kissed, and he is going to find out.

"No." Again there really isn't much to say. Lewis opens his mouth, but instead of letting him talk, I ask my question. "Does your mom still make the best peanut butter cookies?"

My mouth almost immediately starts to water, thinking about those soft cookies that practically melt in your mouth. I haven't had any since the last time his mom made me some on my tenth birthday.

He gives a full belly laugh, and I want to make him laugh like that again. I don't think he was expecting me to ask that question.

"Hell, yeah! I forgot those were your favorite growing up. I'll see if she will make you some before senior year is over. You can ask your question first this time, and then, after mine, you should probably go home so you don't get into trouble."

He has a point, but at this point, I can't get into any more trouble than I'll already be in. I look at him for a long moment, trying to decide what I want to know now. There are what seems to be a million questions running through my head, but what is the right question to ask at this moment?

"When did you realize we weren't going to be friends anymore?" I already know this answer, but I want to see if we both knew at the same time.

The memory floods my mind, and I'm trying hard not to start crying for the little girl that lost two people so close together but for different reasons. I look up at Lewis and wait for the answer to hit me hard in the stomach.

"I knew a couple of weeks after your mom's funeral. I went to your house after school one day, to see if you wanted to play, and your dad answered the door. I think he was drunk. Anyways, he said that you didn't want to talk to me ever again and that you didn't want to be my friend anymore." He sounds like he is in a daze, like he is reliving that day in his mind.

"I remember that day perfectly, too. I was sitting in time out in the living room. I had accidentally knocked over a lamp, and of course, it broke. I heard my dad and you talking at the door. When he came back to the living room, he yelled at me for the third or fourth time that day. He made a rule that we couldn't be friends. If I knew then what I know now, I never would have let my father ruin our friendship." My voice cracks with sadness at the end.

Lewis gives me a sad smile and shakes his head. I feel awful for how our friendship ended and that I let my father get in the way. I wonder what my life would be like had I not listened and still talked to Lewis.

I'm lost in memories of that day. I was spanked for the very first time that day. I was angry after my dad said that he told Lewis I didn't want to be his friend, and then he told me I couldn't be friends with him. I smarted off somehow and stuck my tongue out at him. His face turned red, and I never made that mistake again.

"I'm ready for your question now," shaking off an awful memory.

"Can I kiss you?" My jaw drops, and my eyes widen.

"Really, that is your question? Why would you want to kiss me?" I'm stunned. There's absolutely no way I heard him correctly.

"Poppy, can I kiss you?" He emphasizes the word kiss as he repeats the question.

I look at him, even though my face is heating up with embarrassment. I hear the word "yes," come out of my mouth, without realizing what I was doing.

Lewis doesn't give me any time to change my mind. I feel his warm hand go into my hair at the nape of my neck. He leans in and is gently guiding my head to his, and I feel the softest pressure of his lips against mine. I don't know if he is being gentle to not hurt me or to not make me go running out of his room screaming.

I gasp at how soft he kisses me, which he takes advantage of by sweeping his tongue into my mouth. As the shock wears off, I mimic him. Lewis pulls away and looks at me with what I think is a type of hunger a lion would look at his prey.

I'm confused as to why he stops kissing me. Am I doing something wrong? I don't want to sit here anymore as embarrassment warms my cheeks. The air in the room is getting so thick, making me dizzy. I stand up, take a step away from the couch when I feel Lewis's long fingers circle around my narrow wrist.

"Poppy," he gruffly breathes out my name. He runs his hands through his messy hair, making it messier.

"I think we should get you home before your dad finds out that you're gone. Can we talk before school?"

"Sure."

I don't argue, because he is probably right. I do need to get home, and the longer I'm gone, there's a bigger chance that my father will figure out I'm not there. We make our way to my house with a million more thoughts and questions for Lewis is racing through my mind. I unlock my door; then I turn back to Lewis and give him a lazy wave like all my energy was sucked out of me when I got to my front porch.

He looks at me, with a genuine smile on his face. He swiftly turns around and walks back to his house without a single word or glance

24

back at me. I sigh and watch until I can no longer see his silhouette.

Opening the door as slowly and quietly as I can, I peek in and see that the house is dark. I don't hear anything, and there is no movement from what I can see. I hold my breath as I hear the lock of the door echo throughout the entryway. I don't stop anywhere as I tiptoe my way to my room. I'm trying desperately not to draw attention to myself. I stop at my bedroom door, somehow managing to make my way through the whole house without getting caught. Maybe I'll be able to succeed without my father knowing I left the house and was out past curfew. I grasp the doorknob tightly, twisting the knob slowly, and gradually open my door. All that is left is getting into my room without making a sound.

I lightly push the door open just wide enough for me to slip through, but something in me is telling me not to go into my room. I push the door open wider. I feel the blood drain from my body as fear takes hold of me in its hideous hands. I stay rooted where I stand outside of my room. My comforter and pillows that were once on my bed are now scattered across my floor.

Jennifer Froh

CHAPTER THREE
Lewis

After walking Poppy back to her house, I'm hyped. I'm glad we had to do the rest of the poster outside of school. I wasn't going to ask her to kiss me, but when I was washing our dishes, I couldn't get her lips off my mind.

I make my way to the bathroom to take a shower. I strip off my clothes and leave them on the bathroom floor instead of putting them in my hamper. I get the temperature of the water just right and step under the scalding water. The feel of Poppy's lips and the night plays through my mind.

I got to kiss the girl I have wanted, basically since I learned what girls were. I always wanted to be her first everything, and I got to be her first kiss. The soft moan that slipped past her lips without her realizing she made a sound was my undoing. I knew I had to stop there, or I would have gone further than she was ready for. That moan was the sweetest sound I've ever heard. I should take a cold shower and go straight to bed, but I already made a few mistakes tonight; why not add one more?

I give my body the temporary release I'm craving, but that is only temporary. I get out of the shower and pull on some black boxer briefs. I climb into bed and my thoughts replay the night like your favorite song on repeat while driving the backroads with a pretty girl in your passenger seat.

I remember Poppy as a little girl, and, man, did I crush on her hard. She had this brightness to her that would draw you in, and you wanted to stay, because with the brightness was warm. That made you happy. She began to change when her mom died, but that light hasn't gone away.

Poppy looks so sad and tired most of the time; that is, if I see her at school. Before her mom died, she would never miss school, but since we were about 11 years old, she began missing a lot of school, and she was gone so much, it became normal.

I look at the clock, and if I don't get any sleep, practice will kick my ass tomorrow, and if I'm not on top of my game, Coach will make everyone run more.

♩♫𝄾

I wake up the next morning to the annoying ring of my alarm. I sit up, and everything that happened with Poppy comes rushing to my head, making me feel fucking lightheaded. I swear last night would have been just a dream if I couldn't smell the sweet scent of her perfume lingering in my room.

I throw on some clothes not giving a shit about what I'm putting on. I jog down the stairs to the kitchen. My mom and dad are at the kitchen table eating pancakes. When my mom sees me, a smile lights up her face.

"Good morning, sweetie. We have pancakes, eggs, and sausage for breakfast this morning," she sings in a cheerful voice.

"I don't have time this morning but thank you. Breakfast looks great, though."

I walk to the pantry to grab a granola bar, and then I get a bottle of orange juice out of the refrigerator. I go to the table and take an apple out of the bowl on the table and take a large bite. My mom is the best. She loves taking care of all of us, and she is a fierce woman that protects her family.

"Bye," I say, leaning down to place a soft kiss on her cheek.

Driving to school is quick as we live about five minutes away. I was going to ditch school today, because we would just be going over the student handbook, but after my night with Poppy, I want to see how she acts around me. I want to apologize to her for how I've treated her and tell her that I will never be that way toward her again.

I have time to kill, so I just stay in my Jeep with my music blaring. I'm trying to watch for Poppy's tiny car. A loud knock on my passenger window makes me jump. I look over and see my best friend's goofy face. Jax is the goofy guy of the group, and he is almost never serious. We would do anything for each other, and he's not only my teammate, but he is also my right-hand man on our football team.

"Hey, man," I say, stepping out of my Jeep and shutting the door.

"What's up, man? Are you planning on ditching today? No offense, but you look like shit," he chuckles.

"Nah, man, I have something I need to do today."

"I think you mean, someone to do, right?" Jax laughs at his own joke.

"Something like that," my voice sounds harsher than I intend, but Jax just shrugs and begins to talk animatedly about something I don't want to listen to now.

The good thing about Jax is he doesn't mind my irritable side. He'll continue to talk, even if I don't respond or if I'm in a piss poor mood.

By lunch I never see Poppy in the halls, and that begins to irritate me. Most days, the guys and I leave for lunch, but today I'm going to stay on campus. I just need a few minutes alone with her.

If all she wants from me is a friend, I will be there. If she ever changes her mind and wants to be more... I should brace myself for the possibility that she can't forgive me and wants nothing to do with me.

Lunch is almost over, and the table is getting rowdy. Poppy never comes into the cafeteria. She has sat in the same place since freshman year. I wonder if she is hiding in the library. She usually does after an encounter with me. I ball my fist up in frustration and take a deep breath.

I don't want to sit here and pretend to be social. I pick up my tray and dump my untouched food in the trash can next to our table. I hear Jax say something about Poppy.

"Man, you will never believe who my dad had to kick out of the bar last night. I guess Poppy's father was only there for about an hour before he got completely shit faced and was trying to start fights," he chuckles at the last part.

Jax's dad owns the most popular bar in town, as well as most everything else here in town. I turn around and stare at Jax dumbfounded.

"Man, didn't he get kicked out a few days ago?" one of the other guys at the table asks.

I don't know who asked, but I'm having trouble processing what everyone is saying.

"Yeah man, my dad was saying that he was fixing to ban him from the bar and that Poppy's father is getting more and more out of hand lately," The serious inflation in Jax's voice doesn't sit well with me.

He continues, talking about Poppy's private life in front of everyone like this is no big deal.

"My dad said he has noticed that this has become a trend when his wife died years ago. He is worried about his daughter and has been thinking about checking in on her. I told him how she is pretty much a loner and doesn't talk to anyone. I also told my parents that she is a damn ten and with a tiny body made for fucking. Dude, the look my mom gave me was priceless, and my dad fucking punched me in the arm. I think I have a damn bruise." He starts laughing as if he said something funny. I just turn and walk away, not wanting to hear anymore.

My head is beginning to pound, and my ears are ringing with rage. The kiss from last night disappears, and all I can hear is what Jax told the whole fucking lunch table. I'm now worried for Poppy, and I hope that she is all right. I grab my stuff for science out of my locker and head toward the classroom.

The first bell rings, and I'm the first person in the classroom. Students slowly come into class, but still no sign of Poppy when the second bell rings. and I begin to sweat. I try not to think about the fact that she isn't here. I know she misses a lot of school, but she could be skipping to avoid me. The thought of her not wanting to be around me after last night is really messing with my head.

The bell rings, and I'm halfway to the door when Mr. Franks stops me. "Mr. Jacobs, a few minutes, please." I roll my eyes and turn around to face Mr. Franks.

"Your lab partner will be out of school for the rest of the week. I sent her class work for the week to the office for her parents to pick up. I'm going to grade both of your assignments separately and do a combined grade, so you may want to pay attention in my class and make sure your work is done and turned in on time. If you don't care about your grade, you should talk to Ms. Monroe, because what you do affects her grade as well. You may leave for your next class."

I walk away, knowing better than to say anything else to that arrogant ass. I have gym next, and I know that Coach will let me go in the weight room, and I can blow off steam. I walk in and see that Coach Clarks is here, instead of Coach Denver, but the other students are not in the gym.

"Lewis, I'm pulling you and Jax this hour and for study hall. I want you both to go on the field and work with the fresh meat and teach them plays and how we do our team. They killed at tryouts, but practice is a disaster. I want them ready by our first game."

"Sure thing, Coach."

"Jax and the other players are out there already. We will talk later about why you're late to class."

I go to the locker room and change for practice, but I don't completely pad up yet, since we are not doing an official practice. I walk to the closet where the flag football stuff is and grab the buckets and walk to them field.

"All right, here he is. Ladies, looks like we are doing this the fun way." Jax jogs over to me and grabs my bucket from my hands.

I put my practice equipment next to Jax's and turn to the new players.

"Grab a belt and two flags. This isn't your typical flag football," I holler, attaching my belt around my waist.

Jax tells them the rules, and I set up the cones, thinking about how I should approach Poppy.

"We will be going over different plays and if you lose any flags during the scrimmage that means for each flag equals a lap around the track for everyone." They all exchange a glance with each other, like they must be missing something. I don't finish because I know Jax will have more fun telling them the catch.

"There's more. Oh, and you will not like this part. You'll wear a cheer uniform, poms, and a bow in the hair and run in front of the whole team."

There are a few groans, but they won't know until they must run that Jax, and I will be running with them, just like our captains did with us. Seeing the captain and co-captain doing what them do the punishment for loosing flags to is good for them. This way the newbies can see that, if or when they mess up, we have their backs. The other teammates will be cheering them in the stands. This is always the best photo in the yearbook.

I finish, and we all do some sprints and other warmups before breaking into our teams. Jax is on one side and I'm on the other. We are always paired together, and any chance we get is fun to get a chance to compete against each other.

"Jacobs, you got some girl troubles?" Jax bends into a stance in front of me.

"What's the point of this?" A kicker asks.

"The shit talk or the two hours of lessons before a grueling practice?" Jax turns his head to him.

"Both," he takes a step away from Jax.

"Move back in line!" The kid looks like he visibly shrinks at my command.

"Poppy avoided you after you did your science project last night. That explains why your thong is so far up your ass."

I'm going to have to deal with this shit with Poppy before I let girl shit get in my head, and I fumble at practice or a game. I guess my only option if I want to talk to her today is to go over to her house.

"You see, kiddies, the fact that Lewis is distracted makes for some fun and less resistance on the opposing team," Jax uses me as an example, because for me to be this wound up and my head not right anytime on the field something isn't right.

Jax makes, the call, and its finally time to teach the new players how this team really is.

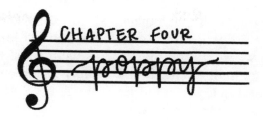

CHAPTER FOUR

Blood rushes to my head making me dizzy. My heart is pounding in my chest, and the air is thickening making it hard to breathe. My stomach turns sour. I've been caught, and my father is waiting for me in my room.

He doesn't pounce when I open the door so that means he is being calculated, and he is wanting to build the anticipation for what is going to happen next. I know what is fixing to happen, and my brain is screaming at me to get the hell out of there.

One of two things happened tonight. He either lost the fight he found at the bar, or he got kicked out. This means that whatever is haunting him is still in his mind and he is bringing that fight here to satisfy whatever he is fighting, and to take it out on me.

"Where the hell have you been, and who the hell were you with?" he fumes in a drunken slur.

I start to stutter, not being able to get my brain and mouth to work properly.

The next thing I know, my face is stinging from the back hand that my father gives me. Trying to stand still and not stagger back is hard. Considering the force of the smack makes me turn my head all the way to the side. I blink away the tears that threaten to spill from over my bottom lashes. I was not expecting that. He gets up so fast I don't even know he is in front of me until I feel a slap on my left cheek.

"DAMN IT! ANSWER ME NOW!" He exclaims in an outburst of rage, his liquor-scented spit coating my face.

"I was next door at the Jacobs' house. Their son and I are lab partners in science class. We had a poster to complete," I whisper so low, I'm surprised he was able to hear me.

Another backhand slaps across my face, but this time my right

33

cheek splits open. The force behind that blow has me stumbling back a couple of steps. Tears make their way down my face on their own accord. I know I'm in deep shit and that school will be forgotten for the rest of the week, if not next week as well. I just hope that he is drunk enough to tire himself out before this gets too out of hand.

"Did I tell you that you could leave my house?" He sounds calm, but I know he is hanging on by a thread.

My father grabs me by the back of my neck and forces me to the floor. My knees hit the hardwood floor so violently, I feel the sting travel from my knees up throughout my whole body. The scrapes on my hands and knees from falling in Lewis's driveway doesn't help.

I'm trying with all the willpower I have left not to yelp out in pain. I feel new tears pulling in the corner of my eyes, and I know I won't be able to stop them. My body tenses, waiting for the next blow.

Instead of a physical blow, he begins chastising me. "You know better than to leave this house unless I give you permission."

I look at his repulsive face and see that his eyes are completely glazed over. I can tell whatever put him in this rage has taken over and, any control he once had is now non-existent.

He takes my shoulders in a tight grasp and shoves me. The force of the push causes me to fall onto my back, my head bouncing off the hardwood floor two times. My legs are still somewhat bent under me, and I faintly register a pop in my left knee. I don't feel any pain yet, but I know that when he stops and I'm left alone in my room, the suffering will truly begin; however, tomorrow will be true agony.

I know better than to move, cry, or make a sound. He is like a rabid animal; anything can set him off. A few moments go by with just the sound of his wheezing, and I begin to think he has tired himself out.

Oh no, I'm sadly mistaken because a few powerful kicks to my sides and stomach have me sliding a couple of inches with each blow. I don't know how long he continues his attack, and I don't bother to count anymore. Counting only makes me feel worse.

Once he is tired of kicking me, he grabs me by the hair and yanks me to my feet. My dad is breathing harder, and he starts to swing his fist wildly, he manages to connect with my face a few times. I can tell that he is getting tired now. His punches become slower, and he is having trouble raising his arms up to extend another swing my way.

He starts to stagger; his footing becomes sloppy. I feel that the end is near. My thoughts are confirmed when my father turns and retreats from my room. The sound of a door being slammed shut causes me to flinch.

I stand there for a few minutes, trying to build my strength up enough to move. I never know if he is going to come back, or if he is going to drown himself in more booze.

The door that was slammed before thuds against a wall, followed by heavy stomping of shoes. I wince with every footstep he takes. The sound of another door being shut makes me jump, and I whimper softly at the pain searing through my body.

The sound of tires screeching outside my window snaps at the tension in my body like a rubber band. I'm starting to feel the abuse that my father inflicted on me. I try to take a step toward the bathroom but stop from the excruciating pain now taking over my knees. All I want to do is crawl in bed and sleep, but before I do that, I need to get myself cleaned up. I don't know if I'm going to accomplish that with the injuries that I have.

I try to push aside the burning sensation in my knees and the aches in my side, so I can wash away tonight's transgressions. Sucking in as deep of a breath, I force one tiny step at a time until I am in the bathroom.

My shower takes longer than normal. I'm trying to not scrub too hard or make any sudden movements. I'd like to go get ice packs, but I know that going down the stairs is not an option for me. I would not be able to go downstairs and back up without getting caught and hurting myself more. Turning off the water, I wrap a fluffy towel around me and walk slowly toward the mirror.

I wipe the fog off the mirror and look at the damage done to me. I recoil from the person in the reflection. Swelling has already started to take over my face along with the coloring of deep bruises forming. My lip is busted, and my cheek split open. I can see the faint outline of my father's hands on my shoulders and shadows covering my stomach, sides, and back that will only darken before morning. My knees are turning a deep shade of purple and blue on top of the gashes I got earlier in the night. I look away from the broken girl in the mirror with a sob stuck in my throat, I can't look anymore.

I put on a simple black pajama set and limp my way to my bed. I struggle to grab the nearest pillow that was thrown onto my floor. I leave the pillow and the rest of my bedding on the floor and just crawl back into my bed. I lay on my back trying to breathe through the agonizing pain. I know this will only bring me nightmares tonight, but my eyes are heavy.

I close my eyes, intending to sleep, but the events from tonight flood my mind. A normal girl would have just been grounded for sneaking out. Even then I should have only been in trouble for staying out past curfew. I shouldn't have been punished this way. I don't try to stop myself from crying this time. I let out my sobs take over my whole body. I know this won't heal my wounds, but sometimes crying shows more strength to let the tears out than holding them in. I used to refuse to cry for the pain I've endured, but I'm not crying from the physical pain I feel, but from everything else in my life.

I know I should fight back and defend myself, but that's hard to do when you're terrified of the outcome. I've thought about running away, but I don't know where I could go. I know that teachers and other people have seen some bruises, whether they are still purple and blue or a faint yellow, but they don't ever say anything about them. I doubt there is anyone who can help me now. Even after all that I have endured from him, I still have hope that I can escape him somehow. I'm just hoping that I can do that with my life.

My father, being the sick and twisted man that he is, will have a sense of satisfaction from my appearance at breakfast tomorrow. I remember the one time that I tried to cover the evidence of his malice with makeup. Let's just say I looked worse after those new bruises started to appear than I do now, but the feeling is always the same.

Around two in the morning, my dad comes, home. I hear him stomping around downstairs. He is taunting me, showing that he is the one in control and can come in here at any moment. His stomping abruptly stops, and then I hear him closing something with more force than necessary. I don't hear anything for a few minutes. The silence is nerve wracking, and it makes the hair on my arms stand up from the goosebumps that are rapidly appearing.

I shudder when I hear high pitched beeps followed by a low hum. He is in the kitchen warming up food in the microwave. I feel some relief, because he didn't immediately come looking for me. The loud ringing of bells signaling that his food is done comes a few moments later. Then, there is a stretch of silence.

I have been lying in bed for close to an hour, listening to any movement my father makes. The silence is awful, because you are often left thinking he is creeping around and will appear out of nowhere. Suddenly I hear a crash of a dish breaking, and then he vehemently swears a few times before he breaks out in a fit of coughs.

My heart starts beating rapidly. He's still pissed, and he wants me to know. I hear the angry echo of his shoes slapping the hardwood flooring leaving the kitchen. The sounds are getting closer to the stairs next to my room. If he was going to his room, he would have used the stairs in the kitchen.

My heart slams heavily into my chest as panic consumes me. He is making his way to my room. To confirm my feeling, I see the shadow of his loafers under the crack of my door. He stands there for a few moments before he shoves my door open making the door bang against the wall.

I don't move, and I won't, until he doesn't tell me to. If I sit up now, who knows what will happen. He continues to just stand there for a few more minutes before I hear a deep chuckle come from him.

"Pops, I know you're not asleep." He stumbles over his words. He uses the nickname he gave me when I was little and hearing him use call me that now in a taunting manner makes my skin crawl.

My father is even more drunk than he was earlier. I didn't even think that was possible. I know he is wanting me to sit up, so he can evaluate the damage that he inflicted on me earlier. I don't want to move, because I'll hurt more when I sit up. He gets this satisfaction or a sense of pride from seeing the pain and bruising he has left on me, and that is something I don't want to give him. Maybe if he is content with his wrong doings, he'll leave me alone until I will have to get up, to make him breakfast. When I shift in my bed to sit up my dad blinds us both with the bright fluorescent light coming from the ceiling fan.

"Well, you look better than I would like. What should we do about that, Poppy?" he taunts. He takes a couple of staggered steps into my room.

"Come here!" he demands, wobbling on his feet, trying to stand upright.

I get up slowly and try to move over to him. He grins at me when he notices that I'm struggling to walk. That part makes him happy. He is a sick human being for being joyful over hurting another person, and he's even worse for taking pleasure from inflicting this kind of agony on his daughter.

The closer I get to him, the more I can smell the stench of sweat and alcohol oozing out of his pores. The faint smell of stale cigarettes is still there, but my father would not reek this bad if he took a shower or passed out in his room instead of going back to whatever bar let him in. I could easily knock him off balance and run but where would I go, and could I really get too far in the state that I'm in now? I have no friends or family that I could run to. Lewis's face briefly pops into my head but what would he be able to do? He is just a teenager like me, and I don't think his parents would like that I bring my issues to their home.

"You look just like her. Why do you have to remind me so much of my Ellenor?" he mumbles, his voice thick with sadness. My father raises his hand, and I am prepared to feel the biting sting of a slap, but the soft movement of him moving my hair out of my face has me truly terrified.

He gives me one more hard look, then shuffles out of my room.

I slowly close my door trying not to draw any attention to myself. I try to get my comforter off the floor, and once I do, I try again to grab my pillow. I was once successful and when I get back into my bed, I lay back down.

I lay in bed but sleep never comes even though I'm exhausted and feel lightheaded from the shooting pain coursing through my whole body.

If I were able to dream tonight, I'd want to dream about a different life. My mom would still be here, my father wouldn't be spiteful and abusive, I could be a normal girl, and maybe I'd even have a boyfriend. A better life where I'm happy and free.

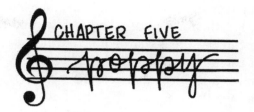

CHAPTER FIVE

The sun peeks through my curtains, and I know I'll have to get up soon to make breakfast. I haven't been to sleep yet, and I'm still not wanting to move. I should have taken some medicine, but my dad keeps all of them locked in the bathroom downstairs, and I don't have a key.

Getting dressed takes me twice as long than normal, and going down the stair is pure torture. I hiss every step I take, while I'm able to grit my teeth before I must act like I'm not in excruciating agony.

I have oatmeal and toast waiting for my father when he finally comes downstairs. I have an empty bowl, a box of cereal, and milk sitting in front of me. I look at what I made, and I see that my father has his coffee, but I forgot to pour him his orange juice.

I limp through the kitchen, frantically getting his juice before he comes downstairs. As soon as I'm seated, my father strolls in, wearing a nicely pressed suit, his hair coiffed to perfection, and he has a smug smile on his arrogant face. He sits in the chair opposite of me and picks up his spoon and begins eating his sticky oatmeal.

When his bowl is half empty, and he has eaten two buttered biscuits he gives me a lazy once-over, seeing what he did with sober eyes. I see satisfaction shine in his eyes, and that's only a small relief, because I don't feel any less humiliated.

"You know the drill. You will be out sick from school the rest of the week, and I will pick up your assignments after I get off work. They will be completed before you return," he says gruffly, picking up his spoon again.

I sit there, listening to the scraping of silverware in the bowl and my father's smacking. My stomach is turning, and I begin to feel nauseous from the sounds my father is making, eating the rest of his breakfast.

When he drops his spoon again, I look up at the loud clanking sound it made. The priggish smirk returns to his face, and this is the time I find out if I get to eat breakfast or not. I would be happy with the simple bowl of cereal I have set out for me to eat.

"You can make a bowl of that cereal for breakfast, and after you are finished eating, I've made a list of chores for you to complete before I get home this evening. You'll find the list on the console by the front door. Order the groceries we need online today, so they can be dropped off on the porch and remember not to leave the house for anything or answer the door for anyone." He pushes back from the table in his typical aggressive way.

I stay where I am until he has plenty of time to drive away from the house. I feel the stress leaving my body at the distance between me and my father. A small part of me is grateful I don't have to face Lewis after our kiss last night, but also, he said he wants to talk, and I'm going to have to miss out on that for a few days.

I scarf down three full bowls of cereal that tastes like cardboard, but I am hungry enough that the bland breakfast is like a feast. I clear the table, then get the list of the console in the foyer. I should have no problems finishing everything, even though I know this was made to be an impossible list of tasks, considering how wounded I am. The list is extensive, but manageable; I just need to start right away.

First, I clean the dishes, and then I go to change into some leggings and a loose t-shirt to clean in, because I put a simple t-shirt style dress on for breakfast. I grab a pen, and then I go to the kitchen to make a list of groceries to order.

Ticking item after item off the list, the morning goes by like a blur. Moving around is making me less stiff, but still nothing dulls the pain. I look at the clock, and I'm excited because lunchtime has already passed. I would really like something else to eat, but I know if I want to be sure that this list and my normal chores are done in time, I'm going to have to skip eating.

I move around the house doing laundry, dusting, sweeping, moping, vacuuming, and other mindless things and as I'm putting away all the cleaning supplies, my stomach growls again. The only thing left is to cook dinner. I look at the small digital clock on a shelf in the laundry room, and I see that I managed to complete everything by 4:45.

I have a little over an hour to get dinner on the table and I'm not going to waste any time. I gather the supplies to make spaghetti. First,

I mix Italian seasonings into some hamburger meat and mix them together, forming meatballs. I'm about halfway through when I'm interrupted by a knock on the door. I'm not sure who that could be, since I selected to have my groceries delivered tomorrow. I didn't want to use the time I needed to clean to put the food away.

I go to the door and look through a small section of the glass on the door. Lewis is standing there with his hands stuffed into his pockets.

"Poppy!" he yells.

"Lewis, go home!" I shout back, trying to keep my voice even.

"Come on, talk to me," he groans.

My father might be home soon, and he can't find him here.

"Poppy, what the hell is going on? You're acting stranger than normal." How would he know how I normally act; he is never around me. "Poppy, open the door and fucking talk to me!" he howls and bangs his fist against the door.

I jump at his sudden outburst, "I can't talk right now."

"Poppy," he sounds more defeated now, but if hurting him gets him out of here, then that's what I'll do.

"I'll try to sneak out tonight. Meet me by the fence in your backyard at 12:00."

"Fine," He lightly taps my door twice before he jogs away.

He thinks I was avoiding him, because I didn't go to school. That makes me laugh, because he couldn't be farther from the truth. I need to finish dinner; Lewis took up more time than I would have liked.

I need to multitask, so I cook the meatballs and boil the pasta water at the same time. Thankfully, I make extra sauce every time, and I have just enough for tonight. I wait for the meat to finish cooking before I add the sauce, and at the time the pasta is perfectly *al dente,* then I add that to the pan with the sauce and meatballs and mix them around. I add a ladle full of pasta water and stir that in to help thicken the sauce a little more. While that simmers on the stove, I get the glasses filled and set the table. I return to the stove and the spaghetti looks perfect. I pop a few pieces of garlic bread in the toaster oven while I take the bowl of pasta to the table.

I'm making my father's plate when the front door opens. In a hurry I add the toast to a small plate next to his bowl, and I scramble to get into my chair as fast as I can before he comes into the dining room.

"How much of your list were you able to complete?" he asks, going straight to his chair, before even looking down at his plate a look of disgust flickered across his face.

"I finished around 4:45, sir," I whisper, not daring to look up at him.

"I'll be the judge of that after I eat," He states before picking up his fork and taking a large bite.

I need to figure out a way to talk to Lewis tonight, so he doesn't come back over here. That would really make things a bigger mess for me at home. I'm so distracted that I barely notice that my dad has finished his plate. The sound of his chair scraping along the tile gives me goosebumps.

I can hear my father moving around the house, but he is back in the dining room before I can even think about what my dad is doing. He looks down at me with a stern look. He is clearly not happy that I did a good job.

"You can eat whatever is left of dinner after you make me lunch for tomorrow. When you are done and everything is cleaned up, come to the living room. We have some things that need to be discussed." He doesn't leave me any room to reply. I clear the table of dishes and go into the kitchen.

I do as my father says and I am happy that there is enough spaghetti leftover that I may be full tonight. I waste no time scarfing my meal down. I'm not leaving him anytime to change his mind, and if he does, I'll already be finished. I practically lick my plate clean; then I put them in the dishwasher. While the dishwasher is running, I take the trash out and wipe down all the countertops. Lastly, I put the dishes up.

I walk into the living room, and I see my dad in one of the accent chairs. He lifts the remote and turns off the tv with one hand while motioning for me to sit on the couch with the other. I walk as fast as I can without crying out in pain. I don't want to delay him anymore than I already have, and I don't want to risk getting in trouble again. Once I am seated on the couch, I face my father giving him my full attention. He has a solemn look on his face which makes me nervous. The last time I saw that face was when he told me my mom died.

"I'll be out of town for business the next few days. I'll have a list for you to complete daily. The rules still apply even if I'm not here. Do you understand me?" He is trying to provoke me.

"Yes sir, I understand," I whisper. I'm not stupid enough to play into whatever game he wants me to lose.

"I won't need breakfast tomorrow; I have a car coming to pick me up at the office in an hour." I nod my head, and I know I'm being dismissed.

I do not wait for him to add anything else. I go to my bathroom; I wash my face first and look over my injuries from last night for the first time today. My face is still puffy and swollen but not much more than last night. The bruising is darker as well as some new bruising that I didn't have when I looked last night. My lower lip is split and could use some cleaning and ointment. I think this one will scar this time because this gash is the deepest cut I've had there.

I clean my cuts and go lay down in the clothes that I wore all day. I feel too drained to change into some pajamas. Plus, I am wearing leggings and an oversized tee so that's pretty much the same, right?

I'm drifting off to sleep when footsteps coming down the hall towards my room alarms my brain, and my eyes spring open. I know he is coming up here to make sure that I'm in bed, but mostly he is mocking me. He likes to prove that he is the one with all the power and that he can do whatever he wants, while I can do anything.

He opens the door. "I put your classwork on the coffee table. You are to complete everything your teachers have sent home before school on Monday." He stalks away leaving my door open.

My father doesn't tell me goodbye or sounds like he will miss me before he leaves to go out of town, which is fine, because I'm looking forward to the space and the fact that, for at least a little while, I'm safe.

I wait for ten minutes to pass after he leaves the doorway of my room before I get out of bed. I open my door and I tiptoe down the stairs, even though I know I don't have to because my father left. I want to see if Lewis' Jeep is still in his driveway.

"Where do you think you're going, Poppy?" I hear from behind me.

I turn around as my father steps out of the shadows by the staircase. I square my shoulders and look up at him with as much confidence that I can muster. I need to think of a lie quickly, He won't wait long for a response. What could I tell him that is a plausible reason for me to be out of bed? I have serious doubts that he would believe anything at this point, nor do I think he wants to.

"I was going to go to the garage to get some more toilet paper for my bathroom," I say in a small voice, trying not to sound rushed or nervous.

"I feel like you're up to something, and I really don't have time for your stupid games. I'm tempted to lock you in your room until I get back. How would that make you feel?" he laughs, spitting all over my face. "Were you going to go see your boyfriend?"

"No, sir," I mumble.

He takes a step towards me, and on instinct, I step back. I'm in deep shit now. He's now an inch away from my face. I gasp, and dear god, that was a mistake. My stomach rolls at my father's foul breath.

"Do you know why you don't have any friends or a boyfriend?" he pauses, "Well, let me enlighten you. No one wants to be friends with a bad girl that took their mom's life!" he taunts vehemently.

He grabs my arm and jerks me around, making me struggle to stay upright. He gives me a powerful shove, making me fall into the side of the stairs. My back connects with the sharp skirtboard of a step making my sore rib cage burn.

I stay where I fell on the floor. I close my eyes tightly and wait for my father's next move. The sound of the front door shutting with a loud bang makes me jump. I cry out in agony from my body jerking from my sudden movement. I'm in so much pain that I just lay there, not wanting to move. The angry screech of my father's tires as he leaves for his trip fills the room.

For the first time in years, I feel safe in my own home, even so, that feeling is fleeting, before being replaced by the throbbing pain that radiates through my whole body. I brace myself as I slowly try to get from my side to my hands and knees, so I can get off the floor. I curse and scream as I reach my hand to grip on the intricate carved baluster to help support me as I get onto my feet. I think I may have a broken rib. I have once, and the pain was like what I'm feeling now.

I somehow manage to get myself to the couch where I plan on sleeping tonight. I know with my injuries that I won't be able to go outside to talk to Lewis, nor will I be able to go upstairs, without causing more stress to my battered body. I try to think of good things before the blackness takes me, and I pass out in the living room.

I wake up on the couch, disoriented. I sit up slowly and look at the clock on the wall. Shit! 12:00 already. I've never slept this late. The first thing I need to do is check my grocery order that I put in yesterday and that was canceled with a note stating that they are short staffed and to resubmit in the morning. I like to go to the store that the Taylor's own, because they have the best quality of food.

I put the order back in, but I add a few more things that I want for myself. I look at all the lists my father set out for me, and they are all the same things but in a different order. If I just do everything, he left for me to do all day before he returns, he won't even know I didn't do them daily, but I'll cross them off each list like I did yesterday. Am I playing with fire testing these limits? Yes, I'm not going to do the same things each day, if I don't have to.

I walk to the piano by the stairs and flashbacks of last night filtered in. I push the images of me crumbling to the floor away while sitting down on the piano bench. I lift the fallboard and place my hands gingerly on the keys. I began to move my fingers, letting them dance across the keys,

I get so lost in the melodies, playing song after song, until I hear a tapping sound over my most recent crescendo. I don't realize for a few moments that someone is knocking at the door. I look at my phone and notice that I have a notification that my grocery delivery is here. I elected to pay with a card, and I included a generous tip, so why are they knocking on my door?

"Hold on, I'll be right there!" I holler, getting up from the piano.

I can see that a guy is on the other side of the window from my size, and I curse myself because, of course, Lewis would come back after I didn't go talk to him last night. When I get close enough, I can tell exactly who is here, and Jax is not a better option.

"Hey, so your card would not go through," his deep voice greets cheerfully when I crack the door open.

"Sorry, I have another card, if you're able to run it," I mumble apologetically.

"Yeah, let me go to the truck and get the card reader."

Jax is only gone for a few seconds before he is plugging the information into his phone.

"Hey, I didn't know you live next to Lewis, and I am over there all the time. Does Lewis know you're his neighbor? I'm sure he does," Jax quips as I'm swiping my dad's credit card, adding a good tip, and signing for the purchase.

Shit, I was hoping he wouldn't realize who I am.

"Oh yeah, we've lived next to each other our whole lives," I stutter trying to get past my nerves.

45

I hand him his phone back and bend down to get a couple of the bags scattered all over my porch.

"Would you like me to bring them in for you?" he asks politely.

I should say no, but I really don't want to carry the bags into the house because doing that will make me hurt even more.

"Yeah, that would be great. Thank you," I stammer.

He doesn't say anything until we reach the kitchen, and he places the bags on the kitchen island. He turns and makes two more trips as I start putting stuff away.

"You're welcome. Would you like for me to put these away for you?" he inquired turning to face me.

I quickly look away from him. He can't see my face. If he does, I know he'll ask questions. I need to make sure that I don't look directly at him, or my hair is covering my face.

"No thanks, I can do that."

I move around the island and try to lead him to the door. I'm almost to the door when I hear a low whistle.

"Damn, is this your mom?" he asks loudly from wherever he is.

I turn around and walk back to the kitchen and see him standing in the hallway. His back is now turned to me, and he is looking at the pictures we have hanging on the wall just outside of the kitchen. I love those pictures. They bring me so many emotions, sometimes sadness for the family I lost, and joy from seeing the love on my mom's elegant face.

"Yes, that was my mom," I reply with a strained voice.

I walk over to where he is standing, looking at all these pictures my mom spent hours hanging on the wall. She wanted them to look perfect, and she was so proud of them. My mom loved showing off pictures of her family.

"SHIT, POPPY!" snaps me out of the trance of memories of my mom. What the fuck happened to you?" Jax asks with genuine concern.

"I was in a car accident," I stammer.

From the glance he shoots me, I can tell he doesn't buy my lies.

He glances up at me while he is still messing with his phone. He is fixing to say something, but instead he pulls his phone out of his pocket. I'm beginning to get angry with him getting into my business. He keeps glancing at me, as his thumbs fly over the screen on his phone.

"JAX, I'M FINE." I yell at him, not realizing exactly how loud I am until I hear the echo of my desperate voice.

He looks up at me, and I see pity written all over him, and for some reason that makes me feel even worse. I don't need or want his remorse. I just need him to leave and never speak of what he sees to anyone.

"Poppy, I feel like you're lying to me, and I don't know what to do, because you look like you got the shit beat out of you. I think you may need help, and I know my dad will know what to do."

"Jax, NO! There is no need for your father to come all the way over here. I am fine. I was in a car accident," I huff.

Neither of us has a chance to reply when a loud knock comes from the door. I jump from the sudden sound. Making a hissing sound from the shooting pain coming from my rib cages, I grab onto my sides and try to breathe through the agony.

I refuse to move and open the door for more people to try to get into my business. Jax, on the other hand, is okay to open someone else's door without their permission. An older version of Jax enters my house. He has a kind face, but there is sorrow clouding his eyes.

"Hi, you must be Poppy. My name is Shane. It's nice to meet you," His voice is gentle almost like how someone would speak to a baby or a scared animal.

I don't respond, because I feel like I'm on verge of breaking down, and if I utter a word then I'll turn into a blubbering mess. That would for sure scare the shit out of them, and then they wouldn't believe me when I need to lie to them.

"Poppy, I'm going to walk my son out to his truck, so he can get back to work. When I return, I would like to talk with you for a little while," He doesn't leave room for any debate, but at least, he is kind in his obvious determination to talk to me.

He walks up to Jax and puts his hand on his shoulder, guiding him out the front door. They don't say anything on their way out, but I see them exchange a couple of looks.

I'm not going to just sit here and wait for him to come back in and interrogate me. I put the groceries up, and Mr. Taylor is still not done talking to Jax. I walk into the living room, stopping for a second to see that they are both talking. With a sigh, I go sit on the couch.

The longer I wait for Mr. Taylor to return the more anxious I become. My knee is bouncing up and down. I pick at the skin around my nails.

Why is he taking so long? Is he waiting for someone else to get here? Did he call the cops? What if Mr. Taylor asks me what happened to me? Do I lie to him, or do I tell him the truth? What if he is meaner than my dad? Maybe Jax should have stayed. At least I would've had a witness or maybe everything will be fine, and I'm just overthinking this. What if he would be able to help me? Isn't that what I wanted? I have had dreams of people saving from my dad and getting me to a better home, but what if they take me, and I'm in a worse position than before? I never should have answered the door.

CHAPTER SIX

When Mr. Taylor comes back in, he sits across from me in the same chair my father sat in the night before.

"Poppy, the last thing I want to do is cause you more trouble by coming here, but I need you to tell me what happened to you?" Mr. Taylor is trying his best to keep eye contact with me, but he is finding that difficult to do, because I'm looking anywhere but at him.

I'm unsure of what exactly I should say, because I know my father would go ballistic if I even hinted that he had anything to do with me being bruised up, and I doubt Mr. Taylor would believe me if I told him I was in an accident like I told Jax.

"I don't know what to tell you, Mr. Taylor," I stutter looking down at my lap. My hair falls in my face, and I'm grateful, because my hair is blocking him from seeing the emotions on my face.

"Poppy, I can't understand how you feel or what you've been through, but I can listen without judging you. I'm here to help you in any way that I can and if I can't, I'll find someone who can." Mr. Taylor looks down at the room around him before finishing, "Take your time and tell me what you are comfortable with."

The room begins to spin, and I'm fighting to hold back tears. When did it get so hot in here?

"There really isn't much to say. I was an accident," I start to fidget with the hem of my t-shirt.

I don't know this man very well, I mean I knew him when I was friends with Jax growing up, but I was only friends with Jax, because Lewis and he became friends playing football. I think the last time I saw him was ten years ago at my mom's funeral.

"Please call me Shane," he clears his throat. "I think I should speak openly to you about what I know of your father."

I go pale and smash my lips in a thin line. I know what he is referring to, because I know what businesses he owns in town.

"Poppy, I own some businesses in town, and among those are a couple of bars." He sounds like his voice is echoing, almost like we are in a cave confirming my own thoughts.

He looks at me to see if I'm listening to him, but something on my face is giving away that I know what he is talking about.

"Mr. Taylor, I mean Shane, I, ugh-" I swallow the lump in my throat.

"Poppy, your father is a regular at both of my establishments. I've been removing him from my bars more frequently for the past year or so for fighting. I kicked him out two nights ago. Do you know which night I am referring to?"

I lower my head as tingles travel all over my scalps, making goosebumps dimple my skin. That's the night I got caught sneaking back in from going to Lewis's house. I wonder if he hadn't been kicked out if he would have been gone all night.

"He has been getting progressively more combative these last few years. I've seen a lot of changes in him since your mom passed away." Something changed the way he is talking to me. I don't know if I showed the horror on my face from his question or what, but he is talking more cautiously and slower than he was before.

The room begins to spin as a chilling sensation runs down my spine. I blink until the fog in my eyes is cleared, and I can see that Shane is looking at me with his eyebrows pulled together and his jaw is set.

"Poppy," he takes a deep breath, "Did your father hurt you?" The way his voice jumps almost makes me think that him asking me that out loud causes him pain.

Fear claws at me, tearing me up. I frantically try to push my hair away from my face, but that's useless, because I tied it in a messy bun. The room goes blurry as I try to hold back tears. I sit here with a kind man asking me if I need help, and I can't answer him because I feel a slight twinge of guilt at betraying my father.

I nodded my head in short jerking movements. I start sobbing from the multiple emotions that are taking over my body. I feel sadness for my dad, relieved that someone finally knows what I've been screaming at people in my head the last seven years.

I flinch at the feeling of Shane putting his arm around me. I was too consumed with my thoughts that I never saw him come over to me. I reacted at Shane's embrace for a couple of reasons, because when he put his arm around me, that hurt from when my father shoved me into the stairs last night.

Shane moves back to his original seat and begins searching my face for any clue on what just happened, but I can tell that he knows the answer to his unspoken question. He just wants me to say what happened out loud so that he can help me.

"Is your face the only injuries you have, or do you have more that I should know about?"

The questions are beginning to exhaust me to a point of dizziness. Everything is happening so fast that processing the events from the last couple of days is nearly impossible. I can't answer him, because my father will only hurt me more if I do.

"No sir," even though I'm talking barely above a whisper my words are echoing in my head.

Shane clears his throat, and I see pain and pity written all over his handsome face. "I'm, ugh, I'm going to make a phone call, but I don't want you to worry. Everything will be all right." He stands up and leaves the and before walking out the front door, he glances back at me.

I don't want to sit here and look around the room awkwardly until he is done calling whoever he feels he needs to talk to right now. My guess is Mr. Taylor is probably calling the police. I limp up the stairs to my room. I have a few pictures in a box my mom had, and I know that I have one with my mom and Shane's wife. If I remember correctly, her name is Roxanne together.

After my struggle to get the box off the top shelf of my closet, I stiffly sit on the foot of my bed, and I look over at one of the photos I keep on my nightstand. I'm about three or four years old. We're sitting in the middle of a blanket that is spread out in the backyard having a picnic. I can imagine my dad is taking the picture, because he isn't in it.

My memory ends abruptly, due to Shane hollering at me from downstairs. "Poppy, where are you?"

Ignoring Shane, I pull the lid off the box and thumb through some of the pictures I saved from the garbage after my father threw them away in a drunken rage a couple of years ago.

I hear footsteps outside my bedroom door before Shane's relieved voice fills my room. "Here you are. May I come in or would you be more comfortable if I stayed in the hallway?" I look at him with my jaw dropped. I don't remember the last time someone asked me how I felt about anything.

"I want to show you something." After I find what I'm looking for, I pull the picture out of the box and move the box next to me on my bed.

I hold up the photo for Shane to take, but my arm begins to shake. Shane tentatively takes a step into my room and walks with careful steps in my direction. Shane's tentative movements kind of reminds me of how someone would approach a wounded animal, so they don't spook them.

He gently takes the picture from me, and my sore arm drops heavily into my lap.

"This is my wife Roxi and your mom at a senior dance in high school," I hear the fondness in his voice when he mentions his wife's name and for a moment my mind flashes to the other night when I had my first kiss.

Shane carefully sits next to me and looks at the picture one last time before he places the photo inside the open box that is now between us.

"My wife and I would like for you to come live with us while your father can get the help he needs."

"I'm all right. He is out of town for a few days, and this was my fault." Shane begins to shake his head, but I continue talking, not letting him interrupt me. "I snuck out the other night, and he was really drunk. I could tell he didn't know what he was doing." The last part is hard to say, because I know that my father knew exactly what he was doing and from the look Shane is now giving me, I can tell he doesn't believe me either.

"Poppy, this is not your fault in any way. You're a teenager. You are going to break the rules and make mistakes. That's part of growing up. The only consequence you should have from that is being grounded,"

I sit there knotting my fingers together. I know my father has needed help for a long time, but I doubt he'll get any. I also know that if I stay here and not take this opportunity to get out of this hostile and unsafe environment.

"What will you do if I choose not to go with you?" my voice quivers as butterflies flutter restlessly in my stomach.

"Poppy, you're not safe here, and like I've said a couple of times before, your father needs to get help. I'll have to call the police and child protective services. They'll want to put you in a foster home or a group home for girls. We can discuss with my lawyers about what steps we need to take to protect you."

I look away from him and let shame consume me. This feels almost too easy, but why do I get this nagging feeling that something is not going to go well, either way, for me?

"I don't want you to worry about your father or his reaction to the fact that you both need help," Shane stops talking when I stand up and shuffle back and forth in front of him.

This is what I wanted, right? Then why is Shane offering me help so hard to accept?

"I want to be here when you talk to him." I know that is probably a bad idea for me to be there, but I want to hear him try to come up with excuses for what he has done.

"I don't know about that. I need to think about your safety here."

"I'll do whatever I need to do to be there. This isn't just about him,"

"Well," Shane combs his fingers through his coiffed hair, "let's just see how you feel when we get to that conversation with your father." Unlike my father, Shane is being firm, and is trying to give me options which, isn't something I've ever had before.

I have so much to think about. The thoughts swirling through my head make me dizzy. What if Jax doesn't want me there? Where else could I go? What's going to happen if I go, but staying could be worse. The room begins to, sway, and before I can stop myself, I blurt out, "Fine, I'll go." I gasp and cover my mouth. What did I just do?

"I think that's a wise choice. Go ahead and pack what you need and want to take."

"I don't think my father would be happy if I took anything from his house." I look around thinking about what I could possibly take with me.

"Whatever he bought you or gifted you belongs to you. Whatever you need after we leave here, my wife would love to go shopping, or I know she would love to take you shopping."

I don't take a long time to pack everything that I would want or need from my room. I'm not taking everything, because I don't know how long my father will allow me to be out of his house. I could just be back here in a few days. The only thing I want to take with me more than anything is my guitars.

"I will be right back," I leave the room and walk down the steps to the living room.

I walk as fast as I can without hurting myself down the hall to my father's room. I try to turn the knob but groan in frustration, because he locked the door. The only thing I can do now is go to my father's office and get the key. I hate having to go up and down the stairs. Let's just say that stairs and limping don't mix.

After looking through his desk drawers, I start to feel defeated, because the key isn't in there. I know he keeps spare keys of all types here, because he loses them all the time when he is drunk. I'm fixing to give up when I see a small wooden box on a bookshelf by the door. I open the box and see tons of car keys and a few little brass ones in a set on a keyring.

I grab one of the sets and go back to my father's room. I'm struggling to find the right key when Shane walks up behind me.

"Poppy, do you need some help?"

"No," I twist the last key in the lock, and the doorknob finally turns.

I push the door open, and the smell that hits me takes me so hard I make a choking sound.

"Poppy, are you all, right?" Shane takes another step toward me.

"Yes," I stammer. "His room smells just like my mom did," I say with a lump forming in my throat. I missed this smell so much.

I take a tentative step inside. The room looks the same as it did when I would lay on the bed and watch my mom do her hair and makeup. I go to my mom's jewelry box, in search of the locket she gave me on our last Christmas together, and I'm disappointed the locket my mom gave me is not in there. I look in a couple of other places, but I come up empty. I think my dad might have hidden or thrown the necklace away.

I walk into the closet, and I don't hear Shane follow behind me. I try to pick up the hard-shell case of my guitar, but the weight of the guitar sends a shock of pain through my sides, and I almost drop the case.

"Shane, can you help me?"

I point to the two cases, and he picks them up, following me back into the hall.

"I'm going to start loading the truck up but take your time."

"I just need to get the stuff from my room and my schoolwork for this week in the foyer." Shane follows me to my room, and I get the suitcase that I packed. Shane slings the duffle and overnight bag I pack, and we leave my room behind us.

A small part of me hopes that I won't have to see this place again. I want to be a badass and flip off all the dark memories that room holds instead; I just turn leaving all those bad things behind me. With each step, I take to leave this place behind, the emotional and mental anguish I have felt since my mom passed lessen. A part of me will miss the good memories I have here, but so much bad has happened that this place will never feel like home again.

Once I am out the front door, I slam the door closed as hard as my injured body will allow. I feel a little of my anger to release after taking some of my aggression out on something that my dad takes pride in. I walk to the driveway and see Shane closing the door to his truck.

"I have all your things you packed loaded in my truck. Is this the last bag?" Shane lightly takes the bag off my shoulder, and I sigh as the pain in my shoulder lessens a little.

I start to walk to the passenger side of his truck when he stops me.

"Poppy, do you have a car?"

"Ugh, yes, I do, but I don't think my dad would like me taking it," I say quietly. I really don't want to talk about the rules I have for my car.

"He gave you that car. The car belongs to you as a voluntary gift, unless there are conditions in exchange for the vehicle. Did he give you any provisions when he gave you that car?"

"I'm only allowed to drive to school or the grocery store, if that counts as conditions," I look away embarrassed.

Shane chuckles. "Go get your car. You can follow me to my house."

I put the code in the pad outside of the garage and watch the door go up revealing my sparkly red Mini Cooper. I love and hate this car. I get the feeling of being free when I drive, but I have always known that I'm anything but that.

"Shane, can I have a minute please?"

"Of course, take all of the time you need."

Looking around, I have a sudden urge to scream. I decide to bottle up the anger, like I do with everything else in my life. I get in my car and start to back out of the garage. I guess need to face what changes are coming my way.

CHAPTER SEVEN

Pulling into the Taylor's driveway, I see a gorgeous house that takes your breath away. Their home is much bigger than mine, and I didn't think that was possible because I thought ours was huge.

This house, if that is what you want to call it, looks out of place in our little town. If you know the history behind their house, then you would understand that this house has been built by the founder of the town and was passed down from generation to generation until an electrical fire two years ago. That fire allowed for Shane and his family to update the house by tearing down what was left of the original home, which, let me tell you, there wasn't much left. They have the money to keep their home in excellent shape and looking better than most in this town.

I walk around to Shane and see that he is grabbing one of my bags, putting them over his shoulder. He then gets both of my guitars out and leans them against the truck to close his door.

"What do you want me to get?"

"If you could just open the door, that would be great," he walks to the massive dark wood door in a giant front entryway that has a beautiful chandelier. We aren't even inside yet, and man, this is already the most beautiful house I've even seen.

I know taking in a teenage girl is not something that he planned, but I really hope he doesn't think I will try anything with Jax. That would make for an awkward conversation.

"Poppy, I know that this might be overwhelming and that you have boundaries, but I want you to know that you are safe here. If you need anything, please let Roxi or me know," Shane opens the door for me.

I don't think Shane expects me to reply to him. We both step into the house, and as he is setting my stuff down by a console with a huge ornate mirror over it, I look around. My mouth is hanging open, and I don't try to muffle myself as the gasp slips past. The parts that I can see are immaculate with a homey feel which I find surprising with how large the space is, but the thing that really sticks out to me the most is the smell.

Whatever is being cooked smells out of this world. I don't know what their rules are for food, but I would do just about anything for just a small taste of what is being made. I feel like I'm drooling, and I reach up to swipe to my mouth, but there's nothing there. My stomach is gurgling more and more as I breathe in that mouthwatering aroma. I try not to feel shame, because I'm sure Shane can now hear how hungry I am.

Shane chuckles behind me. "Come on. I'll let you get to know my wife while I bring the rest of your stuff in."

I look at everything I pass, wanting to take in every detail of this beautiful home that I can. Everything looks like it was specifically created to adorn the walls, and each piece of furniture I pass is carefully selected. Whoever designed this house did a marvelous job of making the Taylor's home feel comfortable and inviting and not like a museum.

We step through an archway into a professional looking kitchen. Pop music being played through speakers somewhere fills the room. The woman dancing in front of the stove seems to be really enjoying herself. One day, I want to be able to dance in a kitchen and cook for the people I love.

Shane gives a lighthearted laugh that catches the woman's attention.

"Hi, honey. Who is this?" she asks, walking over after she picks up a remote, turning the music off.

"Roxi, this is Poppy. She's the girl I was telling you about on the phone." He pauses to kiss her cheek. "I'm going to put her things in the guest room across from Jax."

Shane waves and walks out of the kitchen, leaving me with his wife.

Roxi greets me with a wide smile. "Hi, Poppy. It's so nice to see you after all these years." Her eyes widen, and her voice softens, "You look just like your mom did at your age. It's a little weird. Looking at you takes me back to high school." A fond smile replaces some of the sadness on her beautiful face.

I'm not sure if I should ask if she needs help or if I should go sit in one of the stools. I feel a little awkward to just stand here.

"You can have a seat, if you want." Roxi turns and begins stirring something that is being cooked on the stove. "I want you to know that I understand what you are going through. I came from a broken home, and I spent most of my time at your mom's childhood house, growing up."

"Thank you. I appreciate everything you are doing for me." I tense at the sound of footsteps outside the kitchen archway.

"Mom, what are we having for dinner? It smells fucking good!" Jax's hollers as he steps into the kitchen.

"We are having pot roast. Dinner will be ready in about an hour." She shakes her head but continues cooking.

"Awesome! Lewis and I will be in the den," he turns leaving to wherever the den is.

"Do you know Lewis?"

"Yes ma'am. He lives next door to me." I feel a blush creep up my neck and to my cheeks as our kiss pops back into my mind.

"Oh good. You'll probably see a lot of him while you are here. Please call me Roxi. When I get called Mrs. Taylor, it makes me feel old," She giggles.

We sit in a comfortable silence for a few more minutes until Shane strolls into the kitchen. Shane walks over to Roxi and kisses the back of her head before turning to me, "Poppy, are you ready to see your new room?" Shane asks.

"Sure."

I follow him out of the kitchen to a wide set of stairs. He slows down to where he is walking at the same speed as me.

"Poppy, Jax told me Lewis is here and that he'll be eating dinner with us tonight. If you are not comfortable with him being here, it will be no problem for me to let him know that we are having a guest over tonight."

I blush a little at the thought of him thinking about what I want. "I would rather just get past him finding out I'm staying here now."

Shane scratches his head, almost like he is unsure what to do or say.

Shane walks to the only door that is open out of the four that I can see, and he waits until I walk in before he follows behind me. This room is bigger than the one I have at my father's house. There are two doors to the right, and I am going to assume that one is a closet, and the other is a bathroom. Everything is decorated simply with mostly white.

"You have your own bathroom, the first door on the right, and the closet is the second one. If you think of anything you need, there is a list on the refrigerator you can write it down on, or Roxi would love to take you shopping. You can do whatever you want until dinner time, or if you are wanting to go eat with your friends, that is all right too."

"I don't have anywhere to go, but I have some schoolwork I can do, and I need to unpack some. My father called me out of school for the rest of this week." I see my books and folders for my classwork on a small, simple white desk.

"Okay. Tomorrow, I'll talk to the school about getting your assignments gathered and have Jax bring them home."

I shake my head no. "That won't be necessary, my father brought my homework home before he went out of town."

"All right, I'll let you get settled. If you need anything, just come find Roxi or me. You are welcome anywhere in the house. If you are wanting to go anywhere, please let us know, and your curfews are 11:00 on weeknights and 12:00 on weekends. We will go over the rest once you're settled."

After Shane leaves the room, I unpack the things that I brought with me in about 20 minutes. I shrug off the light sweater I put on before I left my house and look at my guitars leaning against the wall by the closet door.

I haven't seen them in almost six years. I lay each of them down carefully on the large thick rug that is peeking out from under the large bed and open the cases. The stunning wood is shiny and polished, still looking brand new after all these years being locked in the case. My electric guitar is a shiny cherry red with specks of gold glitter that sparkle in the light. I love both of my guitars, but the acoustic is by far my favorite.

There is a quick knock on my door. "Hey Poppy, my dad wanted me to come tell you dinner was ready." I turn around and see that Jax is walking up beside me, but his eyes are locked on the suitcase I placed by the closet door. I haven't decided if I should keep my suitcase in the closet or under the bed. "Are you staying here tonight?" He doesn't sound surprised or mad. Honestly, he sounded like he was joking.

"Probably for a while," I say, and I notice he is looking at my guitar cases.

"Fucking sweet, are these your guitars?"

"Yes, I've been playing for years. I just need some new strings," I chuckle, closing the cases.

"Badass, I can pick some up after practice." Jax helps me put them back against the wall. "Let's go eat, I'm starving. I hope you're hungry. My mom always makes too much food." Jax puts his arm over my shoulder, but when I jerk away, he looks at me concerned.

He looks at me and instead of asking questions, he gently takes my hand, leading me down the stairs. I should be uncomfortable being alone with Jax, but I'm not. I know he won't hurt me.

We are halfway down to the dining room when I realize that I forgot my sweater. "I'll, ugh, be right there. I've got to go get my sweater," I mumble.

He looks down at me with a sad smile, "Don't worry about it. No one will say anything," he says, still leading me to the dining room.

Walking into the dining room, I notice that Lewis's back is to us, Shane and Roxi are seated at the head of the table.

"Poppy, have a seat wherever you want." Roxi puts a napkin in her lap.

Lewis turns around in his chair, and when he sees me his jaw drops, but he doesn't say a word. His expression changes so fast from shock to anger. I look down at the hardwood floor, not wanting to see if he is still looking at me and wait for Jax to sit down.

I jump a little at the sound of a chair scraping against the floor, and I look up to see Jax sitting in the chair next to Lewis. I chose the chair by Roxi. Once everyone is at the table Shane picks up the first dish of food. He puts some on his plate, then passes the large bowl to Lewis. I see that Shane is always the first to grab a new dish of food. Roxi hands me the first bowl that is full of mashed potatoes. I don't put any on my plate. Instead, I place the steaming bowl of fluffy mashed potatoes back on the table.

"Get as much food as you want, Poppy." Roxi leans over to whisper to me, trying not to draw too much attention to us.

I pick the first dish back up and put a spoonful of the fluffy potatoes on my plate. I get a little of everything that Roxi made. We have pot roast with carrots, mashed potatoes, salad and a roll. I can't help but notice that everyone has a lot more food on their plate than mine. Everyone starts talking about their day while eating. They are so calm and comfortable around each other, but I'm a nervous wreck.

I watch as Jax and Lewis practically scarf their food down. I don't know how long I watch them enjoying each other's company and the food before I get the courage to pick up my fork. I scoop up a little bit of the mash potatoes and take my first bite. I have never had mashed potatoes this good before.

I am about to try the roll when someone says my name. I jump and instantly drop my fork. The room goes silent except the sound of the metal fork, clanking against the ceramic plate echoing in the room. Warm tears start to stream down my face as I look at Shane who is asking me a question I can't hear. All I hear is my dad's voice yelling at me for eating without waiting for him to get home for dinner. I'm sucked back into a memory that makes everything and everyone in the Taylor's dining room fade away in a hazy fog.

The memory erases my surroundings, and I'm sitting in my father's dining room as he yells at me and throws dishes at the walls. Once the last dish is smashed, and the floor is covered in food and glass, my father's stomps to where I'm sitting, and he painfully grabs me by my arms. My teeth begin to chatter like he is really shaking me. The only thing that breaks me from the memory is the harsh flinch I make from remembering the slap that echoed across my father's dining room that night.

I hesitate briefly before I finally stutter. "I am so sorry. I know better than to eat without being told to."

"Boys, take your plates and go eat in the kitchen, please. You can come get more food as you want," I faintly hear Roxi.

Behind the blurry mess of tears, I see Jax get up with his plate, but Lewis remains where he is just staring at me with wide, horror-struck eyes.

Jax elbows Lewis's shoulder. He clears his throat and whispers, "Come on, man."

"I am so sorry, Poppy." Shane starts to say, but he pauses and looks at Roxi. "I was just trying to include you, and I see now that I should have just let you talk when you're ready."

I look at him searching his face for any sign of anger. I wipe my face with my napkin. I tentatively pick up my fork again. My handshakes, but I don't let that stop me. I'm starving, and they want me to eat, so I spear a carrot.

Roxi and Shane are patient while I eat. I even got a small helping of seconds from every dish and ate every bite. I know I could eat more, but that is still more than I have eaten in one meal in a while.

I sit there with Roxi and Shane for a few minutes after I clean my plate, feeling embarrassed for my breakdown. I know I should apologize, but that's easier said than done. I stand up quietly and begin to gather all my dishes. I'm shaking, and I know they notice from the sound of my silverware clinking on the plate. Thank goodness, my glass is empty, because with my trembling, I would've spilt my water everywhere.

My embarrassment only doubles when Roxi gently takes the dishes out of my hands.

"It's Jax's night to clear the table and do the dishes." Her kind smile eases my panic a little.

Shane leaves Roxi and me in the dining room.

"The boys are in the den, if you want to go hang out with them. Otherwise, you can go do whatever you would like," Roxi places a light hand on my shoulder before going in the same direction as Shane.

I walk towards the steps to go to my new room, but an open door by the stairs gets my attention. I walk over to peek in, and I get excited when I see a library filled with books. I peek my head in a little further, and I see a sleek black baby grand piano on the far side of the room.

"You can go in." I jump at the sound of Shane coming up behind me. A sharp ache pulses in my sore knee.

I turn around and see Shane walking down the stairs with some papers in his hand.

"That's my wife's favorite room." Shane motions with his free hand to the room.

"Oh, I, ugh, I was just looking." I go to tuck my hair behind my left ear, but I keep forgetting I tied my long hair into a messy bun this morning.

"She loves books and the piano, although she doesn't know how to play it. I got this for her on our first wedding anniversary, because she always had a dream of learning to play, but she put that on hold when she found out she was pregnant." Shane's voice is laced with love, and you can tell that he adores his wife.

I wonder if they would let me play their piano. I think asking to play would be impolite to ask, especially after they have been so kind to take me in and offer to help my father and me.

"If you want to learn to play, Roxi and I will help find you a teacher. There are also tutorials online. You can put your tablet where the sheet music goes and watch the videos."

Shane walks away to the door next to their library. I'm betting that's his office. I take a step into the room, and I instantly feel this invisible magnetic pull drawing me towards the piano. The closer I get, my fingers start to twitch, causing an itching sensation to rapidly make its way through my whole hand.

I sit down on the wood bench and run my fingers longingly over the fallboard. The black painted wood is so smooth, and you can tell by the gleam that they keep the piano polished. I lift the heavy wood of the fallboard that protects the keys. The color of the white is pristine. They aren't colored with age or worn with wear from playing. I lightly place my fingers on the keys. The itching and twitching of my fingers stop as the note flies through my head to the piano, one after another, as I form a mournful melody. I like to play with notes and create my own songs, and this one is a new one for me. As the chords progress, the melody turns hopeful.

The first song fades, followed by another one. This one is entirely different from the first song I played. This composition is light and airy. If the song had lyrics, I would imagine that they would be about love. This piece reminds me of the way my mom and dad used to look at each other, but more than that, the way that Roxi and Shane still look at each other, after all the years they've been married.

I get lost in the freedom of being able to express myself. I glance up still playing, and I'm shocked to see Lewis sitting in an oversized chair. I reluctantly pull my hands away from the keyboard when the song is finished.

Lewis is looking at me with his mouth pulled in a small frown and his eyebrows pulled together. His eyes travel all over my face down my neck, and his slight frown changes into a hard smile as he looks at me. I know he is seeing a lot more of my bruises that I would normally hide under a sweater. I begin to shake as nerves build at the silence in the room.

I open my mouth just slightly, but no words come out. I'm at a loss for words. I didn't seek him out. He came looking for me.

"Poppy, what the fuck happened to you?" His voice is strained, and his teeth are clenched.

"Lewis, what do you want me to say?" I try to swallow my anger, but I just can't stop myself. "This has been my life since my mom died. I had no one, and I woke up every day scared." I try so hard not to yell at him that I am clenching my jaw.

Lewis's eyes widen at my outburst. His breathing becomes more rapid, and his face begins to turn a darker shade of red. Maybe I shouldn't have said anything.

Lewis walks over to me and pulls me into a rough hug. I tense up from the combination of the physical pain that I'm feeling and from the first hug I've really had since I was a little girl. Even though my mind is screaming at me to push Lewis away, my body craves the warmth radiating from his body. I wrap my arms around him and begin to sob quietly into his shirt. Lewis waits for me to stop my blubbering before he pulls away from me.

"Poppy, I'm sorry."

I don't want to talk about this anymore, and I don't want his apology right now. I sit back down and play another song.

"It's about time someone plays that piano. You play beautifully," Roxi says, coming to sit next to me before I can even start another song.

"Badass!" Jax compliments louder than necessary.

I laugh at the simplicity of Jax's remark.

"I didn't recognize any of the songs that you were playing," Shane says.

I fidget next to Roxi. She notices and puts her arm around me. I can't help turning a bright shade of red. "Oh, well, they are my songs."

"You are a very talented young lady. Your mom would be so proud. Maybe one day you can teach me how to play." Roxi compliments me in complete awe.

I look at Roxi and see genuine excitement lighting up her face. "My mom is the one that taught me how to play. I can try my best to teach you something. Is there a certain song you want to play?" I close the fallboard and start to stand up.

Shane moves next to the piano on Roxi's side. He looks happy, and Roxi is chattering on about what songs she would like to learn.

"I look forward to hearing you play more of the piano and your guitars. Just be mindful if people are sleeping. A talent like that should be shared with the world. I would like Roxi to finally learn how to play her piano." They both laugh at Shane's playful joke, and the way they look at each other makes me think there is an inside joke being shared between them.

"Poppy told me she needs new strings for her guitars before she can play them," Jax chimes in with a laugh.

"We will add those to the list of things to get when we go shopping tomorrow. Why don't you go hang out with the boys for a little bit? Lewis can only stay for a little while longer, and I'm sure you would enjoy the den," Roxi suggests before walking out of the room hand in hand with Shane.

Lewis winks and walks out of the room, without waiting for me to see if I want to go hang out like Roxi suggested.

I'm confused by what is going on. Lewis doesn't even ask if I want to do something with him.

"I didn't tell him you're living here for a while. If you don't want him to know, I understand, but he will eventually figure it out."

"I don't care if Lewis knows. He was a big part of my life before my mom died, and I have missed our friendship over the years, but I know it is too late to get it back." I shrug, mostly to make him think I truly don't care, when deep down I do.

"What do you mean he was a big part of your life before your mom died?"

"We were childhood best friends. There was rarely a day when we didn't see each other. I used to cheer for him during all his youth football games."

"I remember. We used to be on the same team. Come on!"

Following Jax through the house, I'm surprised when he brings me to a door that leads to another set of stairs, but this one goes downstairs.

I stop on the last step and look around the massive room. There is so much down here, I almost feel overwhelmed. There's a pool table, a large, overstuffed U-shaped sectional, a huge screen on the wall, and a bar minus the liquor.

"What do you guys usually do down here?"

"We play pool, video games, watch TV, sports, or movies; basically, we just hang out and do whatever we want." Lewis grins and wiggles his eyebrows at me.

I get to pick the video game. They have a lot to choose from which mostly consist of fighting or shooting each other. I don't want to do any of that, so I chose a racing game. I'm not good, but Jax throwing playful insults and a bunch of trash talk makes playing video games more fun.

I don't know how long we play before we are interrupted by Lewis's alarm for him to leave. Jax and I follow him to the living room, but instead of waiting downstairs for Jax while he locks the doors, I go to my room.

I try to get ready for bed, but I forget which door is my closet and which one is my bathroom. I laugh a little at the situation, but the events from the past couple of days don't catch up to me until I lay down for the night, and that's when I allow myself to cry.

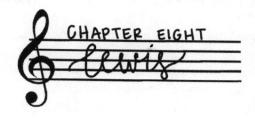

CHAPTER EIGHT

Lewis

Poppy didn't show up to school today, and when I went to her house to talk to her, she basically told me to fuck off. That's probably too harsh to describe what really happened, but when she wouldn't even open the door to tell me to leave, that gives me the same impression.

I need to do a few things at home, but that won't take me very long. I pull my phone out to see if Jax wants to hang out.

LEWIS: you free?

JAX: got to do a few grocery deliveries. Diner or my house after? Jax texts me back almost immediately.

LEWIS: cool. See you at your house.

I'm done with my chores before I hear from Jax, which is annoying, because I'm pretty much out of distractions. I could text Lana and ask if she wants to hook up while I wait, but frankly, she is getting clingy, which is annoying the shit out of me right now. Girls like her are the reason I don't have a girlfriend.

I get in my Jeep, and as I'm fixing to back out when I see Poppy's tiny toy-like car drive past my driveway. I wait long enough for her to get out of the neighborhood before I back out and drive to the diner. I'm at the last stop sign in my street when my phone chimes. I dig my phone out of my pocket, but I don't read the text until I'm stopped.

JAX: headed home. Meet me there!

I toss my phone in the passenger seat without replying, I turn the volume up on my stereo and speed the short distance to Jax's.

When I pull into their driveway and take the round curve all the way around, parking to the side out of the way. I climb out of my Jeep and see Jax waiting for me on his front porch.

"Hey man, you want to stay for dinner?"

67

"Hell yeah! Your mom is a badass cook!"

"All right, I'll meet you in the den, but don't whine like a baby when I kick your ass." He laughs leaving me in the entryway.

Jax goes toward the kitchen, and I head downstairs. Jax is gone long enough for me to get the game set up.

"We're having pot roast." He sits down when he comes in, and before I can say anything, he presses play.

Something must be going on, because Jax's attitude has changed, and he doesn't say as much as he normally does when he is losing. I'm not going to bother asking him what's bothering him, because like me, we won't talk about this unless we want to.

After playing games for almost an hour Jax's trash talk turns from teasing to more aggressive, and I look at him a few times; something is pissing him off.

Jax's phone dings over the sound of the guns shooting through the speakers, interrupts us, I hit pause, and Jax pulls his phone out of his pocket.

"Dinner's ready." Jax almost forcefully puts his controller on the coffee table and gets up to leave.

I turn off the game and follow Jax up the stairs. We get to the living room and Shane stops us.

"Jax, I need to speak with you, Lewis, we'll be there in a few minutes."

Shane looked tense, and not wanting to make whatever is stressing them out more, I head to the dining room and sit in the chair I normally sit in. I text my mom just to let her know I'm okay, and as I'm putting my phone back in my pocket, Shane comes in and has a seat.

"Sorry, Lewis, Jax has to do something for me really quickly." He gives me a tense smile.

"No problem, I was just checking in with my mom." Roxi walks in and places the last dish on the table, then takes her normal spot across from Shane.

We wait a few more minutes in awkward silence before we can hear Jax's footsteps. What gets my attention is the fact that I can hear that he isn't alone. Compared to the heavy sound of Jax's walking, the softer noise of their shoes tapping on the hardwood floor makes me think that whoever is with him is a girl.

"Poppy, sit anywhere you'd like." Roxi's gentle welcome grabs my attention.

Why is Poppy here? I turn in my seat, and my jaw practically hits the fucking floor at the sight of her. What the hell happened to her? She looks like she has shrunk standing next to Jax, but why does she look like someone beat the shit out of her? Anger begins to boil my blood at the thought of someone hurting her like that. She looks lost, with sad glossy eyes that are trying to look anywhere but in my direction.

I'm guessing this is the real reason she didn't open the door for me earlier. She probably didn't want me to see her like this. Poppy really was avoiding me, but not for the reason I thought.

Jax elbows me trying to get my attention as he attempts to pass me the first dish of food. As I am making my plate, I can't help but think about what could have happened to her. I bet her drunken father did this. He has really changed since Poppy's mom died, and the evidence of that is sitting across the table from me.

I'm hoping that she is here, because the Taylors' are going to get her the help that she needs. They'll have the resources and connections to keep her safe and get her whatever kind of help they need. I wonder how her father will react when he finds out that she is moving in here.

I try to act normal as we start eating and carrying on conversations about everyone's day, but trying not to get distracted with Poppy sitting on the other side of the table is hard. Jax begins rattling on about a new game he is wanting to buy with the money he earned after practice filling in for grocery deliveries. Jax's mood is improving, and the tension in his body isn't as tight.

I'm getting some more roast when Shane begins saying Poppy's name, but he stops talking when Poppy drops her fork, and the loud sound of the metal hitting the plate echoes through the dining room.

"I am so sorry. I know better than to eat without being told," Poppy stutters over her apology. Tears begin falling down her face.

Poppy's face pales, and her body tenses. She sways before jerking like she was slapped in the face. Her already glassy eyes widen, and a look of pure horror takes over her beautiful, but bruised face. She looks like she is sucked into a nightmare that she probably lived through.

I'm so focused on Poppy that I don't register Roxi talking to Jax, and me until I feel a sharp jab in my shoulder. Jax clears his throat and whispers, "Come on, man."

We quickly get our plates and leave the dining room. Poppy is crying, and I want to give her a hug, but I think Shane and Roxi can help her feel better than I can.

"Keep your mouth shut about what just happened," Jax says, putting his plate down with more force than necessary.

"All right, man, I won't," taking a seat next to Jax at the bar.

Jax and I eat in silence, and he keeps throwing dirty looks my way.

"Jax, what's up man?"

Jax grunts, but he puts his fork down and turns to me, "I don't know how long Poppy will be here for, but you are going to be nice to her as long as she is, and that includes school."

"All right." We both eat in silence until Shane and Roxi come into the kitchen.

I clear my plate in the trash and rinse it off. "Lewis, I hate to sound rude, but can we have a moment with Jax?"

"Why don't you go find Poppy and see if she wants to play video games." Roxi places a hand on my shoulder.

"Yeah, that sounds good."

I leave the kitchen, and the sound of someone playing the piano fills the living room. I know for a fact that Poppy is the one playing, because no one else in this house can play the piano.

I walk into the library and see Poppy sitting behind the piano. She has her eyes closed, and a soft smile playing at the corner of her lips, and her shoulders are relaxed. Poppy looks at peace, and she has never looked so beautiful.

I sit in an oversized accent chair that is directly across from the piano. I want her to have this moment of peace.

I lose track of how many songs she has played when she finally opens her eyes and notices me. She continues to play until the song ends. She opens her mouth, but she doesn't say anything.

"Poppy, what the fuck happened to you?" I feel like an even bigger asshole, because I know I sound harsher than I want to.

"Lewis, what do you want me to say?" She pauses. The parts on her face that aren't bruised turn red from anger. "This has been my life since my mom died, I had no one, Lewis, I was lonely and scared." I can tell she is trying not to scream at me with each angry word she practically spit at me.

The words she tells me are like a sucker punch straight to my heart. I'm angry that we lived so close to her and never had any idea that this was going on. I can't just sit here and stare at her while she is hurting.

I get up from the chair and walk over to the piano where she is still sitting. I pull her into a rough hug, and I curse at myself for being so forceful, because she is hurt.

Poppy wraps her short arms around me, and she begins crying. I stand there with her pressed against me, staining my shirt with her tears. I wait until she is done shaking to let her go.

"Poppy, I'm sorry." I don't know if the apology is more for what I've done to her or what her father did, but either way, the words don't feel like enough.

I go sit down, and Poppy closes her eyes and begins playing the piano again. Jax walks in and sits in a matching chair next to mine. Poppy begins another song when Roxi practically dances into the room, and Shane follows close behind her.

Every time Poppy closes out one song, she opens her eyes for a few seconds, but this time she stops, because everyone in the house is in the room staring at her.

Roxi moves next to Poppy. "It's about time someone plays that piano. You play beautifully." Roxi is beaming with pride, and I can tell she already loves Poppy.

Everyone begins talking and I take this moment to check my phone. I can feel text notifications vibrate in my pocket going off for a while now, but I've been ignoring them. I have a couple from my parents, but the texts from Lana are annoying the shit out of me.

LANA: Are you free? ;)

LANA: My parents won't be home tonight.

LANA: Lewis?

After the last one with my name is a picture of her in a black lacy bra that can barely hold her tits and matching underwear. I close my messages and tune into their conversation when I hear Roxi say my name. "Lewis can only stay for a little while longer, and I'm sure you would enjoy the den." Then Roxi and Shane leave the room holding hands.

I wink at Poppy and walk to the den. I really can't stay much longer, and if I'm not going to miss curfew again, I need to set an alarm to leave. Poppy and Jax come down to the den with Jax explaining to her what we do here.

We let Poppy pick the game we play, and I noticed that every time she seen a shooting game of some sort, she makes a face, but she ends up settling on a popular racing game.

Jax is calmer this round of games, and he isn't talking a lot of trash, because he doesn't want to make Poppy uncomfortable. He is throwing some harmless insults around, and they're mainly pointed at me, which makes Poppy giggle every time.

Poppy and Jax walks me out and Jax when it is time for me to leave, so I am not late for curfew. The sound of Jax locking his front door cause jealousy to boil my blood, and I realize that I hate the thought of leaving the girl of my dreams here with my best friend.

CHAPTER NINE

My father will be walking in the door from his business trip at any moment. Shane doesn't like that I'm here, but he knows that this is what I want, or what I thought I wanted. I was so busy shopping with Roxi the last couple of days that I didn't have the time or energy to think about this conversation with my father.

"Poppy, are you sure you want to be here for this?" Shane says, while pacing in front of me.

"I think I need to be here." I look at him, and despite his pacing, he looks confident and ready for anything.

"Well, needing and wanting to do something is completely different. If, at any time, you want to leave, you can, and I'll make sure you're safe to do so," Shane says sitting next to me on the couch.

"Thanks." I move my hair out of my face as more nerves make my stomach turn.

"I-," Shane is interrupted by a loud slam coming from the garage door.

"Poppy! Who the hell is parked in my driveway?" my father's angry voice roars filling the room with an echo.

Shane stands up and steps in front of me. I don't bother moving, in a lame attempt not to make my father angrier than he already sounds.

"Hello, Mr. Monroe. I'm Shane Taylor. You may know me from the bars that I own. I would like to discuss a few things concerning Poppy." Shane has his hand outstretched, waiting for my dad to shake his hand.

"I'm going to have to disagree with you." My father looks my way with a smile that creeps me out.

I gulp, I'm in huge trouble.

"What have you done now?" My father taunts me.

"I haven't-" I stop talking. Nothing I say will matter to my dad.

"Mr. Monroe, Poppy hasn't done anything, but the evidence on her face and arms is enough to tell me that you have. Poppy is no longer safe here with you anymore."

My dad attempts to take a few steps to the side so he can get a better look at me, but I move to where I'm completely hidden behind Shane.

"Poppy, I thought I told you not to leave the house." He literally spits at me.

I need to get out of here. I really should have listened to Roxi and Shane's advice.

"Mr. Taylor, you need to get some help, and as I have stated before Poppy is not safe here," Shane pauses, trying to get that to sink in. "Poppy is going to come live with my family while you get the help that you need."

"Who the fuck do you think you are? You have no right to come into my house and stick your nose into my business. I'll treat my daughter how I see fit." My father is becoming more animated while he talks, waving his arms around.

"I could have brought the authorities with me, but out of courtesy of us being friends, I came here on my own." Shane motions for me to sit back down on the couch, and once I have, he sits next to me again. "You want to know why I think I can interfere into your lives? We have known each other for a long time, and I know that Ellenor would be devastated with how you treat Poppy if she was still alive. The best thing for Poppy is for her to come live with my family and-"

"OVER MY DEAD BODY!!!" My father screams, interrupting Shane.

"You only have two options. One is for you to get help and let Poppy come live with me, or I can call the police, and they, along with DHS, will get involved. I'll leave that decision up to you, but Poppy will not be living here until you get better."

"She is a liar, and whatever she said was a lie." My father stomps his foot almost like a child throwing a fit.

"You have changed since Mom died," I whisper.

"You don't get to talk about her! You took her from me! All of this is your fault!" My father plops into the chair across from us in mock defeat.

"Your wife had cancer. Her death was untimely and tragic, and in no way Poppy's fault. She doesn't deserve this maltreatment that she has endured from her own father. Ellenor loved Poppy more than anyone or anything in this world. She would never forgive you for hurting her daughter."

I watch the color draining from my father's face as his whole world comes crashing down on him. He leans forward in his chair and puts his head in his hands.

"Poppy, go pack your things. I need to speak to Mr. Taylor privately." The softness of his voice shocks me, the sad almost kindness doesn't belong to the monster that I've lived with for the past ten years.

My father's head pops up when he hears me stand up, and the tears pooling in his eyes has me stopping.

My father is playing both of us right now. There is no way he really feels remorse right now. I want to call him out, but I want to get the hell out of here more.

"Thank you, sir," I whisper and bolt from the room before he can change his mind.

There's nothing here that I really need, nor want to take with me. Roxi has gotten me everything I could need, plus so much more. I go to my closet and look through my clothes one last time. I take a couple of my favorite sweaters and a few pairs of shoes, but other than that everything else can stay.

I walk back into my room, I'm shocked to see my father standing in the doorway. I want to throw the clothes and shoes that I'm carrying at him, but I resist.

"Poppy, can I talk with you for a few minutes?"

I instinctively take a few steps back, running into the wall into the door jamb of my closet.

"Mr. Taylor is in the hallway," he sounds like a child mocking someone and rolls his eyes.

I still don't say anything. My father comes in and sits at the foot of my bed. He is watching me, and I can see the look of mischief twinkle in his eyes. He is up to something. I walk around my bed and sit on the bay window bench, because that is the furthest place I can sit from my father, but I still feel like he is too close to me as the room shrinks around us.

"Poppy, I don't always know what I'm doing. I let my drinking and anger get the best of me as I grieve your mother's death. I take my anger out on you, and it has taken Mr. Taylor coming here for me to see that I have a problem,"

I sit up straighter, the more my dad talks. Listening to him sit there and lie to me is making me nauseous. I've seen my father at work and in front of a jury, and he is acting just like that. He is trying to appeal to my emotions and make me feel guilty for what he is guilty of.

"I let my drinking and my anger out on you. I know that what I've been doing to you is wrong, but I've dug myself so deep into this mindset I don't know how to get out. Mr. Taylor has given me some numbers of people to call, and I promise you that I'll get better." My father heaves a heavy sigh. "All I wanted was your mother and I knew what kind of dad she wanted me to be, and after she died, I lost all of that."

The more he continues, the more I feel like shouting. I hate this show he is putting on more than all the times he has hurt me. I drop the clothes I still have cradled in my arms. I fist my hands into tight balls. I'm trying hard to not get up and hit him the way he has done me.

"I was blinded by my anger and hate to see what was really happening here," my father continues, not noticing that I'm getting angrier, the more he talks. "I see your mother when I look at you. You look exactly like her, and that rips my heart every time I need to remember that she is no longer here with me."

I sit and wait for the right time to say something. He hasn't finished his speech, yet and I know he is just coming off as remorseful in front of Shane.

"If going to the Taylor's house to stay isn't what you want, then you can stay here, and we can figure out a way for me to get help and for you to stay safe at the same time." For the first time since, he sits on my bed, and my father looks up at me.

"What do you want?" I say with confidence because I know what he wants. He wants me gone as much as I want to leave.

"What the hell did you say?" he howls, standing up facing me. He sinks on to his heels with his knees slightly bent. He looks like he is waiting for the right moment to strike out at me.

Shane, who is standing in the hall, watching us, swiftly gets in front of me. He is shielding me from my father's inevitable attack.

"What do you want? I don't want to hear what you think I would want or whatever it is you think Mr. Taylor wants to hear. I want to know what you want." Talking to my father with this kind of emotion and conviction is easy with Shane in front of me acting as my protector.

"I never want to see you or have anything to do with you again. You can have what you want here, but then I want you to get in your car and never come back. I'll give you one hour." He strides out of my room with angry stomping of his expensive shoes tapping on the hardwood floor. I've grown to really hate that sound.

I stand where I am at with my jaw dropped in disbelief. This feels so surreal. I'm going to be free; I won't have to live in this nightmare anymore. Even though I have some good memories here, I'm more than happy to begin a new life where I don't have to constantly fear what is going to happen to me next.

Shane gives me a one-armed hug. "Don't worry, Poppy. We'll take care of you."

"Thank you. Let's get the last of my stuff, so we can go home." I pause, wait, did I just reference the Taylor's house as home. What if he doesn't like that?

Shane picks up my things off the floor and puts them on the bed. I do one more walk-through of my room and closet, but I am happy leaving the rest here. I didn't pack much, just some books and the rest of my notebooks. I put them in a suitcase and tell Shane that I only have one bag and that I am ready to go.

He doesn't reply, so I wait for about ten more minutes before he comes back to my old room. I don't see anything else that I want. I grab a tote and stuff the armful of things on my bed before turning back to Shane.

"Did you get everything you wanted? Is your laptop or tablet at my house?"

"I have everything I want. I don't have a tablet or a laptop."

"What did you use when you needed one for school?"

"I would use the computers at school to do my homework."

Shane grabs my bag from me, and we walk downstairs in silence.

"You will need to leave your cell phone on the coffee table. That was one of the few conditions he had," Shane says, once we reach the living room.

I place my phone on the coffee table. I'm not sad about leaving my phone behind, because the only number in there is my dad's.

Shane walks as I look around the living room one last time. I see the piano, and I want to get the music out of the bench. I lift the seat up and gather all the sheet music in there.

"I'm going to meet you at home. I need to stop and get you a phone."

77

I'm not sure what to say. I don't like the idea of him getting me a phone, I know they are expensive.

I walk to the foyer and get my purse before turning back to have one last look around the house. We walk out of the house, and after I close the door with more force than necessary, I begin to feel lighter.

"Thank you, Shane. I truly appreciate everything you are doing for me." I give him a rough hug, making my body hurt from not being careful enough.

I hope he can feel how grateful I am. He rubs my back instead of hugging me. I try to push the insecurity of him not returning my embrace out of my mind because I know he is trying not to hurt me or push me further than my comfort level will allow.

"All right, I'll meet you at home. Do you need anything else for school tomorrow?"

"No, I have all I need." Shane gets in his truck but doesn't leave yet.

I walk next door to Lewis's house. We all thought I would be safer parking there instead of my house so if I needed to leave, I could either go into the Jacobs' house until I was safe to leave or drive away. I open my car door and look at Lewis's house. I have some good memories here, but I'm not going to miss this place.

A honk makes me jump, but Lewis's shiny red Jeep pulls up next to me, and I instantly feel a little better.

"You parked in my spot," he jokes.

"Lewis, do you ever feel like you are going to fall out of your Jeep as you speed down the road?"

"Do you feel like you're going to fly out of your mini with the convertible top down?" he laughs.

"Touché, but I wouldn't know. I wasn't allowed to have the top down. I'll have to ask Shane if he is comfortable with me driving with it down."

"What do you mean by 'asking Shane if he is comfortable with it'?"

"Things at home with my father aren't good right now, so I'm going to stay with the Taylors for a little while."

"Poppy," he says, running his fingers through his hair, "I never apologized for the way I treated-"

"Lewis, this has nothing to do with you. It's about my father and me right now. There's just too much to say, and now I really don't want to talk to you about it."

"Can I text you later?" Lewis runs his fingers through his hair making it look messy and perfect at the same time.

"Sure, I'll have to give you my new number tomorrow."

"Sounds good, you can hang out with Jax and me at lunch, if you want."

I can feel him watching me, waiting for a response. The emotions from today are catching up to me. I climb in my car. I know he was trying to be a friend just now, by trying to apologize and inviting me to hang out with him and his friends. Everything is happening so fast, and I feel like I'm falling into a hole with no way out.

My finger hovers over the button that puts the top down on my Mini, and I hesitantly press the little button. My hand is shaking but I press down on the small button and the top lifts quietly and moves back faster than I thought it would. I sneak a peek at Lewis, and he is smiling at me.

I give him a little wave. "I'll think about lunch tomorrow."

I back out of Lewis's driveway, and unlike the first time I left my father's house to go stay with the Taylors, I feel a new sense of freedom lightening the stress I've carried around for the last few years. I guess my mom was right. Senior year is going to be my best year yet.

Jennifer Froh

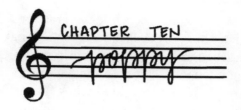

CHAPTER TEN

Two weeks have already gone by, and I'm still trying to learn a new routine and get comfortable with having new rules. I get overwhelmed easily, and I'm a hard time getting out of the headspace where you are told to do something or you're going to be in trouble for the smallest things, but not seeing or hearing from my father since I moved out has helped some of the anxiety. I sometimes think he'll pop up out of nowhere to hurt me or drag me back home.

Roxi and Shane went over their rules and expectations with me the day after I officially moved in, and there are very few of them. I won't break their rules, mostly because I don't want to let them down, but because I want to earn their trust and respect. They could have let me go to a foster home, but they chose to let me stay here. They even brought up the idea of me going to a counselor. I think I will take them up on that one day, but I'm not ready to add another massive change to my life.

"Poppy!" I hear Jax shout from a distance breaking through my period thoughts.

I look up from digging my keys and headphones out of my backpack, "What's up?"

"Where the hell do you think you're going? The field is this way!" Jax is wearing what I've learned is practice gear and is pointing in the opposite direction of my car.

Lewis must have heard Jax yell for me, because he jogs up behind Jax and claps a hand down on his padded shoulder. Both look way too good for just practice, so I can only imagine how they would look for a game. Maybe I'll see if Roxi will go with me, so I don't have to go alone.

"I'm putting my backpack up." I sass, sticking my tongue out at them.

"You can do your homework while we practice." Jax quips.

"I finished all my homework last hour in study hall!" I roll my eyes.

Jax's smile fades, and he begins to jog in my direction. I can hear his cleats making a tapping sound on the pavement. When he reaches me, he bends down until he is a few inches from my face. "Why the hell do we never see you in the library?" Thank goodness his breath is minty fresh, or else we would be having some words about personal space and hygiene.

"I like the tables." I shrug.

"Damn, and you didn't invite me to sit with you," Jax dramatically places a hand over his chest, acting like I hurt his feelings.

"I didn't know you wanted to sit with me, and you would only distract me from my homework." I laugh uncomfortably.

"Well, shit, she does have a brain," Lewis mocks, giving me a flirtatious wink.

I hear someone from the distance blow a whistle, and then, "TAYLOR! JACOBS! YOU'RE LATE! FIVE LAPS!"

When they run in the direction of the field, I finish putting my stuff up. A few girls pass me, giggling about something, but none of us acknowledge each other, and I don't bother looking to see who they are. After I lock my door, I make my way to the football field.

I'm almost to the stadium when I hear the coaches yelling for the team to do drills, and I laugh, because I can hear them, and I'm about halfway through the parking lot.

I get a weird feeling in my stomach and a chill runs down my spine like something's not quite right. I look at my feet as I quicken my pace. I accidentally run into someone, and I look up, and fear paralyzes me.

"Dad!" I swallow hard. "What are you doing here?"

"I'm here to see my daughter." He grabs onto my arm in a painfully tight grasp. "We need to talk."

I can smell the rancid scent of whiskey and sweat on him. My stomach rolls, and I must fight the impulse to vomit. I try to pull myself free from the death grip he has on me, but he yanks me and begins dragging me to a side door of the school. The pain radiating from my arm is getting more intense with every step we take.

My dad pushes the door open with his free hand and shoves me through the door. I fall onto my knees and hands on the hard tile that probably hasn't been properly cleaned since the school was first built. I see my dad's shiny loafers appear on my right side. I take in a shaky breath. My father crouches down and roughly pull me up to my feet by digging his nails into my wrist.

Once I'm on my feet my father pulls me to the first classroom door, and he peeks in to check and see if the room is empty.

"Dad, Let-," my father turns to me with his lips pulled back, in almost a sneer.

"Shut up!" He spits through his teeth with his hand raised threatening to hit me.

He looks back in the room, and without any warning, he gives my arm a violent pull until I stumble in front of him and into the classroom. I feel my father's hands push into me so hard that I fall into the teacher's desk. I somehow manage to put my hands out in time to catch myself before I fall painfully and get seriously hurt.

My father turns around and for a brief second, I think he has come to his senses, and he's going to leave, but he just slams the door closed, blocking my exit with the heavy wooden door.

"Did you seriously believe I was going to leave you alone? You are an absolute imbecile, if you truly thought I wasn't going to come back for you. You humiliated me, and for that, you must pay." My father circles me, sizing me up.

This is going to be worse than anything that I endured while living with him. I need to get out of here, but I think I'll be lucky enough to get out of here with my life. I've never been this terrified of what he is going to do to me before. This is personal to him. I'm having to pay for someone finding out, and he is here to collect his debt. I take a few big steps away from him. He glowers at me and stalks slowly in my direction. I don't know if that is more terrifying than him advancing on me at full speed.

"You ruined my fucking life! First, you took my wife, and now you took my job!" he shouts at me with a red face.

I see a flesh-colored flash out of the corner of my eye, before a sharp slap from Dad backhanding me across my cheek. This is my first piece of collateral to compensate for the losses.

"Did you know I got fired last week!" My father hit me again. "Someone anonymously called my boss about my drinking. They said I was getting out of hand, and they were concerned."

Before my father has a chance to strike at me again, I try to run from him, but he grabs ahold of my hair and yanks me back to him. I yelp at the pain of my hair being ripped from my scalp. He lets go of me long enough to dig my shoulder into my spine. I cry out from the pain, and he gives a satisfied chuckle.

Dad's long slender fingers grasp my shoulders, digging his fingernails in, piercing through my skin. Then he pushes me back into the teacher's desk, but this time, I'm not able to catch myself. I feel the side of my head connect with the hard corner of the desk before I fall to the floor with a painfully loud thud. I reach up, touch my temple and feel my fingers immediately get drenched in warm liquid. I move my hand and try to look at the dark red blood covering my fingers, but they look blurry.

I hear his hoarse voice echo in my head, but whatever insults he is slurring my way doesn't register. My ears begin to ring as pulse after pulse of splitting pain shoots through my head. I put my head in my hands as I hunch over in pure agony.

My father's wrath keeps going as his fists and feet connect with different parts of my body. I'm too distracted from the pain in my head to feel the hits from my dad. His foot hits me powerfully into my side, causing me to fall to my side.

My dad takes full advantage of me falling out of my somewhat protective hunch I was in and begins hitting and kicking me with renewed energy. They are more spread-out landing all over my body. Every time I try to cover my face, my dad pushes them away, clawing at the skin on my hands and arms then followed by a quick hard punch landing somewhere on my face.

After what feels like an eternity, each blow comes slower and slower until they stop. I try to look up at my dad between blurry slits, I'm pretty sure my eyes are swelling. He is looking down at me, and I'm sure if I could see his expression, I'm sure his face would be one of joyful satisfaction. I receive one last swift kick in my left thigh that jerks my body back from the force. My father leaves the room, laughing eerily as I lay there crying in misery.

At first, I don't move, mainly out of fear that if I do, I'll hurt myself more, but I know I need to get out of here before my dad decides to come back. I roll from my side onto my hands and knees with great difficulty. I try to get on my feet by getting on the ball of my left foot, but my foot slips, and my knee hits the floor. Maybe I should just stay here and call for help. I reach to my back pocket, but I don't feel my phone. I curse to the empty classroom; I probably dropped my things when my father grabbed me.

I can't stand up, so I have no other option. I slowly begin to crawl to the door, but with every move, I make excruciating pain shoots through my body.

I make my way slowly to the door; this may be good leverage to help me get myself to my feet. I brace my hands on the door frame for support and clumsily get up to my feet. My legs scream in protest at the weight being put on them, but I take a couple of shaky steps into the hall. My legs shake, and the hallway begins to spin.

I reach out and touch the wall closest to me. I move until I'm leaning against the wall. I walk slowly, using the wall to keep me up. I try not to focus as I leave a trail of blood behind me.

When I finally get to the door that my father dragged me through, my stomach turns, and vomit rises burning my throat. I push the door open and look around, wanting to make sure that my father is not out there.

I don't see anything between the swollen slits of my eyes, and all I can hear is the sounds coming from the football field as the team still practices. I stumble through the parking lot in the direction of my car. I can feel my tears mix with the blood that is staining my face as I try not to panic.

I fumble with the handle on my car door as I try to pull the door open, but it won't budge. I need to go find my phone and keys, but walking is getting hard, as I'm feeling more and more lightheaded, and I'm starting to have trouble seeing out of my swelling eyes If I can't find my keys and phone, I will have no choice but to go to the field, which is not what I want to do. I don't want that many people to see me.

I limp back towards where my dad grabbed me. I can feel the sweat and panic set in, when I don't see anything on the sidewalk. I keep moving slowly and clumsily back in the direction I just came from.

I round the building where the side door is, and I see my notebook, keys, and phone scattered on the grass where my father pulled me into the school. I try, in desperate attempts to get my things, but I fall onto the grass. I reach out and, my hand touches the cool metal of my car keys. I feel around more, and I touch my notebook. I bring my journal over to my side, and then I desperately flail my arm around trying to find my phone. My hand hits something hard, but I quickly find out that the object I found is too round to be my phone. I feel around more, and I eventually feel something else. I pick this new object up, and I can feel the rhinestones that are on my otherwise smooth phone case.

I try to stand back up, so I can get back to my car, but I fall. I desperately try to get up again, but slower this time. I get onto my hands and knees, tuck my notebook into the waistband on my pants and crawl through the limited grass. Crawling through the grass is easier, but the hard pavement makes me want to give up, and lying on the ground, waiting for someone to find me sounds like a better option. I just don't want to give my father the satisfaction in case he is somewhere out here watching me.

My hands and knees are getting scraped on the rocks in the parking lot, but I finally make my way back to my car with far more difficulty than I would like. I reach up and pull on the shiny chrome handle, and I practically cry tears of joy when the door opens. I climb in, and once I'm fully sitting in my seat, I struggle to pull the door closed and lock the door.

Exhaustion overtakes me and I'm beginning to fall asleep, but I need to call for help. I pull my notebook out of my pants and toss it onto the seat. I clutch my phone, lifting it up, but my hand falls back into my lap. I try to call Shane, but I can barely see my small screen from my lap to turn it on speaker. I kick my foot out, searching for the brake pedal to turn my car on, and when I feel my brake pedal, I push down and start my car.

I unlock my phone again. "Hey, Siri, call Shane." Ringing fills my car.

The phone rings several times, and I am beginning to think he isn't going to answer. "Hey Poppy, I am in a meeting. Can I call you back?" Shane's voice breaks the loud trilling sound.

"Shane!" I whimper loudly.

I hear a chair scraping on the floor in the background and the faint sound of Shane telling who he is in the meeting with that he needs to take this phone call, and he'll be back.

"Poppy, what's going on?" I can tell he is alarmed by the rising of his tone.

"Shane, I am in the parking lot at school-"

Shane interrupts me. "Good, you're not hurt then." He pauses and takes a few breaths which I'm assuming is to calm himself down. "Poppy, I really need to get back to this meeting, if this isn't an emergency-,"

This time I talk over him, "Shane, I'm hurt, my-"

Shane doesn't let me finish talking, and I'm slowly getting angry. "Did you get in a car accident? You're at school, go get Jax at football practice. Stay on the phone with me, and let me talk to the coach."

"No, I can't, go to the field. I wasn't in a car accident. My-"

Shane cuts me off again. "How would you get hurt if you didn't get in the car accident? Poppy, you sound like you're slurring."

I just need to finish. I'm getting dizzy, and I just want to go to sleep. My head falls back onto the head rest of my seat.

"Shane, just listen, I-"

"Poppy," Shane starts, but I don't let him finish.

"Please, Shane, please just let me finish. I'm getting really." My stomach rolls, and I fight to not throw up. "I was on my way to the football field when my father grabbed me and took me to an empty classroom. I managed to get back to my car, but I'm hurt and scared." My voice cracks. I want to go to sleep.

"Poppy, I'll be there as soon as I can. I'm in the city." Shane's voice sounds like it's getting further away, almost like he is in a tunnel. Shane is saying something that I'm not able to understand.

I lean over and rest my head onto my car window. I close my eyes and almost fall asleep from the cold glass cooling me. I just need to get some sleep, and I'm sure I'll feel better.

A loud tapping sound scares me. A scream echoes through my car, and I lift my head off my window. I try to open my swollen eyes more, but what I can see is only a blurry haze of white and gray.

"Poppy, it's Coach Denver. Mr. Taylor called me, and he asked if I could wait with you until he could get here."

I fumble around my door trying to find the unlock button.

"Coach, it's unlocked," I yell as loud as my dry throat will let me when I hear the click of the door unlocking.

The door opens followed by a string of curse words.

"Fuck," several more cusswords come out of Coach Denver, "Poppy, I need to get you some help."

"No, I want Shane here."

My phone starts to ring, filling the silence. I rest my head back on the head rest, but I don't answer the phone. I don't have the energy to talk anymore. I hear the rustling of the coach's windbreaker, and the ringing is replaced by a high-pitched screeching.

"Hello! Poppy, are you there!?" Roxi's voice is high pitched, and she is yelling loudly.

"Poppy, your mom is on the phone," Coach Denver encourages.

"Coach Denver, go get my boy. He needs to be with her. I'm sorry, but she doesn't know you! I'm on my way!"

"Yes, ma'am, I'll call Coach Clarks. I don't think I should leave her alone." I hear footsteps, but I can hear a little bit of what he is saying on the phone.

"Poppy! Did he hurt you?" she chokes up.

I don't reply, and Roxi is repeating herself, getting louder each time I don't say anything.

"Mrs. Taylor, I just got off the phone with Coach Clarks. Jax is on his way. Poppy is in rough shape. Most of her face is swollen, and she is covered in blood. I don't know where the blood is coming from. There's no way she isn't in a world of pain; there is no way she isn't," Coach drawls in a lazy southern accent.

Roxi makes a sound like she is also in pain.

"Poppy!" I can hear Jax yell from a distance, followed by the echo of cleats clapping against the pavement getting closer and closer. "Shit! Poppy, I should have made sure you got to the stadium safely." I feel a large hand touch my hand lightly.

I begin crying again, and I lean toward Jax. He removes his hands and lets me lay on his chest. I can feel the hard uncomfortable plastic of his pad, but I don't go back to laying back in my seat. He puts his arms around me lightly.

"Jax, you didn't know this was going to happen just as much as I didn't. The only person at fault here is my father."

I hear the faint sound of Coach Denver saying "fuck," under his breath. I've learned that Coach Denver cusses quite a bit.

"Coach is letting everyone out of practice early, so the parking lot is clear when the ambulance gets here. Everyone is getting ready to head out. Can you keep them from coming over here?"

"Lewis," I whisper to Jax.

"No, Poppy. He isn't coming over here." I can't tell for sure, but I don't think Jax liked that I mentioned Lewis's name.

I feel heavier, and I want to fall asleep. I jerk at the sound of tires squealing next to me in the parking lot.

"Badass driving, Mom." I hear Jax try to defuse the situation, but I can hear the tension in his voice.

"Jax, let me see her," Roxi demands softly.

Jax sits me back on the seat of my car. "Jax, go get changed. Coach Denver can watch over us."

I feel the tender touch of Roxi as she tentatively tries to move hair off my face, but it's difficult since my hair sticking to drying blood. I lean forward again and rest my head on what feels to be her slender shoulder.

Roxi gives up trying to get the hair that is glued to my face from my own blood. She starts rubbing my back and hums soothingly to me. I notice that she is humming one of the songs I wrote.

"I wrote that song about you," I whisper, but I know Roxi can hear me.

"That's my favorite one that I've heard you play. I'm very flattered. Thank you very much, Poppy."

"It's one of my favorite songs to play. Your song is like the one I composed for my mom, but I haven't played it in a very long time. It's been easier to play sad music, but the more I'm around you and your family, the more I want to play happier songs."

"That's true. A lot of your compositions are sad but look at all you have been through. You are a wonderful and strong young woman. You have a true talent when it comes to music. I hope Jax will meet woman half as special as you."

"Hey, whatever woman I land will be a badass, and you'll love her for taking me off your hands," I hear Jax joke from somewhere behind Roxi.

He must have gotten back from the locker room in time to listen to what Roxi was saying. I begin to laugh, but I immediately stop, wincing from the pain.

"Oh! Thank goodness, Shane is here." Roxi doesn't move. She stays, holding me up.

"Poppy! I called for an ambulance," Shane slams his truck door. "I see that Lewis is still here. Jax, after Poppy is taken care of, can you see if Lewis will help you get her car home and back to your truck before you go to the hospital?"

Shane opens the passenger door, and he takes my hand delicately. A few minutes pass where I feel safe and loved. Roxi relaxes when sirens are heard from a short distance.

Shane is talking about what needs to be done with Lewis and Jax. "I want to ride to the hospital with Poppy. Can you guys also get my SUV home?"

Roxi begins humming, and I instantly relax more. "Ma'am, we need to check out the girl," a nice paramedic interrupts my lullaby.

She reluctantly lays me back gently against the seat, and I don't have the strength to hold my head up. I'm tired of having to sit up. I just want to let sleep overtakes me.

I feel light fingertips touch various parts of my face, "Miss, can you tell me your name?"

"Poppy," a finger moves to the gash in my head, and I wince away

89

from the contact.

"Can you tell me your full name now?"

"Poppy Fae Monroe."

"Perfect. Let's get you loaded up, Ms. Monroe. We'll take good care of you,"

I feel my body begin to float as I drift off to dreams of my mom, waiting for me with her arms open waiting for me. I run into her arms, and I finally feel at home. I can't help but think how much I've missed her.

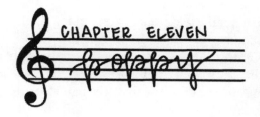

CHAPTER ELEVEN

Waking up in the hospital is overwhelming and scary. At first you are disoriented and confused. The first thing I hear is beeping sounds, and then the smell hits you. I wouldn't say the smell is bad, just not comforting. The room is very stark and clinical, adorned in too much white.

The last thing I want is for someone to ever see me this way. I'm sure there have been many times in my life that I should've gone to the hospital or the doctors, due to my father's violent punishments, but this is the first time I've ever actually made it here. I normally patch myself up the best I can.

I look around, and I see that Roxi is the only one here. She is sitting in a chair next to my bed flipping through a magazine.

"Water," I hoarsely stammer.

"Oh, thank goodness, Poppy. I've been so worried. I'm so happy to see you awake. Let me go get a nurse and I'll see if you can have some water." Roxi has tears in her eyes, but she lightly kisses my forehead before she jogs out of the room.

I'm so grateful that Roxi is here with me. I think if I was alone, I would have been more scared than I was when I woke up. I don't know why Roxi didn't just call for a nurse.

"Hey sweetie, how are you feeling?" a nurse in cranberry-colored scrubs comes in and grabs a clipboard.

If I could roll my eyes I would. I mean, I probably look worse than I feel. I should probably be polite, because she is just doing her job.

"Poppy was asking for some water when she woke up," Roxi says, before I can even answer the nurse.

"Poppy, you had a tube down your throat to help you breathe. What is your pain level on a scale of one to ten?" The nurse hands me a chart with the levels I need to reference, "one being the lowest ten being the highest," she adds.

"An eight or nine." My throat burns, I really wish she would let me drink something.

She asks me some questions that Roxi and Shane can't answer, like if I have any allergies and family history of illnesses that she is scribbling on her charts. She leaves the room but never tells me if I can have any water.

"Poppy, I'm so happy you're okay, considering..." Roxi looks away with glassy eyes.

"I'm sorry you had to see me like that."

"You have-" There is a knock on the door. Then the nurse from before walks in with a Styrofoam cup and one of those plastic hospital cups filled with ice water.

"Start with the ice chips, and if that doesn't hurt or upset your stomach, you can move onto small sips of water." She places them on the table and wheels it over my lap. She then grabs the remote off the side of my bed and adjusts the bed to where I'm in a seated position. "Press the call button if you need anything." She then leaves Roxi and me alone.

Roxi sits on the edge of my bed and hands me the cup with the ice. I pick out a small piece and begin to eat. The ice is helping to soothe my throat, but my thirst is still not quenched.

I grab the handle of the cup and try to lift it, only I don't move but an inch or two, due to pain shooting through me.

"Rox, I brought the stuff you asked me to bring, and I also brought you some food. You need to eat, and frankly you need to get some sleep, too," Shane announces upon his arrival into my room without knocking.

"Poppy, I'm so relieved to see you awake. How are you feeling?" Shane sounds cheerful.

"I'm good, considering everything that happened yesterday." I try to lift the cup of ice water, but the pain is too much, and I give up.

Bless Roxi for her observation skills, because she lifts the cup to my mouth, and she even holds the straw in place as I take several small sips.

"Poppy, do you know how long you have been in the hospital?" Shane's sharpness turns serious.

I begin to worry as I look between Shane and Roxi. "My father attacked me yesterday at school."

"Poppy, I don't know how to tell you this, but-" Someone knocks on the door, and I'm beginning to feel more annoyed with the interruptions.

"I hear Sleeping Beauty has finally woken up." I don't recognize the voice coming from the door. A beautiful middle-aged woman in light blue scrubs washes her hands, then turns back to me. "I am Doctor Lidia Marchall. I'm needing everyone to step out, so I can check on you."

"Um, can Roxi stay with me please?"

"Yes, dear, if that will make you feel more comfortable."

Shane kisses Roxi and me lightly on the forehead and walks out still looking worried.

"Poppy, can you scoot to the edge of the bed?"

I bend my knees and try to lift my butt in the air so I can scoot, but they won't go, as my legs and arms are protesting the weight I'm putting on them. I need to try something different this time. I try to just slide down the bed, but that still hurts. The doctor is watching me closely. She is making me nervous. I do a little wiggle, and I move about an inch, but nothing tremendous. The doctor hits the call button on the railing on the bed, and a few minutes later, I'm still struggling to scoot to the edge of the bed when a nurse comes in.

"Why does she need to move to the edge of the bed? She just woke up?" Roxi questions the doctor.

"I don't normally make my patients move this early after being unconscious for as long as Poppy was, but she is presenting to be more alert and aware than I thought. The sooner she moves around, the sooner she'll get to go home, and I think she would recover better at your house than here with her history."

The nurse climbs on the bed next to me and puts my arm over her shoulder and the doctor does the same, but she stays standing. And they each put an arm around my back, and they lift me up, I scream from the shooting pain starting at my rib cage and shooting through my back until my whole body goes limp.

"We know, sweetie. Go ahead and scream all you want. We are almost there. You're doing a great job." The nurse is trying to soothe me, but I really want to yell at her to shut up.

My head falls back, and I turn my head toward the door, but I find Roxi pausing at the foot of my bed with her right thumb nail being chewed anxiously.

"I need to examine you and check your bandages. Do you consent to me touching you, so I can assess your injuries?" the doctor asks nicely, but professionally.

I look at Roxi, and she nods her head letting me know that I will be okay, but I see the nurse grab a clipboard, and then she stands next to the doctor.

"I will be asking questions, and I need to answer them to the best of your knowledge. There may be some lapses in your memory, I don't want you to worry, because that is common with head injuries, so if you can't remember, just say so."

The nurse does the routine things like my blood pressure and temperature. "Poppy, do you give me consent to do my examination?" the doctor repeats herself.

I nod my head. I'm not sure what to say. I'm really embarrassed about my injuries, and I don't even want the nurse and her to see, even though they are medical professionals.

"Honey, I know this is a very difficult time for you, but I need a verbal confirmation. Do you want Mrs. Taylor to step out of the room for this part?"

I don't like that she called Roxi Mrs. Taylor. That just seems too formal. "I want Roxi to stay, and yes, you can do your examination."

"Thank you. If at any time you need me to stop or take a break, please let me know. There is going to be some pressure, and at any time, the pain is more than a five just give me that number."

She begins putting pressure closer to my hips. The more she pokes around, the more pain I feel.

"Seven," I hiss through my teeth, trying not to jerk away from her when she gets to the bottom of my rib cage.

The nurse is taking notes, and the doctor hits a more tender spot around the middle part of my sides.

"Nine," tears are now falling down my face.

I say a few more numbers before she moves to my shoulders. The pain is around four, so she moves on, asking me questions like what today's date is and if I remember the date of the incident.

I get the bandage on my head changed after some cleaning. The doctor and nurse step outside to go over the notes. Roxi comes and sits next to me on my bed. She lightly takes my hand in hers.

"You're doing a great job." I lay my head on Roxi's shoulder, and all I want to do right now is go back to sleep.

A few minutes later, the doctor and nurse walks back in. They look at each other before the doctor wheels a little stool that tucked away somewhere in front of me.

"Poppy, what I have to say may be overwhelming and possibly scary, but I need you to understand how serious this is, and I want to make sure you are healthy. I need to know some more information from you."

"What type of information?"

"I need to know about what has happened to you previously to the incident that led you here."

"I'll tell you what I can." This is going to probably be about what my dad has done to me in the past.

"First, you have been unconscious for a week and a half." The doctor waits and lets that information sink in. "I have some concerns about previous head trauma and damage to your rib cage. Do you know if you have had a concussion before or how many you may have had?"

"I never went to the doctor's office or the hospital after I was hurt. It was rare when he would go after my face or head at the beginning, but the more often he hurt me or the more he drank, the sloppier or careless he got. I have hit my head several times on the hardwood floors he has at his house or on furniture and stuff like that." I put my hand over my mouth.

OH, NO! WHAT DID I JUST DO!

My reaction to what I said has alarmed all the women in the room. They all look concerned. Roxi sniffles, and I know better than to look at her, because if I see her crying, I will, too.

"Poppy, you are safe here. Your father cannot get to you." This comes from the nurse that is writing something down.

"How do you know that?"

They ignore my question, and Dr. Marchell continues onto her next question. "You seem to have some ribs that are already healing as well as the new injuries to them. Do you know when the healing damage happened?"

"I can't remember the exact dates."

"Poppy, you said dates. Does that mean they were injured more than once before the incident at the school?"

"My sides have always been a source of pain for me. I think I was about eleven since the last time they weren't purple or blue. I had been hurt about two weeks before school, but I don't know if that time broke anything. About a day or two, maybe even both of those days, my father had punished me, and I think that was more severe than the previous injury but not as bad as the ones I just got at the school. Like I said, I can't remember the dates."

"I don't need the exact dates now. We can do that at another time. I'd like to have on file all the past injuries you had as well-."

There is a knock at the door, and two people in dark suits walk in the room not waiting to be asked in interruptions Dr. Marchell. Roxi walks up to them and greets the intruders in hushed tones. I don't know what they are saying, but the older man doesn't look pleased. The woman nods her head curtly, before Roxi walks them to the door. Once they walk out of the room, I turn my attention back to my doctor who has a displeased look on her face.

"Those detectives need to give her some time. Poppy just woke up." Dr. Marchell shakes her head disapprovingly. "Is the same day of your last injury to your head the same day as the last day you had injuries to your side?"

"I don't think so. I mean, they were hurt badly that night, but the following morning something else had happened." I look down at my lap.

Shame and the fear of the reaction my father will have when he finds out that someone knows what he has done to me makes it hard for me to want to continue.

"Poppy, you are safe here. Nothing you tell me will not get you into any trouble. We are all here to keep you safe and to get you better." The nurse pulls up a chair and sits next to the doctor. She is still documenting things that I'm telling them.

"The morning before my father went out of town on a work trip, he shoved me into the side of the stairs. I hit the skirtboard of the stairs on one of my sides, and I can't remember, but I think I hit my head on something, too."

"That's a common side effect of head injuries. Your memory could be fuzzy for multiple reasons, like your brain repressing a bad memory or brain trauma, due to multiple concussions or untreated injuries to your head. I'll set up some tests for you to come in so I can see how you are healing, but also, so I can see if you have any permanent damage. It's too soon to tell right now the extent of what this head trauma will result in since we don't have any other records of damages."

Wouldn't you be able to do a scan and see the damage?" Roxi asks, finally sitting next to me on the bed again.

"Yes, but the damage on her head and brain is significant. From the imaging on her skull alone she has had some crack in a couple of places that appear to be as healed as they are going to be, and if we move to the scans of her brain, most of it is lit up with damage."

"What does this mean? Poppy has cracks in her skull, what could have caused that?" Roxi is confused, but she sounds pained by the questions she must ask.

"The cracks could have come from falling and hitting her head on something like she had stated or being hit over the head with something hard. I don't have those answers, but from the current tests, we are trying to see if Poppy has any permanent damage from her current and past head injuries."

"What kind of permanent damage could be done to Poppy's head? If she does, will it have any side effects?"

"It's too soon to tell. That is why we will be doing tests. From what I have seen in her MRIs, she has some significant injuries to her brain. The spots that are healed appear to have scarring of sorts, and she has some swelling of the brain that I want to keep a close eye on. There are precautions she is going to have to take to make sure that she does not harm her ribs or inflict another injury to her head. We'll go over those before she goes home. At that time, we'll discuss the imaging and other tests that I'll order for tomorrow now that Poppy is awake." The doctor looks at the nurse, and they talk to each other in hushed tones as they move to the other side of the room and write on the white board with some of the new information. They were able to get from me. I see they put my allergies on there too.

The doctor walks out, and the nurse helps me back into the bed. "The detectives are only allowed to have ten minutes. Then I'll come in here and make them leave."

"I don't want to talk to the detectives! I want to go back to sleep or eat a big bowl of pasta," I say as the nurse walks to the door.

The nurse laughs. Before opening the door, she sanitizes her hands and says, "I'll order you lunch. You're on a liquid diet until we can see what your stomach can handle."

"Better than nothing." I know they both can hear the disappointment in my voice.

Roxi fluffs my pillow and tucks the blankets over me, then sits next to me on the bed.

"Can you have Shane come in here for this talk? I want you both to be here, I don't know what they're going to ask, and I also don't want to say things I shouldn't."

"Of course, let me go get him."

The detectives come in, and they introduce themselves, but honestly, I'm barely listening, because a young man comes in carrying a tray, wheeling my food in front of me.

"Poppy, the detectives are here to ask you a few questions. I was assured it wouldn't take long, and then you should be good to rest after they are done." Shane says coming into my room. I can tell he is already trying to help calm my nerves and make it seem like this isn't a bad thing, but I'm not convinced.

Roxi sits on the bed next to me and lifts the lid off the bowl in the center of the tray. I furrow my brows at the bowl of yellow broth, the little cup of clear bubbling soda, what looks to be tea, and a cup of Jell-O. This really sucks. I want something greasy and full of carbs.

"Poppy, you need to listen," Roxi says to me in a hushed tone as she takes the lids off all the boring things I get to have for lunch today.

"Sorry." My apology sounds hollow with no meaning behind it.

"Do you know what day you were attacked?" the short stock man asks.

"Not the exact day or date. I just know that it was after school." I lift a spoonful of broth to my mouth with shaky hands. Roxi notices and takes the spoon from me and helps me eat.

"Do you know where you were?" Again, this is from the man.

I don't answer right away, because I'm mainly embarrassed that they are watching someone feed me, because I can't stop shaking from the pain to feed myself. "Yes, I was going to the football field after dropping stuff in my car to go watch Jax at practice."

"Why were you dropping things off in your car?"

"I did all my homework last hour during study hall, and instead of carrying my backpack around, I put it in my car, because I didn't need anything in there to sit through practice."

"Do you know who did this to you?" This is the first time the woman detective talks to me other than to tell me her name.

"Yes, I know who attacked me." I don't elaborate, because I don't want to say my father was the one this did this to me.

"Poppy, if you know who hurt you, I need you to tell me that information." The woman's tone is firm and almost rude sounding, I think I prefer the man interrogating me.

I look at Roxi, feeling ashamed that someone who is supposed to protect you would be the most dangerous one in my life. She nods her head, telling me that I can talk to them, but I don't know this lady and telling her that my dad beat me up makes me feel more uncomfortable than when I told Shane, or when others found out.

"It was my father." I look away from them. I don't want them to see the tears that are now pooling in my eyes.

"Poppy, Detective Scotts and his partner Detective Whitman are not going to judge you. They are here to help you stay safe," Roxi whispers in my ear.

"Is this him?" Detective Scotts holding up a recent photo that I've never seen before.

"Yes," I whisper, sounding more confused than I sound confident in my answer.

"Poppy, are you sure this is the man that attacked you at your school?" Detective Scotts repeats.

"Yes, that's my father, Jack Monroe."

"Where were you going after you left your car?"

"I was going to the football field to watch Jax at football practice."

The nurse comes in, "After this question, everyone will have to leave. Poppy needs some rest."

"Where were you going after you left your car?" Detective Whitmen repeats what her partner asked me when the nurse leaves.

"I was going to the football field to watch Jax and Lewis practice." I repeat the same thing I said earlier when they asked me this question.

"Where were you attacked?" I was asked, even though the last question was supposed to be my last one.

"I was about halfway to the field when I ran into my father, and he grabbed me by the wrist." I hold up the hand that is wrapped in bandages.

"What happened after he grabbed you?" I feel like I am getting whiplash through this questioning. Each detective is taking turns asking the questions faster and faster.

I tell them as much as I can remember, and unfortunately for me, that is all I remember until I heard sirens in the distance coming to take me to the hospital.

"All right Poppy. We only need you to recount everything that happened. You are going to be pointing to a map of the school and telling what happened when you can remember the time, and where, the best you can. I want as many details as you can give me, and if you don't remember spots tell me as you get to them. I will be writing the details down on the same map you are pointing to." This is the first time Detective Whitmen sounds nice since she started interrogating me.

The last thing I remember before they leave my hospital room is them handing me their cards and telling me to call them if I remember or need anything, before I lay back in my bed and let sleep take over.

♪♫

I wake up a few hours later to see Lewis sitting in a chair playing with his phone.

"Lewis, can you get me some water please?"

"Oh shit! You're awake! It's so damn good to see those beautiful eyes. Let me go ask the nurse what you can have."

Lewis comes back a few moments later with a cup of ice chips and a fresh cup of water.

"Thank you. Where is everyone?"

"Oh, you're too good for me now?" he chuckles and winks at me. "They'll be back soon."

"You're not going to give me any hints, are you?"

"Nope, you want to play a couple of rounds of our question game?"

There is so much that I would love to do, more than get to know Lewis more, but my energy is fading fast. "I think I can handle one question each." I smile and think quickly about what I want to know. "Can I hold your hand?" I don't want to ask anything that I may forget when my brain feels funny.

"That's really going to be your only question?" Lewis looks a little surprised by the slight rise of his eyebrows, but he's giving a full teeth smile, so I know he's pleased by my question.

"Yes, and that wasn't an answer."

"You don't have to ask." Lewis scoots his chair up close to the side of the bed. and he gently takes his hand in mine.

Warmth fills me, and I begin to feel safe. As I relax, the more tired, I become. My eyes begin to close, and I know I'm close to falling back to sleep.

"Poppy, how long has your dad been hurting you?" my eyes pop open at the unexpected question he asked.

This question is too serious and a lot to have to think about, so close to having to talk to my doctor and the detectives about some of the things I've been through. I wish he would've asked me a funny or even a flirty question.

"Lewis," I sigh, "do you remember the day my father told you to never talk to me again?"

Lewis's eyes look stormy, and I can tell he isn't pleased with my question. He jerks his head in a short nod.

"It started that day."

"Poppy, you were only ten. It's been. . ." he stops and looks away from me, like he can barely stand to look at me.

"It has been going on for seven years, Lewis." I finished for him.

Sadness fills me as I see pity and sadness in his eyes. I don't want anyone's pity, but most of all Lewis's.

"Lewis, do you feel sorry for me?" My sudden question has him doing a double take.

"Fuck, no." He breathes heavily and noisily through his nose. "You never asked for this, and you sure don't deserve to be treated that way. Your father should have protected you, instead of hurting you. Poppy, you are the strongest person I know."

I never really thought that I was strong, because I stayed quiet and let him hurt me for years.

"Poppy, I want to take you on a date when you feel better."

"Man, you can't date my sister. That's fucking weird!" Jax yells while plopping down at the foot of my bed. "That goes against the bro code."

I'm sure I'm a deep shade of red now. Jax hears Lewis tell me he wants to go on a date with me. There's no chance I'm going to respond now.

"Mom is sneaking some food up here. I tried to taste it on the way here, but I got in trouble." He rolls his eyes.

"Like you're ever in trouble," Roxi jokes, carrying an insulated bag in one hand and canvas tote in the other.

"What's for dinner?" I ask excitedly, as my mouth waters at the thought of food and not broth.

"Poppy, are you forgetting what Lewis asked you when I woke up?" Jax taunts me.

"I guess a date sounds fun."

"I guess if Poppy wants to go on a date with you, we can break the bro code. We're having spaghetti, salad, and garlic bread."

I look over at Roxi to see that she is amused by our conversation. She is putting the containers out and as she pops the lid off, garlic feels the room, and my mouth begins to water.

The nurse walks in and asks if they can step out, so I can have another checkup.

She takes my temperature, does my blood pressure, and looks at all my tubes connected to me.

"What is your pain level, dear?"

"Other than my stomach hurting because I am starving, I'd say a five or six."

"I see you have dinner waiting for you. I'll only be a few more minutes."

She shines a flashlight in my eyes and listens to my breathing. "Everything looks good. Do you have any questions for me?"

"Can I eat what Roxi brought? Do you know when I will be able to go home?"

"Go slow on the food, and only eat a little at a time. If you feel nauseous or cramping, stop eating and call for the liquid dinner. Let's see if you can keep that dinner down and then see what the doctor says."

"Thanks," I feel disappointed. I know I haven't been awake for a full day, but I am already tired of being here.

The nurse says bye, and after she sanitizes her hands, she leaves the room. The Taylor family walk into my hospital room, but Lewis isn't with them.

"He had to go home." Jax answered my silent question.

I sit in silence as I watch them make their plates. I move the blanket, so I can get up and make mine, but Roxi picks up a plate with steaming food and places it on the table and wheels my dinner in front of me. She gets her plate and sits on the bed next to me. I eat a few small bites on my own, but the aching in my wrist makes me stop.

Roxi helps me, and soon everyone is chatting and eating. I've learned that this is what family is. They show up for me while I'm in the hospital and take care of me. I don't know where I'll have to go when I get released from the hospital, but I really hope that they still want me to stay with the Jax and his family.

CHAPTER TWELVE

Waking up in the hospital has gotten easier, but I still want to get out of here. I want more than anything to be able to go home with the Taylors, where I feel comforted, warm, safe, and cared for. Being here reminds me of when my mom had to stay at hospitals periodically and then the care home, when she got sick.

I remember being six when I visited my mom in the hospital for the first time. All I was told before we went up there was that she would be sick for a very long time, which I didn't understand, because to me a long time at the time was a few hours, if that. I have only experienced the flu or strep from that point, and the longest time I was sick would have been at least a week. I was nine when she could no longer get out of bed. Then, I understood that she had something far worse than anything I ever had.

By the time I turned ten years old, my mom was living in a care facility filled with nurses and doctors to make her better. That's when I knew that things were far worse than I'd ever realized, because my tenth birthday wouldn't only be the last time, I celebrated my birthday, but more importantly, the last one I would have with my mom.

She tried to make my birthday as special for me as she could. Her best friend Macey decorated the cake, brought food, and even made me my favorite cookies. I had my two childhood best friends there. I didn't know that was going to be the last birthday I got to celebrate with her, or maybe I wouldn't have thrown a temper tantrum about not being able to go somewhere fun. That was also the very last birthday that I got to have, because a couple of months later, my mom passed away. My father never acknowledges that day. In fact, he was usually far more drunk than he usually is. I was turning twelve, the first time I tried to remind my dad it was my birthday. To say that it didn't go well is an understatement.

"Poppy. Poppy, are you okay?" Roxi asks, breaking through my thoughts.

"Yes, I was just thinking of my mom."

"Oh, sweetie," Roxi stops folding a t-shirt and turns to me.

"I was just thinking about how she might have felt when she was in the hospital. I'm glad that I finally get to be discharged today."

"I remember sitting up there with her and Macey. A lot of times she didn't like it. She would often talk about how the hospital not home, and the noises and smells drive her crazy. She often cried about how she was sad she couldn't be the mother you needed and that you were going to miss out on things a mom and daughter are supposed to do together." Roxi makes a sniffling sound and begins busying herself by packing my things. "She loved you so much, and being in that care home and the hospital meant you didn't have to see her at her worst moments, because she didn't want you to witness that."

"Sounds like she had a lot of feelings about that matter,"

"Oh, she did. Not to change the subject, but if you want to be able to eat the rest of your breakfast before the doctor comes in for your last check up before we leave, you need to eat." We both giggle and I spear a chunk of pineapple with my fork before I pop it into my mouth.

Roxi goes into the restroom with a little black bag full of my toiletries and the clothes that she brought up here for me to wear home.

"Good morning, Poppy. Are you ready for your last check up?" Dr. Marchell comes in after a single knock followed by a nurse.

I hold up a finger, indicating that I need a minute, because seconds before they came in, I shove a forkful of buttery waffle practically drowning in syrup into my mouth.

"Girl, we love a good breakfast." The nurse laughs while getting what she needs, so she can take my temperature and blood pressure.

"Roxi is the best cook." I push the tray away and scoot slowly to the edge of the bed, so they can examine me.

"We will change your dressings and go through our discharge list, and if everything looks good, you can go home." Dr. Marchell goes to the door after her brief explanation.

The nurse does the normal things like checking my blood pressure, temperature, and when she is done with her part the doctor comes in with a small cart. They both put on rubber gloves, and the nurse hands my doctor a small pair of funny looking scissors. The doctor gently cuts the bandages off my head, wrists, and my knees. They take the tight wrapping off around my midsection before they try to gently pull off the gauze that is taped onto my sides.

I feel a little awkward for me to hold my loose shirt up while looking at the bruising on my ribs, stomach, and back. They at least let me put my shirt down while they feel my sides, which hurts freaking bad.

"Your sides and head are healing slower than I would like, but we will keep a close eye on that. How is your pain level?"

"I would say about a four and a half everywhere, but my sides are at like a six after all that poking."

"Pain levels are improving, but still higher than I would like, but I don't want that to keep you here. I will just say that if it intensifies, then I need you to come in. I'll send a few things home with Roxi." Roxi comes out of the bathroom at that moment.

"Oh, sorry," Roxi turns away and then back in our direction, like she doesn't know what to do.

"I was just telling Poppy that when you sign the discharge papers, you'll get some papers to take home and one of those is care instructions and things to look after, one of those if her pain level goes up bring her in," the nurse hangs the clipboard up and wheels the cart of bloody bandages out of the room while the doctor is talking to Roxi.

"Do you know how much longer until we get all that paperwork and get to leave?" I ask when the doctor starts to walk to the door.

"I'm going to put in what I need to get those papers and then sign them. If I don't get called for an emergency, then you should be out in an hour or so."

I stand up on wobbly feet and go get ready after the door closes with a soft clicking sound. I take a step or two, but I stop to take a calming breath.

Roxi comes over and loops her arm in mine and helps me into the bathroom. She lets me walk in on my own, and thankfully I can use the handrails to help me walk.

Once I get cleaned enough to put my clothes on, I realize I need some help.

"ROXI!"

"YES!"

"CAN YOU COME HELP ME!"

There's a soft knock, and Roxi squeezes through the bathroom door and the door jam. I'm fixing to ask her what she was doing when I notice Jax was sitting on the edge of the bed facing the window, but he looks in my direction and sees me topless, but with my hands covering my chest. His jaw drops, but I don't miss the smile on his face before the door closes.

"What is Jax doing here? I thought he was supposed to be at school today?"

"He came up here to help Shane take your stuff home. Then he'll be leaving."

Roxi helps me get dressed, and when we walk out, the nurse is waiting in the room with a file folder and papers in her hand.

"Let's get these papers signed, so you can go rest in peace." The nurse put the paperwork on the rolling table.

"All right, Poppy, let's get you home." Roxi sounds happy as she helps me sit in a wheelchair.

"That's the best thing I've heard in a while."

Roxi wheels me out, and I can't help but feel relieved that I get to leave. I have a lot of healing to do, but I also have a lot to be grateful for. Shane and Roxi are taking the legal actions they need to make sure that I can't go back home with my father, while trying to take legal actions to have me live with them at their house.

We have a lot to do, but in the very pit of my stomach, I feel like my father will pop into my life at some point, because he is still out there, and the police can't track him down. No matter what happens, my father is in deep trouble, just for attacking me at the school, but also under investigation for suspected abuse and neglect of his minor child.

"We are going to have a big dinner to celebrate the fact that you're finally home." Roxi practically sings we leave the hospital behind us.

I lean my head against the cool glass as my eyes close, and the lulling of the car's movement puts me to sleep.

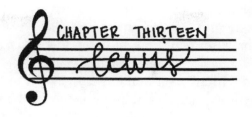

CHAPTER THIRTEEN

lewis

Poppy is coming home from the hospital today. Jax is excited, and he really wanted to miss school today, so he could be home when Poppy does.

I noticed that when he mentioned her name, Lana and a few of the other cheerleaders' moods drastically changed.

Lana has cornered me a few times since Poppy has started to eat lunch with Jax and me. She always asks, "Why is that freak hanging around so much?"

I always just shrug.

Jax comes up behind me on my way to the parking lot after practice. "Hey man, do you want to come over for Poppy's welcome home dinner?"

"Sounds like fun."

We get in our trucks, and my phone rings. I hit the button on my steering wheel, so I can talk hands free.

"HEY LEWIS!" Lana's nasally voice screeches through my speakers.

"Hey."

"You want to meet up at the field?"

"Got plans, talk to you later." I hang up on her and pull into Jax's driveway.

"Dude, dinner is going to be so good. My mom is planning so much."

I follow Jax into his house, and we are hit with the smell of spices and baked goods.

Roxi comes out of the dining room. "Oh, good! You guys are here. Can y'all go wash up and set the table? Dinner will be ready in about five minutes."

"Sure," Jax and I set our backpacks down by the console in the foyer, before going into the kitchen.

"You don't have to help." Jax turns on the water and washes his hands first.

"I don't mind." I look over at the island and I can't help but think that the last time I was here for dinner was the same night that Poppy moved in.

Jax moves, and I wash my hands as he starts to take out plates and glasses from the cabinet. I dry my hands and grab the pile of dishes with silver stacked on them, and he grabs the glasses with napkins tucked in one.

We set the table and Roxi moves around us, placing large dishes piled with food around the table.

Roxi goes into the kitchen and brings out a bowl of mac and cheese with a butter dish as Jax and I get done setting the table.

"Have a seat, I only have one more thing to get," Roxi starts to turn away, but Jax stops her.

"I'll get it, Mom. Sit down and relax." He stops to give her a quick hug before disappearing into the kitchen.

"How was practice today?" Roxi asks, sitting in her normal seat at the table.

"Practice was tough, but those ones are my favorite."

"Sounds like something my boy would say. I'm going to go get Poppy. he is in her room."

"Can I go tell her dinner is ready?"

"That would be great, dear."

I walk up the stairs and stop outside of Poppy's room. The door is cracked. Poppy's room looks dark, except there's a dim light shining somewhere in there probably from a lamp. I knock lightly on the door and wait for a response, but there isn't one. I knock a little louder. "Poppy, it's Lewis. Can I come in?"

"Yes." Her voice is soft, but I don't miss the cracking sound. She might be crying.

I walk in, and Poppy begins sitting up in her bed.

"I came to tell you dinner is ready."

"Thanks." Poppy moves the blanket off her and stands up.

"I'm starving." Poppy slowly gets up and shuffles to the door.

I can tell by the look on her face that she is in a lot of pain. I wait for her to walk down the stairs. She is getting paler under her bruises, like she is getting sick or something like that.

We walk to the dining room, and Poppy sits in the chair on the side she did last time, but in the chair closest to Shane. I look at how sad and delicate she is looking right now, and I'm sucked back to the parking lot after her father dragged her into the school and attacked her. I feel like I'm getting hit in the gut, just thinking about how broken she looked in her car with Roxi holding her.

We make our plates in silence, and I can't help but notice that Shane is helping Poppy make her plate. Her wrists are badly bruised, and I'm sure there might be more damage, but I wasn't ever told the full extent of how bad her dad injured her, and I really don't know, but I think the weight of the dishes are too much for her right now.

"Um, Poppy, my parents want to know if you would like to come over to our house for dinner." I sound like a nervous dweeb.

"I," Poppy takes a small sip of her water. "I don't think I'm comfortable with that." She fidgets in her chair looking down at her plate.

"I get it. We haven't been on our first date yet-"

"No, I just don't want to go to your house, since my father lives next door." she still won't look up, but she isn't squirming as much.

I feel like a dick. I didn't think about her father living next door and how hard going back would be hard for her.

"I didn't even think about that. What do you think about going out to eat?"

Poppy's small hand swipes at her eyes. She's crying. I made the girl of my dreams cry.

After a few moments of silence and the Taylors acting like they aren't listening, Poppy finally whispers, "Can we wait until my bruises fade?"

"We can do whatever you want."

"Poppy, how would you feel if we invited the Lewis's family over here for dinner one night?" Roxi is a genius. I would have never thought of that.

"That will be all right." Poppy picks up her fork and starts eating small bites.

We all begin eating, and Shane asks about practice, and this sends Jax into an animated story about one of the freshmen eating dirt. We are all laughing and having a good time that we stay at the table until Poppy yawns. That's when Roxi asks Jax to clear the table.

"I told my parents I would be home early tonight. Thanks for dinner."

"You're welcome, sweetie. You're welcome here anytime." Roxi leaves the dining room, and Jax walks into the kitchen with several dishes stacked onto each other.

"Poppy, after Jax is done clearing the table, we would like to have a family meeting in the living room." Shane stands from the table and pulls his phone out of his pocket.

"Can Lewis and I walk down the street for a few minutes? We won't go far."

"Yes, stay close to the house."

We step out onto the porch, and the sunset tonight has a purplish pink tint, making the sky look painted than real. Poppy begins walking down the front walkway, and the wind blows picking up her pale blond hair. She looks back and waves at me to walk with her. We get past my jeep, when Poppy stops walking and looks at me with her lips pressed in a thin line. Her fingers begin to play with the hem of her shirt. I've noticed she does that when she is either nervous or has something on her mind.

"Lewis," she takes a deep breath. "I still want to go on a date with you, but I really don't want to be around other people if I don't have to. At least, until the bruises go away. I know it's gotten out about what happened to me, and I am not ready to face the small-town gossip."

"I'm sure I can think of something for us to do," I wink at her.

She walks a few steps, without saying anything. I let her get the lead and some space before I catch up to her and I match my steps with her.

Our hands brush each other and the urge to hold her hand is getting harder to resist. I really want to feel her skin on mine. I shake the inappropriate thoughts that swarm my mind away.

I clear my throat. "Poppy…" I stop talking when Poppy turns to me.

"Lewis, can I ask you something before we go back to the house?" she says fast, almost like she is afraid that if she can't talk now, then she won't get the chance to again.

"Yeah," I bet she can hear the confusion on my face.

Poppy grabs my shirt in her right hand and lightly tugs me. I bend down a little, but she is clearly not satisfied with that, and she tugs my shirt again and again until I'm about an inch away from her face.

"Lewis, can I kiss you?" Her breath tickles my cheek.

I put my hands on her hips, "hell, yeah-"

She cuts me off with a sweet little kiss. Her lips are soft and warm. I try to deepen the kiss, but she winces. I take that as my cue to pull away.

Poppy grabs my hand and my clammy hands cool from how freezing hers is. I see that she is shivering. I should get her in before she gets sick.

"Let's get you back."

"That's probably a good idea, I'm pretty exhausted." As if on cue, a yawn makes her mouth stretch wide, and damn, my mind goes to places, they shouldn't. "Can I call you later?"

"Sure, that would be cool."

We slowly walk past my Jeep and to the front door. I bend down and kiss her cheek. "Good night, Poppy."

Her hand goes to the spot on her cheek, and a smile lights up her face.

"Good night," she says, closing the door softly behind her.

I hear the click of the lock then turn to head towards my Jeep. I notice what appears to be a black SUV idling at the end of the driveway. Something seems off, so I pick up my pace and climb into my Jeep and immediately lock the doors. I angle my phone in my side mirror and take a quick picture. I try to take another one, but the SUV speeds away, making the picture look blurry.

I sent the first picture to Shane, because this is something he may want to know.

Then I text my mom, to let her know I'm on my way home.

I put my phone in my console, and as I close the lid, my phone dings.

SHANE: Thanks for letting me know. Were you able to get the tag?

LEWIS: I got the first one, and then a blurry one as the car sped away.

I added the other picture of the car, and my phone rings with Shane's name flashing on the screen.

"Thank you for letting me know about that SUV. I've never seen it before. I'll get these pictures sent to the detectives. Have you left yet?"

"No, I didn't want to leave when whoever that was did. Do you think the person in the SUV was Jack?"

"Probably a good idea. I do suspect it might also be him. The idea of him also hiring someone to keep tabs on Poppy crossed my mind when he grabbed her at the school." Shane sounds so defeated, and I know that this is taking a toll on him. That family has grown to adore Poppy since she moved in.

"Nah. I will head out in a few more minutes. Thanks though."

"Thanks again for the heads up about that car. Let me know when you get home safely.

I don't know why, but I sit in their driveway for another 15 minutes before I leave. I like that they only live a little over five minutes from my house. I pull into my driveway and look around. After seeing that strange SUV at Jax's house, I can't help but feel uneasy. I don't see anything weird or out of place at my house, but I can't shake this eerie feeling that something is wrong.

I look over at Poppy's father's house, and I see what looks like the same black looking SUV sitting in his driveway.

I take a picture and make sure that Shane would be able to tell that the same car is parked in Jack's driveway.

LEWIS: Do you want me to go next door and get the tag?

SHANE: I don't want you to risk it. The detectives want to meet with us tomorrow.

LEWIS: Let me know if you need anything.

I shut my ignition off and walk into the house through the garage. I can hear the TV from the living room and my parents laughing.

"Lewis, did you ask Poppy about dinner?" my mother asks when I'm stepping onto the first step to go upstairs.

I turn around and look at my parents. My mom is stretched out on the couch with her head resting on my dad's lap as he leans back with his feet propped up on the coffee table.

"Yeah," I don't know how to tell them she is fine with dinner, but not over here. "Ugh, she said it's fine, but doesn't want to come here, because we live so close to her father's house after everything that happened."

"That poor girl, completely understandable. How about we go out to eat?" My mom sounds excited by the fact that Poppy said yes, but her face is saddened at the reminder of what she was living with right next door, and none of them had the slightest idea what was happening.

I chew my lip and contemplate the best way to say this. "Ugh, she doesn't want people to see her bruises-"

"I get that. However, we'd like to get to know her again and spend more time with you before you graduate and move off to college." my father interrupts me.

112

"I know that. Roxi suggested having dinner at her house."

They exchange a look, and I can tell this isn't what they want.

"That should be fine," I can tell my mom's not happy about the arrangements from the clip to her tone.

"Sorry, but I think if you saw her, you would understand. Roxi will be in contact about the dinner."

I walk up the stairs, without leaving room for them to say anything else. I go to my room and shut the door. I pull my shirt off and toss it to the side. I notice that my curtains are slightly open, and I know I didn't have them open. Maybe my mom cleaned them. She does that occasionally. As I'm closing them, I see a bright yellow light shine across the grass coming from Poppy's house. I glance over at Poppy's old bedroom window, and I can see her dad sitting in the chair at her desk. He has a bottle in his hand. He is looking straight ahead, and I know he can see me.

He gives me a creepy smile before flipping me off. I close my curtains tightly. I look around my room feeling paranoid that he somehow managed to come in here and mess around.

Once I am satisfied that everything is how I left it this morning, I get ready for bed. I think Poppy was right to be nervous about coming over here with her father being so close. I'll have to ask her to come over when everything with her psychotic father gets sorted out.

Jennifer Froh

CHAPTER FOURTEEN

I go back in the house, and everyone is sitting in the family room, and my mouth practically waters at the sight of sundaes on the coffee table.

"Honey, have a seat. We are going to enjoy a delightful dessert and a short talk," Roxi motions for me to join them.

Jax stretches out on the couch, and Shane and Roxi are sitting on the love seat. I feel like this is the conversation where they tell me I'll be going back to my father's house, or I'll be moving somewhere else. I don't want to leave, but I can't force them to let me stay.

I sit down, but my knees begin to shake from the nerves. I stand up long enough to tuck my legs under me and sit back down in the armchair, and once I'm comfortable, Roxi hands me a bowl of peanut buttery goodness.

"We want to talk to you about applying for guardianship over you. We know you don't really have any family left, and we don't know how long or if ever you will be safe to move back with your father." Shane sounds like he is conducting a business meeting.

Shane repeats himself a couple of times, because he thinks I didn't hear what he said. I feel like my brain is glitching. Why would they want me to live with them here?

"I would like that very much." I can't help but feel relieved.

"We love having you here, and we all care for you. You're growing up to be a remarkable lady, despite all the trauma you have endured. Your mom would be proud of you," Roxi says with a look of pride on her face.

"Poppy, the police say the chances of it ever being safe for you to go back home with Jack again is very slim." He glances at Roxi. "He has proven that he is more violent than we've originally thought, and you're not safe in his care. Our lawyers think we have a good chance of gaining guardianship, but we wanted to see if that is something you wanted. Since you expressed wanting to stay here, we wanted you to know that there are other steps that we'll be going through to ensure your safety." Shane is talking more formally, and I know that he is trying to be serious, but something about what he just said comes off like he is conducting a meeting.

"We don't want you to think we are trying to force you to make decisions now or make you feel like you don't have choices, because you do," Roxi adds after Shane takes a bite of his ice cream.

I move the ice cream around, in my bowl thinking about everything that I was told. If I can't have my mom back, then I don't want to live anywhere else. I've been in danger from my father for quite some time now. Do they really have enough evidence to keep me away from him, or are people going to listen to all my father's lies?

"Well, is there anything you want to talk about, or do you have any questions?" Roxi asks breaking the silence.

Jax has been unusually quiet through all of this. I almost forgot he was here.

"Jax, what do you think?"

"I like having you here. You're funny and cool to hang out with." He shrugs like he doesn't care if I live here or not.

"I want to stay here, but I also want to know more than anything else that I won't have to go back to my father."

Shane and Roxi exchange a glance.

"Poppy, they checked the security cameras at your school, and they have footage of your father dragging you into that classroom, leaving with what looks like blood on his shirt, and then you leave the same room in the state that you were in. No one else was in that area until the nighttime janitors came in to clean up. There is plenty of evidence against your father." Shane is holding eye contact with me.

I shudder as chills caress my spine. I'm embarrassed and angry that people have seen that video footage, and I don't even know who all saw the surveillance video from the school. I don't like the fact that they saw me at my worst and fighting so hard to get out of there so I could try to find help.

"I'm nervous about what is going to happen. I mean my father has a warrant out for his arrest, and the police can't even catch him. I don't feel safe knowing that he is out there, and I have no idea if or when he'll decide to show up here."

"We are here for you. If you want to talk or to talk to a professional, we can help find you someone." Roxi is literally the best. I know she will always be on my side, no matter what.

"There are some other things we need to go over. I am afraid that this may complicate things and cause you more stress," Shane pauses to let what he just said sink in. "After your walk with Lewis this evening, I received a text from him saying that he noticed a black SUV by the driveway."

I don't understand what he is trying to say or why this should bother me. My father owns an expensive black sedan and not an SUV, unless he suspects it has something to do with my father. "Does it have something to do with my dad?" I ask my thoughts out loud.

"Well, I was highly suspicious, with multiple ideas of how all of this could connect to your dad. I even had the thought that maybe one of the detectives came by to check things out and make sure everything was okay." Shane puts his half-eaten bowl of ice cream on the coffee table. "I talked to Lewis, and the way it sounds to me is that whoever did it, sped off when they realized that Lewis noticed them."

"So, was it a detective or a police officer? Do you think they left in a hurry, because Lewis noticing them could have blown their cover?"

"No, I talked to them, and they didn't have anyone posted here, but the thing is, Lewis saw the same SUV parked outside of his house when he got home." Shane picks his bowl up. "He sent me another picture of it."

"So, he is watching Poppy?" Roxi is concerned, and her face pales from fear.

"I would say that the chances of him watching her are greater than I'm comfortable admitting. I spoke to the detectives, and they'll be here sometime tomorrow. There are going to have to be changes to ensure that we are all safe. First, have the alarms always set, and don't go anywhere by yourself unless it's necessary." Shane is very tense now.

I wonder if they are all worried about what my father is up to.

I begin to shake, and even though I'm trying not to. I can't help but the full body sobs that echo through the living room. Jax sits on the arm of the chair and puts his arm around my shoulders.

"I want to kick his ass. Give him a taste of his own medicine!" I can understand that Jax is angry, but what I've learned is that violence is never the answer.

"That wouldn't help anything. In fact, it would make things worse.

We don't believe in violence in this family, and you're seeing firsthand what it can do. Sorry, Poppy. I didn't mean for you to be an example like that." Shane would be apologetic, but he is right. I'm a good example as to why violence is not okay.

"I think you're right. I've lived with a violent person, and it was a nightmare."

"Very well said. I think we should enjoy our desserts before we must head to bed. We have a lot more to discuss with the detectives and our lawyers tomorrow," Shane winks at me. I think he is trying to lighten the mood.

My sundae is perfect, full of peanut butter cups, caramel, and cookies and cream pieces with a vanilla ice cream base.

"Good night. Do not stay up too late. Jax, you still need to take the trash out." Roxi kisses the top of our heads, then leaves the room with her empty bowl, and Shane follows behind her with his own good night to us.

"Jax, do you want to watch a movie with me?"

"Sure, go pick one out. I'm going to take the trash out quick, then change." He grabs my bowl from me and goes into the kitchen.

I walk to the dark den, and for the first time, the room feels too big and creepy with no lights on. I find the switch and the overhead light shine is nearly blinding me. I turn on the screen and pull up a random streaming service. I scroll until I find a Rom-com that I won't have to focus on the movie plus there won't be anything scary or violent.

Jax comes in several long minutes later with two bowls of popcorn in his hands. He gives me one then takes the controller. After he gets comfortable on his side of the sectional, he presses play.

The movie starts, and Jax begins singing the opening song of the movie. He is pitchy, and his voice cracks a few times. I can't help laughing at his goofiness. I think that is what Jax wanted, because he smiles and stops singing.

I begin to doze off halfway through the first half of the movie, and I faintly remember Jax asking me if I am ready for bed. I don't think I responded before falling asleep.

The next morning, I wake up in my bed, disoriented. I look at my phone and see it is ten in the morning. I groan, seeing that I have several missed texts from Lewis.

POPPY: Sorry, fell asleep last night.

I go into the closet and grab a simple t-shirt dress and head to the bathroom to get ready. I would like to wear leggings and a t-shirt but it's hard for me to get the leggings on myself with how much my wrists and sides still hurt.

My phone dings as I slip on a pair of checkered Vans.

LEWIS: Heading to your house.

I don't bother replying, because he'll probably be here before he even reads a text from me. My stomach grumbles. I'm starving. I walk down the stairs, and the faint smell of bacon hits my nose. I overslept, and I missed breakfast.

"Good morning, sweetie. You look lovely." Roxi is putting a mug into the dishwasher.

"Oh, thanks. It was the easiest thing to put on."

She nods her head, watching me make a bowl of cereal.

"Would you like eggs and bacon to go with your surgery cereal?" I can tell she is joking. "It won't take but a minute."

"No, thank you, but this will be good."

I remember when I went grocery shopping with Roxi for the first time and she let me pick anything and everything I wanted. I didn't get very much, but I did get a couple of different kinds of cereal. I liked them all, but the chocolate and peanut butter was my favorite. I finished that one already, or I would be eating it now. This one is my second favorite, though.

"The detective will be here in an hour. I'm going to make some sandwiches and put them up so when it is lunch time, we'll have food ready. The detectives can eat with us or leave while we eat, but I am going to feed my family, regardless of what they choose." Roxi doesn't sound like she likes the idea of the detectives coming over.

I laugh and rinse out my empty bowl when I finish eating.

"Roxi?"

"Yes, dear."

"Do I really have to go back to school on Monday?"

"Yes, you have missed so much of your senior year already. If it becomes too much, call me and I'll pick you up, but you at least need to try. You're going to ride with Jax, and I'll pick you up."

"People are going to stare at me, and I can only imagine the things that they are going to whisper when they think I can't hear them. It is humiliating, hearing what people say about you in hushed tones."

"If they do, they will have to deal with me, and I can guarantee they won't want that. No one messes with my girl." Roxi is getting riled up.

Warmth spreads through my chest, warming my heart at her protectiveness. I give her a hug and go to the library.

I walk in and sit on the piano bench. I get a sense of comfort being in this room. I lift the fallboard, and I begin playing a sweet and slow melody, but the soreness of my fingers makes playing properly hard. I groan, grab a book off a shelf, and leave the room in frustration.

I don't want to go up the steps to my room, because I'm hurting a little more today. I sit in my favorite chair in the living room. I prop my feet on the coffee table, and I get lost in the random book.

"I thought I heard you play the piano a little bit ago. Why did you stop?" Shane asks, walking out of his home office.

"I tried, but my wrist and fingers are too sore to play properly."

"You just need time to heal. The doctor said there is no permanent damage in your hands and wrists, but just to go slow and give yourself time to mend. Try to be patient."

"I'll try my best, but I finally get to play without fear of getting punished for it."

"Poppy, -" Shane is interrupted by the doorbell ringing.

"We can talk more about this later, if you would like."

I nod my head to show him that I don't care if we pick this conversation up later. Lewis walks in, briefly greets Shane before turning to walk further in the house. He sees me sitting in the living room and comes and sits on the couch.

"Hey, why the long face?" He gives me a goofy smile.

"My fingers and wrist hurt, so I can't play the piano right now."

"I can see why that would be upsetting to you. Music is important to you, but until you can play, you're more than welcome to hang out with me."

A tiny smile lifts at the corners of my mouth. "I don't always want to play video games and watch movies."

"We can do whatever you want." He wiggles his eyebrows at me, lifting my legs up sitting on the edge of the coffee table.

A giggle slips past my lips at his flirting, and I sit up on the edge of my chair. Lewis leans in and gives me a light kiss. He tries to pull away from me, but I grab his shirt, deepening our embrace. I could kiss him forever, and that would still not be enough. The doorbell rings, interrupting us, and we pull apart breathlessly.

Shane walks back into the front room, he glances at Lewis and me, giving us a knowing smile. I must be a bright shade of red, because he chuckles softly under his breath. I seriously hope he didn't see us.

"Hello, detectives. Please come in and make yourselves comfortable while I go get Roxi."

I look around the room, and I notice that no one lets Jax know that the detectives are here.

After everyone sits down, they begin talking about the SUV, and I begin to tune everyone out. I could care less about what they suspect my father is up to. Talking about what my father is possibly up to and where they suspect he is, doesn't change the fact that he is still out there, able to get to me. I feel a light tap on my shoulder from Jax.

"Do you know where your father would go?" Detective Scotts repeats with an annoyed tone.

"I can imagine he won't want to be very far from the house he shared with my mom. You can either have someone stake out the house or show up more frequently but randomly, so he doesn't learn the pattern."

"What do you mean by learning our pattern?" Detective Whitmen asks with more curiosity.

"Well, that's how he figured out when the best time to grab me at school was. He watched me and started learning my new routine."

They begin talking about restraining orders, and honestly, that's a waste of time. Jack is not going to care about that. If he wants to get to me, he will, and a piece of paper isn't going to stop him. They all agree that they think I'm in danger and that my life is threatened if my father is around. I told them I was treated like that, to some degree since I was ten. I got more than one disapproving look from that remark.

They ask me several questions, but mostly I think they were trying to understand why I never tried to get help until now, and I don't have a good answer for those questions.

"If you need anything or see your father, give us a call. We do not care where or what time it is."

Jax goes out the front door, looking down at his phone.

I must look confused, because Shane whispers, "He is going to run to the store for Roxi."

Jax comes in a few seconds later. "Hey, there is a black SUV circling our cul-de-sac. I've never seen it before."

My spine straightens, and my vision blurs. I feel the strong urge to move. I can't just sit here anymore. I walk out of the living room and into the library on shaky legs.

I sit down at the piano bench again; I need the comfort of music right now. I feel numb, so hopefully, I won't feel the pain this time. I begin to press down on a key and then another. I play as each of the Taylors come in. Lewis comes in, and after my third song starts, the detective comes back in.

"That is a remarkable talent you have," Detective Whitmen compliments.

"We called the police with a sighting, and they'll be searching the nearby surroundings for him. We took a video with the tag, and a clear visual of his face. I think the next step is to show this to your lawyers, petition to relinquish your father's rights, and for the Taylors to get guardianship of you. We'll be in touch, and please contact your lawyers, the sooner the better," Scotts says with urgency.

They leave, and I begin to feel lightheaded. I want to go back to bed. Roxi looks at me with concern written all over her.

"Let's eat, and then you can get some rest." Roxi comes up next to me, helping me up from the hard piano bench.

"A nap does sound good right now," I say with a small smile.

"I want you to go to your room and make yourself comfortable. I'll bring your lunch up to you," Roxi murmurs lovingly.

"Lewis, can you help Poppy to her room?" She winks at him. "I'll bring both of you some lunch."

Lewis looks so happy about being volunteered to help me to my room.

"When are we going to go on our date?" I take a deep breath, trying to breathe through the nerves.

"I've got a few ideas. How does Friday night sound?"

"I think Friday is perfect. Lewis,"

We quit talking, because focusing on getting up the stairs for me right now is a challenge. We are slow, and I find moving at a snail's pace is getting old.

I walk into my closet, when we get into my room and shut the door behind me. I change into a nightgown, and then Lewis helps me in bed, and my heart skips a beat when he tucks my comforter around my legs.

"Lewis, do you think I am causing more issues in their lives that they didn't need or want? I'm terrified that one of them is going to get hurt because of me." I play with the soft fabric of my bedding.

"They would do anything for you, and I know they all want you here. It's hard not to want you, Poppy. I'm sorry everyone has been doing such a shitty job of treating you like you deserve. I'm sorry for not being better to you after your mom died."

"I don't want you to apologize anymore. I forgive you, but I am working on trusting you again. Lewis, I really don't want to talk about that right now." I look up at him, and he doesn't look mad or shocked by what I said. "I just want to know that I'm not intruding on them and causing unnecessary drama in their lives."

"You are doing no such thing, and I don't want to hear you doubt yourself again, young lady!" I jump a little at the sound of Roxi's voice. "You did not ask for your mom to be sick and pass away. You also didn't deserve your father mistreating you for all these years. You are family, and I don't ever want you to feel less than you are worth, because you are worth more than anything in this world." Roxi walks into the room and clearly from her response, she heard my emotional dump I was spewing at Lewis.

I giggle. "Not more than Jax."

"Maybe more than Jax at this point. You're not giving me gray hair like him." She winks and laughs at her own joke.

"I'm sorry, Roxi. I don't like that I am bringing all this chaos and drama in your life."

"They come and go throughout our lifetime; it's how we handle the bad times that truly matters. You can stress out and let it dull your experiences and affect everything in a negative way, or you can take all the darkness with grace and learn from it. So, how are you going to deal with all these curve balls?" She pins me with a knowing eye.

"I guess I have a lot that I need to think about, then. I promise I'll try to make you and Shane proud."

Roxi hands me my plate and sits on the bed next to me. I take a bite of my sandwich and eat a few chips when Lewis kisses my cheek.

"I'll text you later. My sister is coming home from college for a couple of days."

When Roxi and I are finally alone, I take the opportunity to have some much-needed girl talk while I eat my lunch.

"I think the only way my life would have been normal was for my mother to never die, but she did, and I can't be mad at her for that. She didn't choose to leave me."

"You're right, but I also think she fought for you. I just want you to remember that you are allowed to feel however you want."

"Do you think I will ever be able to forgive him?"

"I can't answer that for you, but I don't want you to live with that kind of anger and hate in your life, so I hope one day that you can forgive him for yourself."

"Lewis is going to plan our first date together for Friday evening. Will you help me get ready?"

Roxi looks up at me with tears in her eyes. "I always wanted a daughter to do that with, Poppy. I would love nothing more than to help you." She hugs me tightly.

Roxi pulls away from me and lets me eat the last few bites of my food while she moves around my room straightening up.

"Do you need anything else before you get some rest?"

"Am I allowed to take anything for my headache?"

"Yes, let me go get you something."

Roxi walks out of the room with my plate and returns with a cold glass of water and a small bottle. She hands me my glass, then takes two pills out and gives those to me, too.

"Get as much rest as you can. If you're not up for dinner, I'll put a plate up for you."

I lay back on my pillow, and Roxi bends down to place a kiss on my hair. I snuggle down into my fluffy pillows and in a few short moments, I drift into a dream world where my mom is still here, and my life is perfect.

CHAPTER FIFTEEN

poppy

I'm so happy today is Friday, not because I get to have my first date in a couple of hours, but because Jax just dropped me off at home before going back to school for practice. This week was exhausting and hard to handle. I only got through half a day of school on Monday and Tuesday. Then Wednesday Jax got permission to take me home the rest of the week during study hall.

The teachers were no help with keeping them quiet. I could hear all their hushed giggles after saying something awful. They gave me looks of pity and cooed at me in a sickly baby voice that made the hair on my arms stand up. I even had a few flashes of people trying to get pictures of the bruises that are too dark for makeup to cover. I could have caked on more makeup or gotten a color-correcting serum, but I don't want that much product on my face.

I got lucky, though, Jax and Lewis would take turns walking me to each class, and Jax would order us lunch at the diner, so we could go grab our food and eat in his truck or Lewis's Jeep. Lana was more of a bitch to me when she was able to see me alone, which wasn't a lot, mainly in the restroom. I still laugh every time she would get in my face to threaten me away from Lewis. She thinks I'm afraid of her, but after all I've been through, she is like a little yappy puppy that never shuts up.

"ROXI!" I accidentally slam the front door, because I'm so excited for this evening, "I'm home, where are you?"

"I'm in the kitchen, sweetie. Go take a shower, and I'll be in your room shortly!" she hollers with her normal exuberance.

I don't waste any time making my way to my room. I take a shower, making sure to be quick. I wish I had the time to stay under the hot water a little longer. I would love nothing more than to be able to loosen my aching body more.

I walk to the mirror, wrapped in my fluffy oversized towel that Roxi insisted I get. I grab a folded washcloth out of the basket on my counter and wipe the condensation off the mirror. I lean forward to get a closer look at my face. The bruises are healing nicely, even though they are still dark, and the small cuts are in desperate need of some ointment. The rest of my body isn't healing as well. The discoloration on my sides is the same, but the damage done was worse than the others.

Roxi breezes into the bathroom, humming a light melody.

"Roxi, I don't know what I should wear or anything, because Lewis won't tell me anything about our date."

"Oh, honey, you're going to have such a good time. I'm so excited, I've always wanted to do this." She goes back to humming.

I look at her with my brows pinched together and my lips pressed in a tight line. What is she talking about?

"Sweet Poppy, I always wanted a daughter to do all the girly things together, like help her get ready for her first date. I gave up that dream when I had Jax, and I knew I couldn't have any more children. I'm not sad about not being able to have more kids anymore, because I love Jax, and I wouldn't trade him for anything."

"I'm so grateful to have you help me with this. I always thought that this was something my mom would have done with me. but since I can't have her, there is no one else I would want to help me."

Roxi's face pales, and the realization of what I just said sinks in. I didn't mean for that to sound like I don't want or appreciate her help.

"Roxi, I didn't mean for what I said to come out like that. What I'm trying and failing to say is that I'm happy that I have you to help me, because, without you, I wouldn't even be able to go on a date. You are truly the mom figure I need in my life, and I know that my mom is looking down on us, sending you millions of thanks for taking care of me and everything." I hiccup from the thick emotions bubbling up my throat. "I love that I get to have this memory with you."

Roxi's cheeks turn pink, and a tear or two falls down her cheek, but she doesn't say anything. I pick up the wrapping for my ribs and she gently takes the gauze bandages from me. I leave the bathroom long enough to go to my closet and put on my underwear and a robe.

"Are you ready to wrap your sides?" Roxi asks me when I come back into the bathroom.

I nod my head, and I start crying silently. I really messed up something special with Roxi, because I don't know how to talk to people about how I feel.

"Honey, don't cry. I'm not upset about what you said. Most girls want to do this with their mom or their friends. I also understand that since she isn't here, I get this opportunity. This is a big step in growing up, and I just want you to have a good experience and to have a good time."

"What was it like getting ready for your first date? Did anyone help you?"

"I didn't have anyone to help me." Roxi puts the first piece of the wrap on my belly button, and I hold it in place as she begins to slowly wrap it tight around me. "My mom wasn't really present in my life at that time, and I didn't have any girlfriends, either." I move my hand when she overlaps the bandage on starting piece to hold the bandage into place.

"You're the greatest person I know. Who wouldn't want to be your friend? Did you go on your first date with Shane?"

"Thanks, I think you're great, too," Roxi glances at me in the mirror. Her lips are smashed into a tight line. "No, I was in middle school when I went on my first date." She shivers. "I didn't really have any friends at that time. All the girls that said they wanted to be my friend only wanted to use me to try to get close to my older brother."

"Did you marry the man of your dreams? I think you did. I used to daydream about princes, boys, and what my future husband would look like."

"What did he look like?" Roxi asks as she finishes with the bandages, but I don't mistake that she basically dodged two of my questions.

"At first, I didn't care what he looked like. I just wanted him to treat me the way my dad treated my mom," I tie my robe closed, "When I started to like boys, I always pictured Lewis or Jax as my prince. I eventually started to just picture Lewis, and I haven't been able to think about anyone else since."

Roxi gasps at me for a moment when I mention Jax's name, but only for a minute or two. I don't want her to have to worry that I'm going to try something with Jax while I live. Maybe I should say something.

"I felt the same way about Shane when I moved here. Shane and your mom were always together. I was jealous, and when your father asked me out, I couldn't help but say yes,"

"Wait, Jack, as in my father?" My voice rises at this new discovery.

Roxi laughs. "It wasn't until me and your mom became friends that I found out they were only friends. I was so shocked and angry."

"I knew my parents were high school sweethearts, but I never knew she was friends with Shane."

I love that even though I'm learning about Roxi, I also get to hear new stories of my mom.

"Oh yes, they were so close that everyone thought that they were going to end up together." Roxi's laugh echoes off the white tile in my bathroom. "I wanted to hate your mom so much, but when she marched up to me demanding that we be best friends, I quickly learned that it's not possible to dislike her."

Roxi starts brushing my hair.

"Roxi, will you tell me the story of your first date with Shane?"

She stops brushing my hair and looks perplexed as she scratches her head.

"Well, I have your mom to thank for us being together. We were having a sleep over at her house and doing all the girly things like facials, painting our nails, and girl talk. She looked me dead in the eye and asked me who I liked. I was mortified. I didn't want to tell her who I was crushing on. The last thing I wanted was for her to think that I was her friend because I wanted to get close to Shane."

"Was Shane the only reason you became friends with my mom?"

Her cheeks turn a deep shade of pink, and she fidgets with a brush before finally putting the brush on the countertop.

"I think she knew, because girls were always using her to get close to Shane. It was a lot like the girls that would be friends with me, so they could try to get with my brother."

"What do you mean by which one?"

"She wanted to know if I was interested in Heath or Shane."

"Wait, who is Heath?"

"Heath was your mom's brother. He died when he was 20, and your mom was 17 years old. He enlisted and died while away on assignment."

"That's so sad. I never knew she had a brother. I didn't know you had a brother, either. Will I get to meet him?"

Roxi looks so sad that I feel like I kicked a puppy. I'm really ruining this night for her.

"I wish you could, sweetheart. He passed away when I was 13. He was on his way home from a football party when a driver hit him and then drove away. There was a witness, and they said the other driver was most likely drunk, because they were swerving before running a red light."

"That's awful, I wish I would have been able to meet them. Was she mad when she found out that's why you wanted to be friends with her?"

"Yes, at first, she was, but she eventually broke down and said she only wanted to be my friend, because she had a crush on Jack, and that she was happy I liked Shane instead of her brother. It turned out that we loved our friendship more than trying to use each other for boys, but that was just a bonus in the end."

"What happened between my mom and you then?"

"Are you asking why we stopped being friends?"

I nod my head. Roxi sections my hair, then picks up the curling iron, checking to see if it is hot.

"We went to different colleges after high school. Email and phone calls had gradually stopped, and we lost touch. She met Lewis's mom while in college, and after we all graduated, we moved back here to start families. I loved raising my Jax with friends that had kids the same age. You used to be the boys' biggest cheerleader during their games, but since you lived next to Lewis, you guys were closer to each other."

"So, I was right. I used to be friends with Jax, too." I'm in complete shock. How do I not remember that very well?

"Yes, Lewis used to tease Jax that you were in love with him, and Jax would taunt Lewis right back. Macey and I would joke with your mom that she needed to have another daughter."

"Yeah, I'm glad that I didn't have any siblings. I wouldn't want to have anyone else suffer like I did."

"I guess it was a blessing in disguise, but I still miss Ellie every day."

"What was your first date with Shane like?" I ask again. I'm curious.

"Your mom told me to meet her at the diner after school one day, but when I showed up, she wasn't there yet. I went to our normal booth and sat down. I ordered an extra thick chocolate cherry milkshake and fries to snack on while I waited for her, but she never showed up."

"What do you mean, she never showed up? Also, what does this have to do with your first date with Shane?"

"Shane sits on the opposite side of the booth a few minutes after I

129

get my order with two envelopes in his hand...." she trails off with a dreamy smile lighting her face.

"So, Shane knew it was a date?"

"NO, NOT AT ALL!" Roxi is getting excited and very animated, waving the hot curling iron in the air. "Ellie was the mastermind behind it, and to this day, I'm grateful that she set that whole date up without either of us knowing. As I was saying, he showed up with the envelopes, and when he saw me, he came to the table and sat down. He handed me a letter with my name scrolled on the front. Not once saying a single word to me. We never said more than a few words to each other when we all hung out, but the other letter had his name scribbled on it. The notes gave us instructions on what to do and that she wanted us to take a chance on each other, because she said life is too damn short not to make a move."

"My mom sounded like a badass."

"She was. I loved my first date with Shane. We did everything the letters said. It was a whole day of activities. We were also not allowed to show each other our letters until we got married. I still have them somewhere; I'll show you sometime. I think you will get a kick out of them, and you can really understand what our date was like, because there isn't enough time to cover half of it."

"I would love to see them one day. Thank you for sharing that story. It makes me less nervous for my date tonight."

"I'm happy to help. I love talking about this, but it makes me miss my friend and the good old days. I did ask Shane if he really wanted to go on the date before we left the dinner. Apparently, your mother had her own motives, and Shane was the one to convince her to approach me about being friends. He said he wanted an excuse to talk to me, because he was too nervous to ask me out, but I wasn't convinced at first, because I knew he was hooking up with plenty of girls before me."

Roxi finishes the last curl and then combs her fingers through them to break them up when my hair is cooled down. I need to start thinking about what the hell I should wear. None of my clothes are exactly comfortable unless I wear a dress, but I don't know if I should do that or leggings and a cute, loose top.

"Roxi, what should I wear?" Maybe she will know since she knows what we are doing.

"I have a few ideas that we can go over after we do your makeup. Lewis will like whatever you decide on, so I wouldn't worry about it too much if I were you."

"Okay…um, Roxi, I don't want to wear a lot of makeup."

"I think just the simplicity of a tented gloss or ChapStick and mascara would be perfect."

"I like that idea. I also think a gloss could be fun," I begin to think about Lewis, and if we'll kiss, or what if he tries to do something else. My foot begins to shake from a new set of nerves.

"Poppy, you're going to have a good time tonight. I think you're really going to love what is planned."

"I can't help but be nervous. Lewis is the only person I've ever kissed, and what if he wants to kiss me again tonight or what if he tries something else?"

Roxi turns off the curling iron and hands me a tube of mascara, "Poppy, you don't have to do anything you don't want to or that you're not ready for, but as a mom, I will say if you go that far, please wait and let me take you to the doctor, so they can discuss your options to stay safe."

My cheeks flame at the mention of Roxi's subtle hint at birth control. I'm nowhere ready for that, but I like that Roxi wants me to come to her when I'm ready.

I put the mascara on and turn to Roxi. "Thank you."

We walk to my closet, and Roxi pulls a couple of leggings and two pairs of jeans out for me to look at.

"I'm leaning more towards leggings. I don't think jeans will be comfortable, no matter what we'll be doing." I look at the leggings she chose, and I like the option of the ones that have manufactured rips in the knees. "You don't think a dress, or a skirt would be a good idea?"

"These will be easy to sit and move around in, but if you want a dress or skirt, we can make it work."

Hmm, she may have a point. I have a cute romper that would be super cute, and I've been wanting to wear, but I might wait until I can have a date outside of the house to wear it, and hopefully that will be before the weather gets too cold.

"I think these leggings would be perfect." I choose the ones with the rips that I originally liked.

Roxi gives me a playful grin before turning to the rack that we took the time to organize by color.

"This is a hard choice. Any of your tops would be perfect." Roxi hums and taps her chin in thought.

As I scan the colors, I slip my leggings on under my robe. I struggle for a moment from the pain in my wrist.

"I think red would be the right color, because it's both of our favorite colors."

I take a simple red peplum top with spaghetti straps, and then I go to move to the white tops and grab a white flowy bohemian style blouse that has tiny red flowers embroidered throughout the top. I pick this, because the blouse is slightly sheer and if I wear a cute I bralette underneath, it would be flirty without showing too much.

Roxi looks at both tops and then looks at the leggings I choose.

"I think you should try both on with the leggings, but both of those are going to be cute. Also, make sure that they are comfortable with the bandages."

I walk to the drawer that my underwear is in, and I choose a simple white bralette with a little lace trim. Roxi walks out of my closet while I change into the new bra and the red top.

"I like the simplicity of the red with the peplum flare and the flirty slim straps, but I still want to see the other option, too."

I look in the mirror and agree with what Roxi is saying. The top is dressier than the more casual leggings I chose, but they kind of balance each other out to a perfect amount of, I'm casual, but flirty.

I try on the white flowy blouse and look in the mirror. I like this option, because the loose flow of the thin material doesn't rub against the bandages around my midsection.

"I like how this feels around the bandages better than the red one. What do you think?" I walk back into my room, and Roxi beams at me.

"Where is your black sweater with the lace on the bottom?"

"It's in the dirty laundry."

She begins to chew on her lip. I give her a slow spin, "I like the one you are currently wearing, because it feels good around your bandages, and you want to be cute and comfortable. I don't think you'll need to wear a sweater with that top, either."

I walk to my jewelry box and put on simple jewelry consisting of two gold bangles, my mom's locket, mini gold hoop earrings, and my normal gold rings. Roxi hands me some lip gloss that will give me the perfect tint of red and tons of sparkle. I'm very happy that it's not the overly sticky kind of lip glass. I slip the tube in the small pocket in my leggings, in case I need to touch up later.

"Should I wear shoes?"

"Oh yes," Roxi goes into my closet for a couple of minutes, "I think these gold sandals will be perfect!" Plus, they will be easy for you to slip off, if you need to," Roxi walks back out with a pair of sandals I've never seen before.

"I didn't know I had these. I love them!"

"I bought them while you were in the hospital. I did a lot of online shopping to help me pass the time. You have a few more new pairs of shoes in your closet and some other things I've ordered, but they haven't made it here yet," Roxi laughs with a slight blush in her cheeks.

"Thank you. I'm sure I'll love it all. You have great taste, and I think you know my style better than I do." We both giggle.

I'm so glad that Roxi looks like she is having a good time, because I know I am.

"You look beautiful." We both turn to the door when we hear a man's voice.

Shane is leaning against the door frame looking like a proud father.

"Thank you." My face heats up from a simple compliment, but he'll never know how much his kind words mean to me.

"So, this is where the party is. DAMN, POPPY! I may have to steal you from Lewis for myself!" Shane elbows Jax in the side.

"Damn, Dad, I was just trying to tell Poppy she looks good."

Roxi shakes her head, and I blush from all the embarrassingly good attention I'm getting. We are joking and laughing as we make our way to the living room. Lewis will be here any minute. Shane is asking Roxi if she wants to go out to dinner with her, and Jax says he has a date to go pick up in a little bit, so I'll be here alone with Lewis.

The doorbell rings, and my stomach drops. I begin to sweat a little, and my hands shake with anticipation. Lewis walks in, and I wish I got a picture of his face, because the expression he is making is priceless.

"Poppy, you look-," he stops and clears his throat a couple of times. "Um, Poppy, you're beautiful."

I don't get to reply, because I'm interrupted by the sound of what I'd describe is an animal dying, but the sound is just Jax laughing and making an absolute fool of himself.

"Dude, I've never seen you speechless or even this nervous in front of a girl before. THIS IS PRICELESS! Please tell me someone is recording this."

Shane smacks him across the back of his head, but other than that, we all just ignore him.

"Are you ready to start our date?" I hold my hand out to Lewis and, when he takes mine, his warm skin warms me, making the nerves intensify but in an oddly good way.

♩♫♪

My first date was better than any girl could have ever asked for. There were twinkly lights hung in the den and a small picnic set up on the floor in front of the big screen on the wall.

"We can watch whatever you want, but I have the one we talked about the other day ready, if you want. My mom made us dinner, and I think you'll like the extra surprise she threw in there for you."

I look around the room with watery eyes. I can't believe people would go to all this trouble to make my first date so perfect. I look at the ottoman and see that there are a bunch of goodies. I sit down at the picnic, but my name keeps going to the Tupperware bowl with my name scrawled elegantly across a piece of tape.

"My mom asked if there was anything you would want for dinner. I told her she can make whatever she wanted, but we absolutely need to have her peanut butter cookies. She made them today before I came over to get this all set up with my dad, Jax, and Shane."

"This is perfect. Thank you for going through all this trouble. I'll have to thank everyone else, too."

"This is nothing. I wanted to do more, but Roxi and my mom said you would think this would be everything. I don't understand what they mean by that, but I wasn't going to argue with them. It wouldn't have been a fair fight, two against one."

We sat down to eat the burgers that Macey made, and let me tell you, they were delicious and super juicy. Our meal lasted, I think, an hour, because we talked and laughed so much that we lost track of time.

After we eat, Lewis cleans up the trash from our dinner and moves the ottoman back in front of the sectional. I sit in one of the corners of the large sectional and lay back with my legs straight in front of me and my feet crossed at the ankles.

"Would you like anything?"

"Um, the peanut butter cups, popcorn, and water."

"No cookies?" he leans forward, grabbing everything I asked for.

"Just one, I want to make those last as long as I can."

He chuckles, taking out two cookies, then puts the lid back on.

"Hey! Those are my cookies!"

"Don't worry. My mom put a couple of chocolate chip ones in there for me." He laughs, sitting back on the couch next to me.

I begin to feel butterflies in my stomach when Lewis's leg touches mine. He presses play, and as the opening credits roll with a good throwback song that Roxi constantly dances to in the kitchen plays through the speakers, Lewis stretches, and he puts his arm around me.

We stay like this for about half of the movie before Lewis manages to pull me closer into his side. I look up at him through my lashes, and I see that he is looking down at me with a mischievous smile playing at the corners of his lips and eyes dilated as he inches closer to me.

Lewis is inches from my face. I lick my drying lips, and Lewis takes that opportunity to kiss me. I gasp in shock, but I gain composure quickly kissing him back.

I grab hold of his shirt and hold him there. I never want this kiss to end. Stars shoot in my eyes, and fireworks go off in my mind. I feel Lewis lightly grabs my narrow hips pulling at me. I move closer to him, and he moves his hands until his hands are cupping my thighs right under my butt. He picks me up, making me squeal.

Lewis laughs, setting me down. I adjust to where I'm straddling his lap. We sit there staring at each other for a long moment as we breathe in ragged breaths. I put my hands on Lewis's shoulders. He takes this as a cue and cups my cheek with one hand and moves the other on to my hip. He gently pulls me to him, and we begin kissing again.

I get a flash of nerves, because I have never made out with someone before. What am I supposed to do with my hands? When am I supposed to breathe? Do I keep my eyes closed the whole time? I think Lewis can tell something is wrong, because he pulls back an inch.

"Do you want to stop?" He looks at me, and I giggle, because I can see my gloss smeared on and around his mouth.

"Um, no," I tuck some of my hair behind my ear. "It's just that I have never done this before, and I don't exactly know what I'm doing."

Lewis pecks my lip.

"Trust me. I like everything you have been doing." He chuckles. "Don't overthink it and just do what you want."

"I think I can handle that."

Lewis reaches up and holds my chin; then he begins to kiss me again, stealing my breath from me for the third time tonight.

When we finally pull apart, we notice that the credits are rolling. I climb off his lap with shaky legs. I shiver as the cool air of the den chills my hot body from being pressed up against Lewis. We clean up the den fast, and I walk him to the front door.

"Good night. I had a wonderful time tonight." I lean up, and Lewis meets me halfway.

He thinks I'm going to kiss his lips, but I duck and kiss his cheek instead. If I kiss his lips again, I may not let him go home.

"Me, too. I'll text you when I get home."

He leans down and gives me a sweet kiss on the cheek. He turns to walk away, but I stop him by grabbing his hand. I stand on my tippy toes, and he bends down, meeting me the rest of the way like he can read my mind.

Lewis breaks our last embrace of the night and leaves me flustered in the doorway. I lock the door, and I go to my room.

Shortly after I'm in bed, I hear my phone dinging.

LEWIS: I'm home. :)

POPPY: Sweet dreams!

A soft knock comes from my door, and Roxi peaks her head in.

"Come in." I giggle.

"I don't mean to pry, but I can't wait until morning. How was your first date?" Roxi comes in, wearing a silk robe.

"ROXI! It was perfect!" I scoot over and lift the covers for Roxi.

She climbs in bed, and we sit back on the soft headboard. As the hall light shines on us. I can see the excitement in her eyes, and I know she must feel like she's back in high school.

"Oh yes,"

"I couldn't imagine a better first date."

"So, did you watch any of the movie, or did you make out through the whole thing?"

My face heats at being caught not watching the movie.

"Oh, I'm sorry, Poppy. I didn't mean to pry." Roxi starts to get up, but I put my hand on hers stopping her.

"It's just funny that you knew we made out."

"I was a teenage girl once." Her smile is playful, almost like she has a secret. I bet she and Shane still make out.

"I was so nervous to make out with Lewis, but I don't think I was bad at it. Would I know if I was a bad kisser?"

"You would know, but I think we all have these questions at that stage in our lives. I know I did." Roxi knows exactly what I need to hear to feel better.

"Roxi, I have so many questions that I don't know where to begin. Can we have a girl's night sometime soon, so we can talk about boys and everything in between."

"Nothing would make me happier. Goodnight, sweetheart." She stands up, and after I lay down, she kisses my forehead.

I don't miss the huge smile on her face and the tears welling in her eyes before she closes my door. I hope she is happy, and that is what is making her teary-eyed. I plug my phone into my charger and then bury myself in my blankets with the thoughts of kissing Lewis again fills my mind.

Jennifer Froh

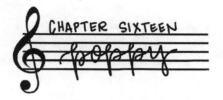

CHAPTER SIXTEEN

I haven't seen or heard from my father since that day at school, which I find hard to believe, because a month has almost gone by. He is still out there, because he still manages to evade the police. I have this feeling deep in my stomach that he is planning something and biding his time before he shows his arrogant face to wreak havoc, ruining all the happiness I've had lately.

I never knew that I could be surrounded by so much love and be able to return those feelings after everything I've been through. The Taylors have been nothing short of amazing, and I know that I am truly lucky to be able to have them by my side throughout this whole mess, but I think I need to see a therapist. I can't escape the nightmare, and I've been having triggers and anxiety attacks that I try to hide.

I have freaked out at the table during meals several more times, and each time, I get sucked into the bad memories of my father's abuse, like I did the first time. I know every time I panic, I scare everyone and that they don't know what to do or say. I hope that I can have a normal meal without any freak outs tonight because tonight, is my first official meal with his family as Lewis's girlfriend. We've been planning this night, since Lewis asked me if I would go to his house for dinner.

As I apply a thin layer of sparkly gloss to my lips, my face flushes from the memory of the first time, I let him touch me under my shirt. Lewis's touch makes me feel like I'm on fire and that I'm going to burst into flames. Roxi has assured me that feeling is normal when you are with someone that you truly care for. She told me she still feels that way with Shane. I've learned so much from her, and I love that she is honest and open with me. Her advice comes from a place of understanding and experience.

"There are cinnamon rolls for breakfast, if you would like one. They are still hot," Roxi says, when I walk into the kitchen.

I go to the cabinet and grab a plate. I find the glass baking pan and lift the foil that is covering the gooey cinnamon rolls. Immediately, I'm assaulted with the mouthwatering scent of cinnamon and butter. I lift a heavy sticky cinnamon roll out of the pan.

"Macey, Lewis, and his father will be here shortly." Roxi fills a glass with milk and sets it in front of me. "Lilah was able to get away from college for a couple of days, so she'll be here, too."

I can't remember the last time I saw her. I know that she'll look at the yellowing bruises that are slowly disappearing, but I try not to think of them anymore.

Roxi turns on some music and starts to clean the kitchen as I eat my yummy breakfast. I love watching Roxi in the kitchen. She dances, no matter what she is doing. You can tell she is having fun and the smile, on her face is so infectious.

"HHEELLOO!" Macey sings, dancing through the kitchen's entryway.

When they notice I am still in the kitchen, they waste no time shooing me to go hang out in the den. Thankfully, I'm done eating, and I was washing my plate. I can hear the cackling of their laughter from the living room. I want a friendship like that one day, but I think that will come after high school. All the girls at my school are just wanting to get close with me to be with Jax, and then there are the ones that are jealous that I was the girl that Lewis decided to be with exclusively. They aren't so nice to me. In fact, they are downright mean, but Lana is the most vicious of them all.

Going into the den, I see Jax, Lewis, and a gorgeous girl that could be Macey's twin. Wow, Lilah has grown into a stunning young woman.

"Wow! Poppy, you are beautiful! I see why understand why Lewis won't shut up about you now!" She is cheerful and reminds me of Macey.

I look away from the attention that she is throwing at me. Jax is looking at Lilah with a lopsided grin on his face, admiring the vivacious woman standing in front of me.

"It's so good to finally see you after all these years. How is college?"

"I love it so much! I feel like I don't have any free time between studying and my sorority. Even though I'm only an hour away from home, I can barely make it home. When I can, it's not for very long."

"I'm glad you were able to get away for dinner. It's nice having another girl closer to my age to talk to. I can't wait to go to college. I've been counting down for a very long time."

"Do you know where you want to go?"

"I have a few schools picked out that I would like to attend. I don't know. I guess it depends on where I get accepted to and who has the best program for what I'm wanting to do."

"Well, if you need any help with applications or anything, let me know."

We play board games until Shane comes down to tell us dinner is ready, and by that time, we are all more than hungry. The boys practically sprint to the dining room. I can't help but laugh at their excitement.

We gather around the dining table, and I see that we have pot roast and all the fixings. Roxi is a southern cook, meaning there's lots of butter, at least two to three sides, and some kind of bread with each meal. We pass plates around the table, and everyone is talking and laughing. I'm sitting next to Lewis and Jax on my normal side of the table while Lilah is on the opposite side between her parents, so that Roxi and Macey can talk to each other.

I'm fixing to take my first bite of food when a thunderous pounding comes from the front door. I drop my fork and slide out of my chair until I'm hiding under the table. A few seconds go by; then we hear glass breaking and hitting the floor from what sounds like a window being smashed.

There is a string of curse words followed by my name being howled through whatever my father broke. The hairs on my arms stand, and a chill creep down my back.

"Ladies, go upstairs and lock yourselves in Poppy's room. Then, call the police," Shane demands in a harsh tone.

We run through the kitchen to get to the stairs, in hopes that my father can't see us. Roxi is the last one in. She slams the door and locks it behind her. She is breathing heavily as she sags against the door. Macey looks around my room and spots my cellphone on the nightstand. She picks my phone up to call the police.

I sit down in my desk chair before I look around for Lilah, and I'm not surprised at the sight of her when my eyes connect with hers. She looks a mess with food caked on her nice sweater and her face blotchy from the sobs that are slightly shaking her body. She looks like she has seen a ghost, with all her color drained from her face and the look of fear widened eyes.

Why did he have to come here? I feel like he knows when I'm happy, and I begin to let my guard down a little when he suddenly appears in my life full of rage.

"Why is Jack showing up now?" Macey questions hanging up the phone.

"I have a feeling he is trying to scare Poppy, and possibly us, too. This could be a way to try to draw you out of the house. There's no telling with him," Roxi says, leaning on my desk beside me.

I haven't referred to Jack as my father in the past couple of days. As I spend more time away from him, the more. I begin to understand what my life really consisted of. He is only Jack to me now. He no longer feels like a dad to me. Sometimes thinking about the fact that I no longer hold any good and healthy feelings toward my relationship with him hurts. I shake my head, trying to clear the negative cloud from my head.

"Lilah, let me go get you something clean to wear." I get her one of our school shirts and flash her the best reassuring smile I can muster.

"How were you able to live through that for all those years?" I wasn't sure I heard her correctly, but from the gasps I hear from the other two, I know I did.

"I'm so sorry for how rude that was. Lilah, we do not ask people questions like that." Macey berates her already hysterical daughter.

"Macey, I didn't take any offense to the question. I ask myself that all the time. The simplest explanation I have is, I thought that I deserved everything that he did to me, plus it was all I knew for a very long time. The complicated part of it is that I didn't have anyone else in my life, so there was no one I trusted enough to go to or anyone I thought would believe me."

"We lived right next to you, and I know I never noticed anything. I was living my own life, not paying attention to what was going on around me. I never even suspected that there could have been a problem, and your friendship ending like it did with Lewis after your mom's death should have been a huge red flag. I'm so sorry we didn't check on you after that." Lilah is now panting, and her eyes are puffy and bloodshot.

Macey gasps, but she sounds like she hiccupped. Her eyes are watery, and she clasps her hand over her mouth.

"Poppy, I'm so sorry that we never came to check on you or that we were oblivious to what was happening right next door. Had we known, I swear we would have gotten you the help you needed." Macey's voice cracks, and she begins taking ragged breaths to control the sobbing she is trying to suppress.

"Macey, you don't have anything to apologize for. I'm where I need to be."

Macey pulls me into a tight hug. I don't tell her that she is hurting me, because I think that would make her feel worse. Lilah finally goes to get cleaned up. We are quiet for a few minutes before we hear some commotion from downstairs. Jack is cussing and yelling my name. I hear someone's voice mentioning that the police have been called. The door slams so hard, we hear the clinking sound of glass hitting the ground.

I go to my window in time to see Jack peel out of the driveway. If he's here when the police show up, then he will be arrested, and I don't think he wants that.

Lilah walks out of the bathroom, more composed than she was before.

There's a knock on the door, followed by Lewis's dad's voice. "All right, ladies you can come out now. It's safe."

I'm astonished by the looks of everyone when we get downstairs. The guys are all in a rumpled mess, like they just got done fighting, and the window closest to the front door is completely smashed.

"Jack was highly intoxicated, and he wanted to see 'His ungrateful daughter,' as he referred to Poppy. Jax and Lewis tried to hold him back, but he managed to get loose a couple of times, and he would swing at everyone and everything that was in arms reach. He got a few hits on us, but nothing we couldn't handle." Shane shrugs, like what happened was no big deal.

"I'm so sorry dinner is now ruined."

Everyone tries to assure me that nothing is ruined and that we still have a delicious meal waiting for us. I know we have games after dinner planned, but I really don't want to do that now. I just want to hide in my room until the reality of my life disappears.

We get Lilah a new plate, because hers landed on the floor, and soon after we start eating, we all begin to talk and laugh like nothing happened. The crummy feeling I have never goes away, but our laughs do a good job of covering my souring mood like a band aid until everyone leaves.

When I go to bed, I lock my door, even though Shane and Jax nailed in a board where the window was. I still don't feel safe with my father being on the loose and the police not being able to catch him.

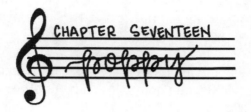

CHAPTER SEVENTEEN

"Roxi, what time is my doctor's appointment this afternoon?" I ask before putting a forkful of waffle in my mouth.

"I'll pick you up right after lunch, unless you would like to go out to eat somewhere."

"Lunch would be great!" I grab my phone that is next to my plate. "I need to tell Lewis I will be out for the science lab."

POPPY: Hey Roxi, is taking me to lunch before my docs apt.

Jax comes in and walks to the pantry grabbing a granola bar before heading out of the kitchen. His brows are furrowed, and his lips are smashed in a thin line.

"What's wrong with Jax?" I ask, and my phone dings with a reply from Lewis.

LEWIS: Have fun. I'll see you at school.

I reply with a simple kissy face emoji and then turn my attention to Roxi.

"He's been like this since Lewis's family came over for dinner, but today is worse, because we won't let him go to the meeting with the lawyers." Roxi begins washing a coffee cup. "He was willing to skip practice, but Shane had to put his foot down and tell him he can't miss practice to go."

"I get it, but he has obligations with the team, and it would be really hard for me to go to his game and cheer him on if he has to ride the bench, just to go to the lawyer's office so we can prepare for court coming up."

"You're the best. If anyone can cheer him up, I bet you can."

"Poppy. Are you ready to go? I need to get to school a little earlier than normal today." Jax scowls at me but turns again toward the front door.

I guess he was hoping that I was just going to follow him out of the kitchen while I am eating the fluffiest waffles ever made. I reluctantly put my fork down with a sad sigh. I pick my plate up, but Roxi stops me.

"Go on. He's in a mood today. I'll take care of this."

I rush to give Roxi a hug before jogging out of the kitchen to catch up with Jax. I grab my stuff out of my favorite chair and turn to see Jax waiting for me in the foyer.

"What's up?" I say opening the front door.

"I am pissed," Jax stomps onto the front porch, like a toddler that didn't get candy at the grocery store. "They won't let me go to the lawyer's office with you guys after school. I know I have obligations to my team, but I think they would understand that this is an unusual circumstance, and I'm needed there with you," He grumbles as he gets into his truck.

"Jax, I really want to go to the rest of your games and cheer you on. I already missed so many of them, and I don't want to miss anymore. What if I video the meeting, and we just hang out together this evening."

"Just us, no one else?"

"Just you and me," I promise.

"It won't be the same." He sounds like a brat, but I can't help but laugh at his sulking.

"I know it's not, but I really do want to go to the rest of your games to cheer you on, and I can't do that if you're benched." I put my seatbelt on and turn back to Jax. "And think of it this way, when we watch the video, you'll be able to crack all the jokes and won't have to worry about the possibility of getting grounded again." We laugh because the second time we all sat down with the lawyers, Jax made so many inappropriate wise cracks that he got grounded.

"I like that you want to cheer for me, and, honestly, I want that too. I guess if you can film the meeting, then I'll go to practice, but you better cheer for me louder than your boyfriend." He has a taunting tone at the end, and his nose is scrunched like he just smelled something rotten.

"You got a deal. What are we going to do with all this extra time?" I say as he pulls into the empty school parking lot.

"Since I interrupted your breakfast, I should treat you and Lewis to breakfast burritos."

"Sure, I could go for some food." As if on cue, my stomach

146

grumbles.

He does a couple of donuts in the parking lot; he is going so fast that the force of his turn and speed pushes me into the door. He laughs like a villain and peels out of the parking lot with his tires squealing and smoke rising from where his tires are.

"I have always wanted to do that in the school parking lot."

My phone rings interrupting our laughter. "Hey, Lewis!"

"I went to your house to surprise you and take you to school, but Roxi said that you guys already left."

"DUDE! MEET US AT THE DINER! BREAKFAST BURRITOS!"

"FUCK, YEAH!!" I hold the phone away from my ear before I lose some of my hearing from these heathens yelling.

When I don't hear anymore screaming, I put my phone back to my ear. I hear the end of whatever it is that Lewis was saying.

"Ugh, what did you say?"

"I'll be there in a few minutes. Order for me if you get there before I do."

"See you in a little bit." Lewis hangs up on me, and I look at Jax.

"Lewis wants us to order for him." I rub my head where a headache is starting to form. "Do you know what he gets?"

"You mean to tell me you don't know what your boyfriend likes?" He gives me a wolfish grin. "You, okay? You're rubbing the side of your head, and you're turning pink." Worry creases his forehead.

"Yeah, my head is hurting."

Jax pulls into the parking lot and once he is stopped, he turns to me, but I on too busy trying to see if Lewis is here to notice at first. "Do I need to call my mom or take you to the doctor? You're still healing from a head injury."

"Let's eat and see how I feel."

We walk in and go up to the counter to order.

"How many burritos this morning, Jax?" the pretty waitress behind the register asks in a high-pitched voice that resembles the sound of someone baby-talking.

I know she is flirting, but how can guys find that attractive? I would never go up to some guy I thought was hot and change my voice to be ear splittingly high. I swear, if the octave goes up any higher, my windows will crack.

"I want the normal plus 2 more."

She finally looks at me, and from the look of shock on her face, I'm guessing she isn't used to Jax not flirting back.

"Lewis will be joining you?" her voice has this kind of rasp to it that has a natural sexiness if she doesn't change it.

I purse my lips and slant my eyes in her. Why the hell is she wanting to know if Lewis is coming or not. I look around at the tables, trying to decide where I want to eat. I look back at Jax. He is shaking from laughing so hard that he isn't even making a noise.

"What?" My tone is clipped; my irritation and headache are just getting worse.

"You're jealous, and it's cute. She does have a thing for him, so I get it. I think they hooked up at a party once."

My brows furrow as much as they can, and I feel my face heat in anger. I cross my arms and shift my weight from one foot to the other.

"Dude!" Lewis and Jax do this handclap shake thing, "What the hell did you do to piss off Poppy?"

Jax wiggles his eyebrows, "Kit is working this morning, and I may have mentioned that you hooked up with her. Wasn't it like the best night of her life?" Jax changes his voice at the end to imitate a girl's voice and rolls his eyes as he is being extra by flipping fake long hair.

"Poppy, it was last year at the end, and-"

"I don't want to hear about it!" I huff.

I feel Lewis wrap his arms around me, and I instantly melt into him with my head resting on his chest. I love having a tall boyfriend. I shouldn't let what Lewis did in the past bother me, but I can't help it.

"You're funny and cute when your claws come out. Don't worry, Poppy. Your pants are the only ones he wants to get into now." Jax puffs his chest up, and you can tell that he is pleased with himself. "But if you ask me, I'd say you're way too good for him."

That waitress comes back out of the kitchen a few minutes later; she sees Lewis, and the seductive flirty smile she gave Jax earlier comes back, but bigger this time. She hasn't seen me in his arms yet, and I can't wait to see her reaction when she does.

"Lewis, it's so good to see you." Her voice goes back into nails on the chalkboard territory.

I watch silently as her eyes slowly move down Lewis, checking him out. When she finally notices that Lewis is hugging me from behind, her eyes turn into thick slits, and her cheeks begin to turn red.

She turns her attention to Jax.

"I thought she was with you since she rode with you."

"Oh no, those two are the ones bumping uglies now. She has him locked down." I snort, trying to hold back a laugh at what Jax says, but when I see Kit's reaction, I can't but laugh.

Her jaw drops, and her face turns pink. She walks backwards until her back hits the revolving door that I assume leads to the kitchen. We move to the side; I don't know why we haven't sat yet. I mean, we ordered, but I'm wondering if the guys are waiting to pay.

I turn around again, but this time I rest my cheek against Lewis, burying my face into the soft dark blue t-shirt he is wearing. I close my eyes and silently beg my head to stop hurting.

"Lewis, take Poppy to my house," Jax says in a low voice just loud enough for us to hear.

I'm confused why he would want me to leave. I haven't gotten my food yet.

A bell rings, alerting Ms. Promiscuous that a customer is here, but when I hear the voice, chills go down my spine that has my eyes popping open. I know exactly who's here.

"Well, well, well." The hairs on the back of my neck instantly stand from the goosebumps breaking out all over my body. "If it isn't the little brat that is ruining my life."

Kit comes forward, plastering another fake smile on her overly made-up face. "How may I help you?"

"Yeah! The order is under Jack Monroe!" His voice is clipped. Even if he wasn't my father, you can tell there is more than annoyance laced in his tone.

He talks this way when he wants to intimidate someone, and I can see that Kit feels intimidated because she looks like she physically shrinks under Jack's stare. Welcome to my world. It was never a fun place to be.

"Of course, let me go check on that for you." Kit rushes to the window and talks to the cook. She returns to the register, empty handed.

"It is being packed up for you right now. Is there anything else I can get you?"

"Yeah, some plasticware would be great."

She goes back to the window when the cook rings a bell letting her know that there is an order ready.

She finishes checking Jack out, then hands him his bag. Jack turns toward us where Jax and Lewis now have me practically sandwiched between them as they act as a shield from my father. Lewis has me pulled to him with my back pressed firmly against his back as Jax is standing in front of me with his feet shoulder-width apart, his arms crossed over his chest. This stance makes him appear bigger than his already large frame.

Even though I'm being blocked by Lewis, that doesn't stop the moron that is my father from opening his damn mouth.

"I'll get you, little girl, and when I do, it will be when you least expect it."

He tries to walk out of the diner backwards but fails when he crashes into a table. I bite into Lewis's shirt, but I accidentally nip him in a sore attempt to conceal my laughter at my father stumbling. Lewis's hand goes into my hair, fisting a tight grip close to the nape of my neck, but he doesn't react any other way. We stay that way until my father is leaving in the black SUV that has been spotted at Jax's house more than once already.

My mind begins to race, and I completely tune out my surroundings. I feel like time has frozen, and the pounding in my chest intensifies as the seconds go by with none of moving.

Lewis pulls lightly on my arm trying to get me to move. When he figures out that is not going to get me to do anything, he scoops me up in his arms and carries me to a booth. I hear Jax's voice get further away, but I heard him say "Dad," so I'm guessing he is calling Shane.

Lewis sits me down and gently pushes me until I'm next to the window, and he scoots in next to me. He is halfway in the booth; I wonder if he is trying not to crowd or overwhelm me right now. I tap his shoulder softly, and he looks down at me with one eyebrow raised. I pull at the sleeve of his shirt, and thankfully he gets the hint and comes all the way into the seat. His thigh is pressed against mine, making me feel safer after the little run in with my father.

I love the feeling of his body warming me up. I look behind me, and my eyes connect with a wall. I sigh and sag into Lewis's side, and he puts his arm around my shoulders, pulling me closer to him. Two big burritos in foil slide in front of me. I'm just staring at them; these are massive. How do they think I'm going to eat all of this? I look to see how many Jax has, and my eyes almost jump out of my head. He has four of them, and so does Lewis. Lewis slides a Styrofoam cup toward me, followed by two tiny plastic cups. One is filled with salsa, and the other is filled with queso.

I pick up the burrito and peel back the foil and take a big bite that is mainly tortilla, but damn, it's so soft and warm. A moan escapes past my lips, and Lewis shifts in his feet and one of his hands swiftly disappears under the table. I'm fixated on his movements, and my eyes watch as he adjusts himself. I am pleasantly surprised by his actions and slightly embarrassed at the same time.

Jax howls with laughter and breaks the spell I was under. I pick up the burrito I have bitten into. I tear a piece of the tortilla off and toss it at Jax, hitting him in the chin this time. Lewis howls with laughter.

"Kids! Is anyone hurt?" Roxi yells from the other end of the diner, in what one would mistake as pure panic.

Shane puts his hand on her shoulder, but she shrugs him off jogging to where we are. I look at Shane, and he is trying to hide the fact that he finds Roxi amusing because of the situation we are currently in, since we accidentally ran into Jack.

"Are you okay?" Shane asks when he reaches our table.

We all nod our heads, still stuffing burritos into our mouths.

"Poppy, do you want to go home, or are you feeling up to going to school?" Roxi is thankfully no longer yelling, but the pitch of her voice is still higher than normal.

"Mom, I think Poppy needs to go home or to the doctors early. She was rubbing her head early, and when I asked her what was wrong, she said her head was hurting." My jaw drops. Jax totally busted me.

"Come on, honey." Roxi waves me to her, and Lewis stands up so he can get out of her way because I'm sure she would have moved him herself. "Let's get you to the car while we wait for Shane to talk to the boys." Roxi take my cup of salsa and queso and the burrito that is still in foil off the table and takes them to the counter.

She is saying something to Kit, and after a few seconds, I scoot out of the booth and hug Lewis, and Shane and I give Jax a high five. "Boys, the detectives will be by the school this afternoon to get a statement from you. Lewis, your parents are going to be present for your talk. Jax, we asked if they would stand in as the adults when you go in for your record of what happened this morning." Shane runs his hand over his face, and the lines in his forehead deepen.

"When will I have to do mine?"

"We'll stop by the station on our way home from the lawyers' office. Jax, we'll be home later than we thought."

"POPPY!" I hear Roxi calling me so we can leave.

"Jax can come have dinner at my house tonight," Lewis volunteers.

"That would give me some peace of mind. Thank you, Lewis," I wave to the guys and walk to Roxi while they finish their talk, but they grab their food and follow me to the parking lot.

Roxi and Shane go to wait in the truck for me, and I sigh and look at Jax. "I was fine going to school. I already missed so much."

He shrugs, but deep down, I know he did what was best.

"Can I give you a ride back home?" Lewis asks, shoving his hands into the front pocket of his jeans.

"No, finish breakfast, and make it to school before both of you are late and have to do sprints at practice." I stand on my tippy toes, and Lewis bends down to meet me the rest of the way as I kiss him bye.

This kiss feels different from what they usually do. Lewis kisses me like he's starving, and I am the only one that can make the hunger pains go away. I grab his shirt and pull myself closer to his body; I want to feel as much of him as I can.

"You guys should just fuck already. It would make everyone feel better!" Jax hollers out of his truck window.

When did he get in the truck?

I pull away from Lewis's shaking body. I look up at him, and Lewis is laughing, while I'm embarrassed. What if Roxi and Shane heard Jax? I bury my face in Lewis's shirt, wrapping my arms around him. Lewis hugs me back before walking me to Shane's truck.

"Text me later." Lewis kisses my cheek and walks to his jeep.

I climb into the truck and drive the short distance home.

"I'll call the doctor when we get home. She may want you to come in sooner." I nod my head and look out the window.

I wonder if there will be time for a nap. I'm beginning to feel crumby.

I'm feeling more than drained by the time I get home. Today was a lot all at once. I want to go to bed, but I promised Jax we could reenact the meeting. When Roxi called the doctor, she wanted us to go up there right away, and I did tests. We were there for the whole morning. I pull my phone out, so I can tell Jax we are home, and if I'm lucky, he'll come right here.

POPPY: Let me know when you get home.

JAX: Sweet, you're home. Be there in ten.

I walk up the stairs to my room, because I want to change into my favorite pajamas, but I start to get this funny feeling in the pit of my stomach that something is not right. I get to my door and see that it is closed. I don't remember closing my door. I rarely do when I'm gone.

I twist the knob and push the door open. I'm not prepared for the sight before me. My room is in a state of disarray as things have been thrown around. I run downstairs ignoring the pain pulsating through my head, and the first place I go to is Shane's office, praying that he's there.

Shane isn't here, and I don't know what to do. My room is an ungodly mess, and I know no one in this house would do that. Shane's office seems to be in order, and nothing looked weird when we came into the house. I take a long deep breath in, but when I try to take a calming breath out, an ear-piercing, almost blood-curdling scream, comes out instead.

I hear the sharp taps of footsteps, and I feel the nape of my neck get moist with sweat. I begin to get sucked into a memory of my dad pacing in front of my bedroom door, wearing expensive loafers, one stormy night before barging into my room with fury clouding his bloodshot eyes.

My scream dies out at the loud crack of thunder rings in my ears and lightning shoots behind my eyelids and, just as violently as that night and the fear I felt crawling to the bathroom after my father leaves me on the floor in an unrecognizable pile of pale blonde hair. I crumble to the floor of Shane's office, crying as the memory keeps slamming into my mind over and over in an unbearable loop. I can't break free from my father and his endless abuse.

"Poppy, what's wrong?" I hear Shane murmur from somewhere close by.

"My room," I manage to stammer.

"Okay, I'll go check it out. Roxi, wait here with Poppy."

"Mom, I am home, and Lewis is with me!" Jax announces like he often does, but his unwelcome announcement breaks the silence that was comforting me.

I lift my head up enough to see that Roxi pokes her head out of the office door, and she waves the guys over to us.

"What's up?" Jax asks, not picking up on the fact that something may be wrong.

"I don't know yet, wait here until your father comes back downstairs."

"I went upstairs to change, and my room was a mess."

153

Roxi turns to me. "What do you mean, a mess? When we left for your appointment earlier, your room was tidy."

"Everything appears to be thrown around, like someone was looking for something or was in a hurry."

Shane returns red-faced and boy, I've never seen him so mad. Sirens fill the quiet room; red and blue lights bounce off the walls outside of the office.

Shane goes and answers the door. "Thank you for coming. Poppy's room is the only one that is in disarray. The rest of the house seems to be untouched as it was this morning."

"We are going to do a full sweep of the house, and then we'll want to look for evidence and take pictures of the room that was tampered with. While we clear the house, we ask that you all remain in here," Detective Scotts instructs.

They don't take very long clearing the house. They come in to get our statements, and I go first, and then they ask a couple of questions to Lewis and Jax, but they don't know anything, since they just got here, and then they finish with Shane.

Detective Whitmen adds, "Log anything that might be missing and send us that list."

We go to my room so we can clean up, but I really don't want to be in here. Roxi and Shane begin picking up my clothes, while Lewis and Jax begin straightening up my furniture and desk that was knocked around or turned over.

I stare in my closet, and my stomach rolls when I find the box I keep my mom's things in has the lid off with the contents scattered around the floor. I fall to my knees picking up one thing at a time, mentally noting what was in that box. I look through the contents again, and I'm missing three pictures, one was my mom and me in the hospital the day I was born, one while my mom was pregnant, and the last picture I got with her while she was alive.

I move some of the laundry off the floor and put them in the hamper, and I continue to pick up more when Roxi comes into the closet.

"Honey, I found these crumpled up under one of your pillows." She holds out what looks to be three little balled up paper.

I take them, and one by one, I see the missing pictures with creases and tears in them.

I begin tearing up, and Roxi pulls me into a hug when she sees what I have.

"I know someone that can restore these. I had some old family pictures that barely survived a fire, and she was a miracle worker and was able to save the important part of the pictures. I think she can save the parts with your mom and you in it."

I pull away from her, and she gently takes them from me. She walks out of the closet with the pictures held against her chest. Once she is gone, I finish my closet, and I note that nothing else was taken.

"We don't think he took anything out of here, but we would like you to double check. Also, the stuff we were sure where they went, we put them on your desk," Roxi gives me a weak smile, but I know she must be scared, because I know that I am.

I stand there, letting a brief flash of relief surge through me, before the sinking feeling of dread consumes me. I'm terrified about what is happening in my life, as well as what is happening in the Taylors' lives.

Lewis hugs me. "Poppy, what can we do to help you?"

I lay my head on his chest. "All I need is this."

We stay there while everyone leaves us in my room. I don't move, and neither does Lewis.

We stay that way until Roxi comes back. "Poppy, pizza is on its way, but Lewis, your parents want you to go home." She gives him a sad smile but giggles when she sees that Lewis's shirt sticks to my face when I pull away from tears that managed to escape.

I don't blame them for wanting their son home where they know that he is safe. I have brought so much shit into all these people's lives. Maybe everything would have been better if I stayed with Jack.

Lewis gives me a kiss on the cheek; then he leaves with his shoulders hunched. I can tell he doesn't want to leave, but if I'm being honest with myself, I'm kind of grateful that he can't stay and see me try to hold myself together through dinner.

"Would you like to switch rooms?" Roxi asks, as we go to the dining room.

"Maybe for a couple of nights."

The doorbell rings, and Roxi goes to answer the door while I go sit in the dining room. The table is already set, and I have a glass of water on the table. I take a sip with shaky hands as everyone else sits down.

Dinner is unusually quiet, and I know it's my fault, but I also think no one knows what to say right now. Jax ate with Lewis, but he somehow found some room for half of a pizza. Shane and Roxi are picking at their food like I am.

When we are done, Shane clears the table, even though I'm supposed to do the dishes tonight, but I wasn't going to argue with him.

"Jax, will you go to my room with me, so I can move a few things to the guest room?"

He walks silently toward the stairs but waits for me to catch up before he climbs the stairs.

"So, did you get the video?"

"Yeah, I'll show you after this."

"Sweet. You want to watch a movie after?" He sounds excited since he first came home.

"Yeah, let me change, and I'll meet you in the den."

Jax gives me a side hug before he walks away, closing the door behind him. I sit down on the bed and let myself cry for a few minutes.

Jax isn't in the den when I get there, so I make myself comfortable on the couch and pull up the video on my phone. Then I find a comedy for us to watch.

Jax walks in and hands me a big peanut butter and cookies and cream sundae; then he flops down on the long side of the couch. I video cast the lawyer's meeting on the screen, and he watches in complete silence, listening intently. I notice he makes a few faces, and he stands up, opening his mouth like he wants to say something, but he just sits back down with his lips smashed and his face turning red.

The video stops, and I exit out of the video cast and the title screen for the movie reappears. Jax sits there with a blank expression on his face for a few minutes and seemingly out of nowhere, he jumps off the couch.

"This is fucking great! Poppy. You're going to be safe! Your father will lose his rights." He sits down, when he realizes that, even if my father gets his rights fully terminated, it won't be at this court date, and not until after I turn 18, because there is a system. "You're going to technically be in foster care until you age out. Is there nothing my parents can do to change that?"

"No, but it's definitely better than going back to Jack, and your parents are taking classes to get certified to be my foster parents."

He sits back down defeated, like he has done after getting his ass kicked at a video game.

"So, what did the doctor say?"

"I'm healing well, and I only have to wear the wrap on my sides when I am doing any kind of physical activity, or if I go anywhere, I have a chance to be jostled around. My headache from earlier is probably a side effect of all the untreated head trauma I've had. We'll be doing more tests, but until we figure out what is going on, I was prescribed meds to help with the bad headaches."

"It's good that you're slowly getting better, but the headaches, when are you supposed to hear back from those?" Jax frowns, running his finger through his dirty blond hair. "I told Mom we're having movie night, and we're crashing in the den tonight. She just said to be sure to get enough sleep for school tomorrow."

We make ourselves cozy with pillows and blankets as the guys on the screen make fools of themselves. We laugh, but eventually Jax's loud snores fill the room. After all the events of today, I'm frightened and anxious, with no hope of getting any sleep. I don't know how I'm going to function tomorrow. I wish Jax would have stayed up with me to keep my mind off all of this, but he needs to sleep, or practice will be hell for him tomorrow.

Jennifer Froh

I feel dazed and my stomach rolls as I push my oatmeal around my bowl. I notice that Jax has sat down at the island bar in the kitchen next to me. I'm struggling to keep my head up to stay awake.

"Poppy, how are you doing?" Roxi rushes over to me from the entrance to the room. "Are you not feeling well? Is your head hurting again?" Roxi presses warm hands to my head, checking to see if I have a fever.

"I couldn't fall asleep last night. It's hard not to think about Jack coming into your home and destroying my room, and then court is today, which means I'll have to see him," I eat a small spoonful of the sweet sticky oatmeal, and my stomach lurches, "I think it's time I talk to someone."

Roxi hugs me and rocks gently, trying to soothe me, but the movement is only making me more nauseous.

"Is there anything to keep in mind while I'm looking at a therapist?" Shane walks in with a coffee mug in his hand. He goes to get a refill before leaning against the counter across from me.

"I'm not sure. I've never been to therapy. Maybe a woman that has some specialty in this kind of thing."

"Of course. I need to grab some papers from my office. We'll meet you two outside." Shane dismisses us and puts his mug in the sink.

The tapping sound from my heels echo behind me as I make my way to the living room. I am vaguely aware that Jax is following close behind me. Roxi helped me get ready this morning and she said I'm court ready in my black dress, red blazer, and matching red heels.

I'm feel Jax close behind me as I walk onto the front porch. My phone vibrates in my blazer pocket.

LEWIS: I'll be at the courthouse shortly, see you soon.

I put my phone away without replying. I just need to try to get through this morning and get past seeing my dad and whatever potential doom the court decides for me.

I stop dead in my tracks next to Shane's truck. Jax must not have been paying attention, since he bumps into me from behind. I stumble forward and catch myself on Shane's truck before I fall.

"Poppy, what the hell?" He's clearly annoyed by the clipped tone of his voice. I interrupted whatever he was doing.

"Jax, Shane's tires are flat." I know it's just in my head, but I sound like I'm talking in a tunnel as every word I say echoes in my mind.

Jax moves me out of his way. He bends down to look at the tire and he mutters under his breath, "Fuck." He stands up and walks to each of our cars in the driveway.

"Hey Shane, can you come out here please?"

"THIS IS BULLSHIT!! ALL OF OUR TIRES ARE FUCKING SLASHED!" Jax kicks a rock on the ground, stopping where he bumped into me.

Jax's muttering increases in volume, and soon he is shouting curse words to no one in particular.

"What's going on?" he asks, eyeing his enraged son.

"All of our damn tires are fucking slashed!" Jax's face turns red, and he kicks another rock.

Shane's posture changes to straight and rigid from relaxed. He pulls his phone from the inner pocket of his suit jacket.

"Son, see if Lewis wouldn't mind giving you guys a lift to the courthouse." He puts his phone to his ear. "I also need to get us new tires as soon as possible, and I should probably get them checked out for any other kinds of tampering."

I stand there without knowing what I should say or do.

"Lewis will be here in a couple of minutes." Jax shoves his phone in his pocket and turns toward me. "This is bullshit! You know your deranged father did this!" Jax points at me before pacing again.

I wince at his harsh tone and at his vulgar words, because I know he is right; my father is responsible for this. Why can't he just leave me alone?

"I'm sorry." I'm trying to hold it together, but my surroundings begin to blur. My lungs burn as I try to suck in air. It feels like someone has them in a vice grip.

"Jax, you need to calm down. The detectives think it might be a ploy to get us not to show up to court. We will be on our way shortly.

Roxi is getting us a car, and I'm calling the lawyers to let them know about what happened as well.

Lewis pulls up. Jax goes over and opens the passenger door, pushing the seat forward so I can climb into the back. He is mad but still helps me climb into the car. Before I sit back, I poke my head through the front seats and plant a swift kiss on Lewis's cheek.

"Thank you for coming to get us."

"No problem." Lewis pulls out of the driveway, and Jax is back on his phone. "Do you have any idea what is going to happen this morning?"

"They are going to put in a request to start the process of revoking my father's parental rights from him. They feel, with the evidence of my bruises when I first moved in with Jax's family and my father's attack at the school, as well as his continued harassment, the court will grant a protection order in place, and they may even start the process of terminating his rights."

"That doesn't feel like enough after all of what he has done." Lewis hits his steering wheel with his palm.

"They've had enough to arrest him, but they of course had trouble locating him. It seems like whenever they get close to catching him, he manages to get away somehow." There's been so much going on that the detectives have found. "My father has lost his job and is dangerously close to losing the house. He has made a lot of awful decisions, and they seem to just be getting worse as time goes by," I add, after deciding to be completely honest about what is all going on.

Jax turns in his seat and looks at me with his jaw dropped. Lewis pulls into the parking spot at the courthouse.

"He's a damn coward, hiding and running away. Someone needs to get a hold of him to face the consequences of what he's done, since he can't own up to his own damn actions." Jax is back to ranting and damn, I hate that he doesn't know any of this and that he is learning all of this just now.

Lewis nods his head in agreement, "Yeah, pretty much."

"Dad and Mom are here and waiting on the steps. He also wants us to park in the garage from now on. Reminder me later, and we'll get you a garage door opener for your car."

"Oh, you don't have to do that."

"It would be pointless for you to punch in the code or go through the house to open the garage."

"Oh, well, if the door is locked. I'll just wait outside for someone to come home, and I can go in the garage when they get here or text Roxi that I'm on my way to your house, and she can open the garage for me?"

"Why would you do that? You don't have to wait to be invited in."

"Um." I climb out of the backseat of Lewis's Jeep and begin to walk to the courthouse.

"Poppy, what's the big deal?"

"Well, I don't think I should get a garage door opener or a house key."

"What do you mean? You have a house key."

"No, I don't."

"Fuck, why haven't you said anything?"

"I'm not going to ask for them. That is rude, Besides, I haven't needed one before."

I reach the steps and see Shane and Roxi standing with Mr. Steen, my lawyer, and his assistant or partner, I'm not sure what Ms. Runes is.

"Good morning." Mr. Steens greets us, and he is in too good of a mood for what is happening today.

"I have been in contact with Mr. Monroe's lawyers, and they assure me that he will be in attendance today," Ms. Runes add cheerfully.

I don't think that is anything to be so happy about.

Lewis's family is joining us on the courthouse steps. They give me an awkward side hug as Lilah comes up the steps out of breath with crazy windblown hair.

"Thank goodness. I made it in time."

"Thanks for coming. It means so much for my family and me to have your support."

"Of course." Macey walks over and hugs Roxi, rubbing comforting circles on her back.

After they pull apart, they wipe tears from their eyes, and we walk into the stone building, and I go through a metal detector and sit on a bench close by while I wait on everyone else.

My lawyers return from checking in. "We will be in courtroom one. They'll let us in shortly," Ms. Runes says to Roxi, who is sitting next to me on the bench.

"Poppy, as a reminder of how this is going to go, they'll open the doors, and then we can enter. We'll be on the right side of the courtroom while your father and his team will be on the left. Do not talk to them or acknowledge them unless you are on the stand, for any reason. You also don't have to talk unless the judge asks you a direct question. Ms. Runes or I will be doing the talking and the pleasantries when we go in." Mr. Steens puts his briefcase on the floor next to his foot.

I look around and notice that my father is not here, nor are his lawyers. Maybe they are instructed to wait somewhere else.

We sit there for about 45 minutes, but to me, all the time that has passed feels like so much longer before the dark wooden doors open. A guy in a police uniform says that we may enter if we are here for the *Monroe vs. Monroe* temporary orders hearing. Everyone goes in, but I remain where I am sitting.

"Just take your time. I'll wait here with you until you're ready." Roxi has been my rock through this whole ordeal, and I wouldn't know what I would do without her patience and compassion.

"I guess I'm as ready as I'll ever be." I stand up and smooth my dress down.

I walk down the aisle that splits the two sides, and the walkway seems to be getting longer and longer, almost like I've seen in horror movies. I feel like everyone is watching, but they aren't. People are turned to who they are talking in quiet conversations.

"Poppy, we're unable to sit with you, but we will be right here behind you." Shane motions to where they'll be. When I finally get to the table, I need to sit with my lawyers.

My lawyer goes over a few things. Then they ask me if I have any questions or if there is anything that I may not understand.

My father's legal team comes in, and boy, they look pissed. I wonder if my father has done something else. "They don't look happy," I whispered to Ms. Runez. "Is my father considered a no-show, since his lawyers are here, and he isn't?"

"Not yet, but if he isn't here by the time the doors close, and the judge comes in, then he'll be a no show."

I watch three police officers enter the room and stand next to the door. They rest their hands on their belts looking around the room.

"They are here to arrest your father; odds are there are a couple of them outside as well. He'll have to come in wearing cuffs if he shows," Mr. Steens explained.

We wait several more minutes, and then the bailiff announces the judge. I'm tapped on the shoulder, and Ms. Runez motions for me to stand up.

The judge enters. Then we are told to sit back down. I glance to my left and see that my father is still not here. The police officers that are in the back are exiting and closing the doors quietly behind them.

The judge begins talking, and I suddenly realize that they are ordering Jack as a "failure to appear." Then, he asks if either party would like to say anything.

"Your honor, we would like to petition to terminate the parental rights of Mr. Jack Monroe, request a protection order on Ms. Poppy Fae Monroe, and request to start the process of granting guardianship to Shane and Roxanne Taylor, who are currently acting as caregivers and foster parents to Ms. Monroe."

There is some more talking, and I'm not quite sure what is happening. I am told that we are breaking for lunch and then our legal team will be meeting with my dad when we get back.

Lunch is a blur of the smell of garlic and chatter from our crowded table. The day is moving by faster than I thought. The morning went by; then lunch is suddenly over. I'm now sitting in the chair as the judge tells me that the protection order has been granted, and they can move forward with the petition to revoke my father's parental rights, if he refuses to do what the court is going to mandate. I'm told he will have to serve his time, and while he does that, he can do the counseling, group, and even parenting classes.

I'm also told that I have choices for the first time in my life, and he has no doubts that the Taylors will be a wonderful family for me, but he's adamant about listening to what I want.

Lewis is taking us by the house to change afterwards and then we'll be going to school in enough time to get to the last three classes plus practice.

Lewis is watching me in the rearview mirror, and I can tell that he is concerned about me after court. I push the thoughts away as I look out the side of the Jeep, watching the building pass.

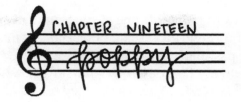

CHAPTER NINETEEN

We park in the school parking lot, and I can't help but think that this is the last place I want to be right now. Roxi convinces me that going to school after court would be a good idea, because getting back into my routine would be good for me, and she also reminds me of how much school I've missed this year, and we are still in our first semester.

There are only eight minutes left of what our lunch would have been if we hadn't eaten a little over an hour ago.

Jax gets out of the Jeep, slamming the door behind him. He doesn't even bother to see if I want out. I climb through the middle of the front two seats.

I sit where I am facing Lewis, and he shifts as much as his big frame will allow in the limited space of his Jeep. I lean over the console, and he meets me halfway. I swear I'm addicted to this boy's kisses and the electric current that pulses through me just from his touch. He deepens our kiss, but I still want to be closer to him. I shift in my seat, and Lewis takes that as a cue to help me over the console and onto his lap. I shift until I'm straddling him, and I give him a shy smile as we begin to make out in the school parking lot.

Our hands begin to roam, and Lewis's lips leave mine, and he begins a teasing trail of wet kisses from my cheek to my neck. My hands run down his shirt until I feel the hem, and my fingers tease the flesh hiding just above the waist of his jeans until my hands are exploring the muscles that his shirt hides. I feel his large hands go up the back of my shirt and he rubs lazy circles on my back driving me wild.

Someone lays a long lazy honk on their horn, interrupting us.

"GET A ROOM!" the person that honked yells at us.

Lewis looks out the window. "Damn sophomore is going to pay for that," he chuckles, flipping off one of his teammates.

I can't help the giggle that escapes me, and that makes Lewis laugh. I climb into the passenger seat, flip the visor down, fix my gloss, and attempt to smooth my hair down. I hop out of Lewis's Jeep once I'm satisfied that I don't look like I just hopped out of Lewis's bed.

I walk around to the driver's side, and Lewis is still inside, but now his head is leaned back against the headrest, and his eyes are closed. I tap on the window and mouth, "What are you dining?"

He rolls the window down, "I need a moment."

I smile triumphantly up at Lewis. "Need a cold shower?" I tease.

"You damn well know it. The claw marks on my chest are proof you need the same, but unlike you, I can't hide it." My cheeks flame at his words.

Lewis sits there for several more minutes, "Lewis, if you plan on staying in there longer, I'm going to say bye now. I don't want to be late for class."

He gets out, and I can't help the bubble of laughter that is tickling my tongue from spilling out as I watch Lewis adjust himself before getting his backpack and slamming his door shut.

"Yeah, laugh it up," but he chuckles with me.

We stop by our lockers before we part ways to go to class. The class goes by slowly, but that is usually how it is when all you're doing is book work.

The bell rings, and I don't see Lewis or Jax in the hallway. I turn in the direction of the stairs that lead to science, when I hear someone yelling my name. "Poppy! Hey! Wait up!" I stop, and with better judgment, I turn and see Lana, the head cheerleader, waving her arms in the air and marching towards me.

I brace myself for whatever this encounter is going to be. Lana is a bitch on a good day, but she never talks to me unless it's about Lewis and how I need to stay away from him. I'm feeling feisty today after the morning I had, so let her try something.

"Hey, Lana. What's up?"

"I just wanted to let you know that Lewis and I are going to winter formal together next week, and if you don't back off, I'll make you." She puts her hands on her boney hips and stomps her foot a few times while she talks.

She looks like a bratty child, and I can't help but laugh at her tantrum.

"Does Lewis know about this?" I cross my arms and shift my weight to my left leg, making my hip go out.

"You think he wants to take a walking punching bag to formal?" She is practically yelling at me now.

I look away from Lana, because I have the urge to slap that smug face of hers. I've never wanted to hit someone as bad as I want to hurt her, and that says a lot, considering what my father did to me. My eyes connect with Lewis, and I can only imagine the expression he sees, because his smile fades.

"Since I'm so nice, this is the only warning I'm going to give you. LEAVE LEWIS ALONE! He is mine, and I know that him dating you is some kind of joke."

I know he is still too far away to hear what she is saying, but with the surrounding students getting quieter to hear what she is saying to me, it won't be long until he does, and I can't wait to see his reaction.

"Let's see what he thinks of your plan."

"Lewis is going to kiss more than my feet when he thanks me for getting rid of you. Did you know that I'm the only girl he hooks up with more than once? Would you like for me to tell you why?" She's gloating now, and the smile on her face gets wider, "Once he's been between your legs, he'll drop you and then laugh about it in the locker room. I have texts from him that prove that he still wants me. Would you like to read them?"

Lewis bends down to where his face is only two inches away from Lana's ear, and I know she can feel the warmth of his breath on her. I would be mad at this seemingly intimate move, but the anger shining in Lewis's eyes tells me all I need to know.

"Lana, you better not come near my girlfriend again. I don't like your bitchiness and clinginess. We fucked once, and that was one time too many. Keep this shit up and I'll let the guys know what it's really like to hook up with the head cheerleader." Lewis stands up and moves until he is next to me.

"Lewis, we had a great time, I-"

"I told you one night, and I would give you no more. I made the mistake of letting you hang on me, but I'm stopping it now. Don't talk to Poppy again."

Lana stands up straight, tears streaming down her cheeks. She runs into the girl's bathroom that is down the hall. I know that Lewis was harsh with his words towards her, but honestly, I could care less. She started all this drama when she approached me.

"She's a bitch," Jax says, eyeing me. I know that is his discreet way of checking to see if I'm all right.

"I'll be right back." Lewis kisses my cheek, and he leaves me in the hall with Jax. I notice he walks in the direction of the bathrooms.

I look at Jax, and I see that he is on his phone again. I notice he has been glued to it lately.

"What's up with you and Lilah?" I couldn't help but ask.

His head snaps up, and he gives me a deer in headlights look.

"What are you talking about? Why would you say anything about Lilah?" His head snaps up, and I know two things with that reaction.

One, I was right. There is something going on with his feelings for Lilah and two, him being distracted and stuck in his phone has something to do with it.

"Well, a couple of things; I know you couldn't take your eyes off her at dinner. I also noticed that you amped up the jokes, trying to make her laugh. Your charm was on in full force, and I know it wasn't for Lewis and me."

"Well, SHIT! I can't get anything past you. Would I be a shitty friend if I made a move on my best friend's sister?"

"I think if you 'made your move' on his sister without discussing that with him first, then that would be wrong," I don't know how I feel about this new conversation with Jax.

"What do you think?" He sounds nervous.

"Like I said, talk to Lewis about it before you do anything, because my opinion doesn't matter, but it does matter what Lewis thinks, and don't forget to add in how Lilah feels about you." for some reason, I can't bring myself to tell him how I feel, because the jealousy I'm feeling is confusing me.

The bell for science rings, and I'm officially late. "Shit! I've got to go!"

I run to class, and when I get there, Lewis's seat is empty. I don't know where he is, and I can't help but wonder what he is doing, because when he left me in the hallway with Jax, he was going in the direction that Lana ran off to.

I'm doing an easy lab, and the bell rings before I'm even done. I clean up and leave class. The hall is crowded, and I look for Lewis the whole way to my next class, but I still haven't seen him.

I don't know what's going on, and I'm starting to get annoyed. Today has seriously sucked. The teacher comes in and tells us to gather our things, and we'll be collaborating with the music class that I get to take next semester.

"All right, class we are going to pair up, and unfortunately, we have an uneven number. I need either one group of three or a volunteer to do a solo," Mr. Menders says at the front of the room.

My hand instantly goes up at the word "solo."

"All right, Poppy, you can do the solo. The workload is the same, so I just wanted to warn you." Ms. Harting smiles, and I can see that Mr. Menders is pleased that I chose the solo.

The rest of the class goes by with the instructions of the project, and then we are given a list of supplies they need us to get. I can't wait to go shopping for this with Roxi. Maybe we can stop-in tomorrow when we go look for my formal shoes. We got my dress but not the shoes and accessories.

"Poppy, a minute please?" Mr. Menders stops me on my way out. "I know you will do wonderfully on this project, but I'm interested in what instrument you're going to choose."

"Oh, that's easy. We will have to compose four to six songs as our final. The ones in Ms. Harting's class will write the lyrics, and the ones in yours will compose. You didn't give us a limit on instruments, and there is nothing about if we can record the other instruments, but I'll either do half of the songs on the piano and the other on guitar. I need to see more about what our six topic areas and genres are, before I decide what instrument I want to pair with it."

"I look forward to hearing about what you choose to do when you have to turn that in by Monday."

"Do you need a pass?"

"No, I have study hall."

I walk in and check in with the librarian and see that Jax is at my table.

"Where's Lewis?"

"I don't know. I haven't seen him since the Lana thing."

I put my headphones in when Jax looks back at his phone. The bell rings, and I pack my things up.

"Lewis got caught in the hall when he was on his way to science with no hall pass. Do you want to stay for practice or go home?"

"I don't have my car."

"I got my car during the sixth period. You can drive mine home, or I can take you home after practice. I want to hang out with Lewis and talk to him about Lilah."

"I'm nervous about driving your truck home. What if I scratch it or something?"

"Then you scratch it." He shrugs, but his eyes crinkle, and his lips smashed in a line.

"I would like to go home." Jax hands me his keys, and I hug him before we separate.

I go to the parking lot and look for his blue truck.

I climb in and shut the door. I put the key in and turn on Jax's truck. The loud roar of the engine fills the cab with the low sound of county music playing on the radio. I adjust the seat and mirrors before putting my seatbelt on. With a sigh, I slowly drive out of the school parking lot, trying to maneuver this massive vehicle carefully through the parking lot. There are still a lot of other cars trying to get out of the parking lot, plus other students walk, running, or goofing around.

The whole way home, I stress out and decide that this is absolutely the last time I want to drive this damn thing again.

I get home, and I push the button on the visor, and at last, the garage door opens. I park and get a brilliant idea, and I know that since Jax is at practice, he won't reply right away.

POPPY: I made it home, and there is only a minor scratch from pulling into the garage.

I text him before I turn off the truck and hop out. I reach up and grab my bag from the middle seat.

My phone dings with a response as I enter the door leading to the kitchen.

JAX: You had my truck for 5 minutes! What the hell did you do?!

POPPY: Well, I scraped the wall pulling into the garage. :)

JAX: if you're not hurt, then it's no big deal.

POPPY: Your truck is fine. I was only joking, but good luck with your talk.

I walk into the house, and the mouthwatering scent of rich chocolate makes my stomach growl. I walk straight to the counter, and I see Roxi cutting what looks like gooey brownies in a glass pan.

"Hey, honey, I made brownies. Would you like one?"

"Yes, please. they smell so good."

Roxi gets a glass and fills it with milk and dishes a large brownie onto a plate. She places them in front of me and opens a drawer that is closest to the kitchen entryway. She slides two more things to me; one of them is a key and the other is a garage door opener.

"We're so sorry. We never thought about giving these to you sooner."

"It's all right. I didn't really need them before. Roxi, are we still going to go look at shoes and accessories for formal tomorrow?"

"Yea, I'm so excited for shopping and girl time."

"Do you think we can stop by the music store? I need to get some things for a school project."

"Of course. I'm going to do some laundry before dinner. Are you going to be eating here? I know Jax texted and said he and Lewis are eating at the diner."

"Yes, today was kind of a lot, and I kind of want to veg out in front of a movie in the den for a little while."

"Let me know if you need anything, and I'll come find you when dinner is ready."

I go down to the den, and I put on a classic musical and sink deep into the fluffy cushions of the couch. Roxi comes into the den carrying a tray as I'm picking another movie.

"I made pizza, and I thought maybe we could have a girl's night, since Jax is out with friends, and Shane had to go pick up a shift at the bar since one of his bartenders called in sick."

"I can't think of a better way to end the day, after everything we went through this morning. What movie do you want to watch?"

Roxi picks another musical, and she sings through the whole movie. I join in on the few songs that I remember. I haven't had this much fun in a long time.

After the movie, I help Roxi clean up, and I go to bed.

I lay in the guest room bed, looking around. This is not my room and I miss it. Jax knocks on the door jamb before leaning against it.

"How did your talk go?"

"He is pretty pissed at me right now, and it got a little heated." The look he is giving me is like 'are you serious, right now?'

"He'll get over it."

"I'm going to just go to bed. I'll see you in the morning." I've never seen Jax look, or sound so upset.

"Good night, Jax." I whisper into the dark after he is already gone.

I start to drift to sleep when my phone rings, and I see Lewis's handsome face flashing on the screen. I don't want to hear what he has to say about Jax's feelings for Lilah, but I know he needs someone too.

"JAX HAS A THING FOR MY SISTER! CAN YOU BELIEVE THAT?" Lewis yells through the phone before I can even say hello.

"I mean, I'm not surprised." I sigh, sitting up. "Do you know how she feels about him? I think her feelings may be mutual."

"Why would you say that?" I hear a banging sound on the other end of the phone. "There is no way my best friend and sister can have feelings for each other."

"There are worse guys for Lilah to go out with than Jax. He is great and has a fantastic family."

"What's your point?" Another loud bang echoes in the background. "I don't want them together!"

"Why? Jax is the best!"

"I'm tired of talking about this. I'm going to bed." He hangs up without waiting for me to respond, which is a good thing.

He is being an asshole, and frankly, he doesn't want to hear how I think it is stupid that he is basically throwing a fit for nothing. At least, Jax was grown up about this and talked to him about how he felt first and didn't see Lilah behind his back.

Lying back down, my thoughts go back to my room. I really love the room Roxi helped me decorate. I want to move back into my room, so I'll wait a couple of more days before I try to sleep in there again. If I can sleep at Jack's house where he used to hurt me then I should be able to sleep in my room here, because all he did was mess it up.

I can't help the thoughts of court and what my future will look like, but one thing I know is that I'll never have to live with Jack again. The judge wants me to think about what I want for my future and then come up with a few ideas and plans that could get me there and present them to him when we go to court in three months. I need to talk to Roxi and Shane before I do anything else.

I want to work in music somehow, but I'm not sure of the path I want to take. I would love to write music for a living and maybe even become a producer or something, but I don't want to be performer. I wonder what schools have a music program that would help me on the path of getting a good internship at a record label or something like that. Maybe even one day, I could own my own record label.

Tomorrow, I'll start making a good change or do one good thing to change my life and get on the right track. Tonight, I'll try to sleep, and if I'm lucky I won't have a nightmare.

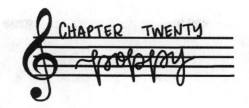

CHAPTER TWENTY

Winter formal is tomorrow, and all the girls have been squealing about it all day. Their loud screeches of excitement have given me a dull headache, so I can only imagine that when prom comes, I'm sure the squealing will be much worse.

Roxi had made Jax and me appointments to get our haircuts. She'll pick me up at the salon around 4:30. After the hair salon, we're going for manis and pedis then out for dinner. I'm excited, but I also have no clue what to do with my hair. I have never been allowed to pick my haircuts before, and Roxi told me I get to. We've been online trying to look at reference photos. She has even texted me "suggestions" as she would refer to them.

This is so new to me that I can't help the nerves that make my knee bounce, as I sit in the hard plastic chair that Coach Denver brought in here for me to sit in, when I'll have to wait at school until Jax is done with practice to go home. Waiting in here is my least favorite part about not being able to do what I want, since my father is still hiding.

I've received three threatening letters from my father since court two weeks ago, and I did get to read them before they were taken for evidence against my father. I was shocked by what I read, but I wasn't hurt. The letters have all said the same thing. "You'll pay for what you did," but I haven't seen my dad though.

The door opens, and Coach Denver walks in. "Poppy, what are you still doing here? Jax left about ten minutes ago."

"What do you mean, he's already gone. He's, my ride!" My heart beats harder and harder in my chest, as panic causes me to sweat.

I look at my phone. Our appointment starts in 10 minutes. Jax hasn't even called or texted me asking where I am.

"Poppy, where are you? Our appointment starts soon," Jax

173

questions loudly, sounding concerned.

"Well, I'm wondering the same, since I'm sitting in the coach's office, waiting for you to take me to our appointment."

"What are you talking about?"

"Jax, we rode together. You left me here?"

"No, we didn't-"

"Yes, you did. We rode to school together, because Roxi is picking me up at the salon." I don't like having to interrupt Jax, but he is frustrating me, because he has been distracted with the Lewis and Lilah situation.

"Shit! I forgot!"

"Ha! You think? I'll call Roxi and see if she will pick me up, since you're already there."

I hang up on him and immediately call Roxi.

She picks up on the second ring. "Hey, Poppy, I'll be heading to the salon in like 5 minutes." She sounds so excited, and I can't help but smile at her enthusiasm.

"Roxi, can you come pick me up at the school. Jax kind of forgot we rode together."

"Of course. Is there an adult there that can wait with you?" I hear a jingling sound and a door closing in the background.

"Coach, do you mind waiting with me until Roxi gets here?"

He gives me a thumbs up while he is putting his laptop in a black backpack.

"Yeah, Coach Denver said he can."

"Perfect, I'm on my way. Can you guys wait in front of the school?"

"Yeah, I'm sure that will be fine."

I hang up and grab my bag. "I need to wait out front for her?"

"That's fine. I'm heading home, once you're with Mrs. Taylor." Coach grabs his backpack, and we leave the office.

As we walk, Coach clears his throat several times. "Ugh, Poppy. Can I talk to you before you leave?"

"I don't see why not." We walk out of the heavy metal doors that lead to the parking lot.

"Would you be interested in being a football manager? It would be very simple; all you would have to do is take notes and stats for the rest of the practices and games. You would be on the sidelines with the team."

"Don't you already have two student managers on the team?"

"Yes, I guess you would say you would be more of a student"

assistant than a manager."

"Can I think about it and let you know tomorrow? I have a lot going on, and I need to talk to my guardians about it first."

"Of course, just let me know whenever you can."

Roxi pulls up, and I thank the coach again before getting in the car. I fill Roxi in on the way to the salon about what he asked me.

"It's up to you, sweetie."

"I want to see what Jax and Lewis think as well. I know that football is their thing, and I don't want to get in the middle of it." Roxi parallel parks on the street outside of the salon.

"They won't care one bit if you are the manager or not. Just make the choice for you," she says, unbuckling her seatbelt. "I love that it takes no more than 15 minutes to get from place to place in this town."

We enter the salon, and I go sit in an empty chair next to Jax while Roxi checks me in.

"I'm sorry Poppy. I wasn't thinking."

Roxi joins and gives Jax the mom looks. Let's just say I am glad that Roxi is not pointing that look in my direction.

"Come on, Mom, don't give me that look. I feel awful enough." Jax looks away from his mom. I can see that his face is red to the ears, and he looks sad with his mouth downturned in a frown and his brows furrowed.

"Since you have a big weekend ahead of you, we will talk on Sunday, and don't you dare think I'll forget." Roxi shakes her head and picks up a magazine before sitting down next to me.

I glance up at Jax, and he rolls his eyes, then winks at me. Oh, he put on a good show for Roxi. I thought he was truly upset.

"What do you think I should do with my hair?" I whisper to Roxi. I'm still very nervous with having so much control of what I can do with my hair.

"That's up to you, sweetie. You need to experiment and find your style." She closes the magazine, places it on her lap, and turns to me. "If you want highlights, full color, fun color or colors, a full cut, or a trim you will look stunning, no matter what you choose. Just make sure it's what you want to do."

"What if I don't like it? Formal is tomorrow."

"Maybe start small, and then we can come back next week or so and get our hair done together."

That is a lot for me to think about in such a short time.

"I think I'll keep it simple and start small. I'm thinking of trim, fresh layers, and some bangs." A girl walks by with bright purple highlights under her hair, and I like the idea. "Maybe after we come back, I can add some bright red like that." I point to the girl with the purple in her hair.

"I think peekaboo highlights would be fun for you. We'll make an appointment before we leave."

A beautiful young woman comes up and greets Jax and Roxi. She has dark shaggy hair with lime green streaks framing her face.

"Who's first?" the lady asks.

"Poppy is going to go first," Roxi answers, giving Jax the side eye.

"Go for it. Yay, girls' night," Jax mutters sarcastically with a small shake of fists like he is celebrating, but he doesn't even look up from his phone.

Could Jax be jealous that Roxi and I are getting to have this time together and do things that he can't with her?

"You can remember we have a girl's night, but you can't forget that you are giving Poppy a ride to the hair salon? I really don't understand what is going on with you lately." She shakes her head, then joins me in the back of the salon.

"Mom, I am sorry. I just wasn't thinking." He walks up to her giving her a big hug.

"Don't apologize to me. I'm not the one you forgot." She huffs and shrugs his arms off him.

Jax walks off with his shoulders hunched. I can tell that he doesn't like when he thinks he disappoints his mom.

"Poppy, my name is Amelia, and I'll be doing your hair. What are you wanting to get done?"

"Well, I was thinking of a trim and some layers. Do you think I could pull off bangs?"

"You have the face for them, but it's really about confidence. What kind of look are you going for? What vibe are you wanting for your overall cut? It could help us determine the type of bangs. You could go for something edgy, girly, or simple."

"Maybe something simple to start out with, and then experiment a little after the formal."

Amelia examines my face, and her red painted lips spread into a wide grin.

"What do you think about some wispy curtain bangs? Let me pull up a reference photo super quick."

She types on her phone, then scrolls for a few minutes with her long sparkly nail tapping against the screen. She hands me her phone, and I see a blonde girl I have seen on TV. I never would have thought of doing this to my hair.

"Those are perfect, and I like the length of them."

"We will start longer and cut them until we get to a length that you like but also won't bother you."

Amelia is chatting, and I don't realize we are done until she is unsnapping the cap and brushing any hair that got on me off.

"Let me get my book, and I will schedule Poppy in with you on your next appointment."

Roxi pays and tips her; then Jax is called over to get his haircut.

We walk next door to the nail salon and look at all the options we have while we wait for our turn. There are a lot of girls from my school here already getting their nails done or waiting for their turn.

"Any of your friends here that you want to hang out with while we wait?"

"I don't have any friends outside of Lewis or Jax," I look away from Roxi, embarrassed.

"If anyone doesn't want to be friends with you it's their loss."

"It honestly doesn't bother me. They didn't want anything to do with me until I moved in with you guys and got close with Lewis and Jax. After Lewis and I started dating, they would either be meaner to me than they were before, or they went back ignoring me. There are still some girls that try to use me to get close to Jax." I shrug, mainly because I don't want to have any fake friends.

Roxi's jaw opens, and her cheeks start to turn a light pink. If smoke was able to come out of her ears, it would have,

"Bitches! That's all girls are." She angrily crosses her arms over her chest.

"I agree," I say, laughing.

Our names get called, and we are sat at tables on the opposite side of each other. This is new to me, and I would have preferred to be next to Roxi. Maybe I'll get lucky, and we get to do our pedicures with each other.

When the lady is done doing my nails, she moves me to a pedicure station. These chairs are mostly empty now. I look over and see that Roxi is standing up.

"Can I sit with my daughter?" I hear Roxi's raised voice, and she point her freshly painted finger to me.

I turn pink when a few of my classmates look at me but I like that she referred to me as her daughter. The lady that will be doing Roxi's nails nods her head, and Roxi comes over, climbing into the chair next to mine.

"What did you get?" I ask when she is situated.

Roxi thrusts her slim hand in my direction. Her nails are almond shaped painted in a wine red with matte finish.

"Those are perfect! Simple but has the right attitude with the deep color and finish."

Before I can reply, Roxi grabs my hand and gasps.

"Poppy, I love the gold. That will look so good with your dress and heels."

I went with a pale natural pink as my base color. I asked for gold details, and the girl surprised me with gold flaked glitter that faded perfectly into the pink.

We talk and laugh the whole time we are getting pampered.

"Roxi, we need to do this more often," I say when Roxi pays.

"Poppy," Roxi swipes under her lashes with her thumb, "I would love nothing more. How do you feel about eating at Mancini's?"

"I love that place!'"

We get in her car, and Roxi makes sure it's clear before pulling out in the street. She makes a U-turn and gets stopped at the first light we come to. I look out of the passenger window and see my father in the car next to me.

An ear-splitting scream slips past my lips. The look he is giving me is almost murderous. I slouch down in my seat, but I know it's pointless, because he has already seen me.

"It will be all right. He won't do anything that will draw attention to himself." Roxi's words should be reassuring, but it was shaky and not convincing. I don't think she is convinced that he won't try something.

The light turns green, and Roxi stomps on the gas. My father speeds up to keep up with us. I look at Roxi, but her eyes are locked on the road in front of us. She appears to be calm, but her knuckles are white from how she is gripping the steering wheel.

I look back out of my window, in time to see my father smirk at me, right before he jerks the steering wheel in our direction. I scream again as his SUV scrapes the side of Roxi's car.

My heart drops, because Roxi wouldn't be going through this terrifying event, if it wasn't because of me. I begin feeling more and more angry at my father for trying to hurt Roxi. She doesn't deserve this, and neither do I.

Roxi slams on the brakes and presses a button on her dash by the air conditioning, basically at the same time. I look over to see her blinker on, but she put on her hazard lights flashing on the side mirrors. The car behind us lays on their horn as they come to a squealing halt, barely having time to stop so they don't rear-end us.

She waits a few minutes, and then she starts driving again. The light in front of us turns red. I hold my breath. I really don't want to have to go through that again. I hear an engine rev, and then my father's car shoots across the intersection almost hitting another car as he runs the red light. I know it's illegal to run a red light, but for once, I'm glad my father isn't the smartest guy around.

"Poppy, are you okay?"

"I'm all right." I breathe a heavy sigh, sagging into the seat.

My heart is pounding, and my palms are clammy. I am anything but okay, and I think Roxi knows that. I think we both are a little more than shaken up right now, but neither of us is going to say it out loud.

"When we get to the restaurant, I'll call Shane and see what he wants us to do. I may have to call the detectives as well."

I shake my head, trying to shake this feeling of dread and panic. I see the restaurant up the street and adjust restlessly in my seat. Hopefully, Roxi and I can mend this night and still have a good time.

Roxi pulls into the closest spot she can get to the door and gets her phone out of her purse.

"Shane," Roxi yells, covering her other ear with her hand. "Jack just hit my car while Poppy and I were on the way to dinner."

My ears begin to ring, and the building outside Roxi's car begins to turn in a swift circle, almost like you're looking in the washing machine while it's on. I can see that Roxi is shaking her head, but she goes blurry from tears forming in my water line.

Roxi replies to whatever they were talking about, and then she turns to me. She gives me a sad smile then holds her arms out to me. We hold each other awkwardly over the center console until both of us are calmed down a little more.

"I have to call the detectives, and then we can go eat."

I pull my phone out of my purse to help distract me as Roxi talks on the phone. I see a few from Jax, apologizing again for leaving me at school. I reply telling him to stop beating himself up and that I forgive him. As I am locking my phone, a new notification pops up on the screen.

UNKNOWN NUMBER: DO NOT GET TOO COMFORTABLE WITH "YOUR NEW FAMILY," YOU WILL BE MINE AGAIN SOON ENOUGH!

I look at Roxi, and I begin sobbing silently in ugly gasps, not being able to catch my breath. She's looking out of her driver's side window but turns to look at me when I hiccup. I hold my phone out for her, and she takes it, looks at the screen, and then curses at the phone in front of her and to the detectives she is talking to.

"There is a nasty threatening text from an unknown number to Poppy on her phone."

She listens to what the detectives say and then looks at me with a sad smile.

"Detective Scotts wants you to screenshot that text message and email them to him. They will send me that information, and they also advise not to reply and to block the number."

I rub my forehead as black spots appear in my vision, each time I blink. I wait while Roxi finishes her conversation. She lets me sit there in silence for a little while.

"Poppy, are you ready to go eat?"

"Ugh, yeah, let's go."

We hastily walk into the little bistro, and we get seated right away and after we get settled into the booth, we both begin to relax a little.

"Thank you for having a girl's night with me. I'm sorry that Jack is ruining everything."

"He is not ruining anything; I will not give him that power. We are going to continue to have a great evening as if that didn't happen. I've been looking forward to this all week, and I know you have, too."

"I really have." We get out of the car, and when Roxi meets me on the sidewalk I loop my arm in hers, and we walk into the restaurant. "You and Shane have really changed my life in such a short amount of time, and I'm really happy that I get to do this with you."

"Thank you, Poppy. That is nice to hear. You have changed our lives too."

We walk into the busy restaurant and wait for a few minutes before we are seated.

"Do you think that I will be able to live my life without this drama and heartache?" I say when we get seated, and our drinks are ordered.

"Yes, I do, but unfortunately, while your father is still on the loose you won't."

"I'm afraid that they'll never be able to catch him."

"Are you ladies ready to order?" Our conversation is interrupted by the kind waiter.

After Roxi and I decide that we want to order two different dishes and share, we tell the waiter what we want plus two empty plates. He leaves, and I fidget with my napkin.

Roxi turns to me, giving me her full attention, and soon we are laughing and having a good time. Our meal arrives, and after what feels like too soon, we are ready to go home. Roxi said she has a few things for us to end our evening with and that I'll love them.

"This night is about pampering, and what is a girl's night without face masks and a chick flick?" she asks, driving her scraped up car home.

Jennifer Froh

CHAPTER TWENTY-ONE

Poppy

Lewis is here to take me to dinner. We'll meet Jax at the restaurant with his date. I walk into the living room, and I see Shane standing there looking proud.

"You're absolutely beautiful." Shane hugs me, and I turn to get a look at my date for the first time.

The sight of Lewis makes me catch my breath, and my mouth goes instantly dry. If he looks this good in nice jeans, a dress shirt, and nice jacket, that makes me even more excited to see him for prom. It's not fair for someone to be that damn good looking, but I'm the lucky girl that gets to have him all to myself.

"Wow, Poppy, you look…" He rubs the back of his neck.

We all laugh at his reaction. I think it's cute that he is at a loss for words. Normally Lewis is charming and knows exactly what to say to girls. Trust me. I've seen him flirt with a lot of girls before we started dating. Also, you don't get the reputation as a player if you're shy.

"All right. Get together! I want to get some pictures." Roxi breaks the silence, and for once, I'm glad she is so good at reading the room.

I feel Lewis pull me gently to his side. I look up and see that he is looking down at me. The way he is looking at me makes my stomach tingle. The way he is staring at me should make me uncomfortable, but I just feel more alive and beautiful under his gaze.

We pose for several pictures before we are told to leave, so we don't have to keep Jax waiting for dinner longer than he is.

When we get to the driveway, I stop short. Lewis's Jeep is decorated in our school colors with streamers, balloons, and chalk written on his windows.

"It's tradition for the cheerleading team to decorate the football player's vehicles, if they have one."

"Jax's truck wasn't decked out."

"No, he flipped shit the first year he got his truck decorated, so instead, they do his locker, which he still hates."

Lewis opens the door and helps me into his Jeep. He is the perfect date.

"You look good, I was too embarrassed to say anything in the house."

Lewis laughs so loud it echoes in the car.

"I'm so excited. This is our first date outside of the house. Also, I get to watch you guys play tonight,"

"It should be a good game, as long as none of my teammates overeat before the game." He laughs.

"Why is that funny?"

"Someone barfed last year on the sidelines, losing the game for us."

"Is Mexican food a great choice before a game?"

"Probably not, but Lana is refusing to eat anywhere else."

"It's not about her, though. You guys need to eat something that isn't going to affect your game play."

"We will. Their grilled veggies and rice are good."

I'm still not convinced that spicy food and football are going to mix, but I have seen Jax eat a giant bag of those spicy chips everyone loves and drink a giant blue slushie, then hold nothing back at practice without puking at practice.

We walk into the restaurant, and I spot Jax easily, but he doesn't look thrilled to be here. In fact, he looks bored, scrolling on his phone. However, as soon as his date spots Lewis and me she begins shooting daggers at me.

"Why is Lana glaring at me?"

"She is still pissed at you for what happened in the hall."

"She approached me. She has a great date tonight; she should be happy."

"They really didn't want to go with each other. She wanted to go with me, and he wanted to take Lilah."

"Why didn't he take Lilah?"

"Let's talk about it later," he huffs, clearly getting a sour taste from this conversation.

Jax looks up at him from his phone, and his shoulders relax as a playful smile appears on his face. He is up to something. When he gives me that wolfish grin usually ends with me embarrassed.

"Hey! It's about time you got here. Couldn't keep your hands off Poppy?" My face heats at his joke, but we hear a clear "ugh!" come from his date.

"It took me a little longer to get ready than I initially thought."

"I was ready when my date picked me up. You should learn to think of the other people that your poor time management skills affect. I mean, seriously, learn to manage your time better," Lana sasses.

"Lana, retract your claws, or you can forget about having a date to the dance. I will not tolerate you being a bitch to Poppy."

"Fine." She crosses her boney arms over her hot pink dress.

Too bad, she has such a nasty personality because she would be pretty if she was nice.

Lana gets her phone out, and when it's time to order, she goes last. My jaw drops with how rude she was to the waiter. After that, the conversation stays between Lewis, Jax and me. She just busies herself with her phone until we leave.

♩♫♩

Lewis walks me to the girl's locker room for me to wait in while the guys get ready.

"Come in, Poppy. Since you don't have to get ready for the game, you can wait in here with me. We will head out in about ten minutes." Coach Leslie shuffles a few papers, then looks at me with a sad smile.

"The girls that are on homecoming court will be wearing their dresses during the game. I told them to get something they can still cheer for, but some of them didn't listen. I know she is talking about Lana. Her hot pink strapless dress barely ends at the curve of her, but I'd be surprised if she somehow manages not to flash the crowd tonight.

"At least, it's not as formal as prom."

There is a knock on the door, and one of the younger cheerleaders pokes her head in. I've seen her while the cheerleaders practice on the track while the football players use the field. She is a good tumbler and a great dancer. She is also the top of the stunts they do, and when she gets tossed, she goes up high. She almost looks like she is flying.

"Coach, there is a man in the hallway, and he reeks. It's really bad, but he is asking for his daughter."

"Did he say who his daughter is?"

"No, ma'am."

I sit up straight in my chair and watch as Coach Leslie raises one hand, and then you hear a few girls shush one another before the room goes completely silent. Coach begins pointing at each girl getting a head count.

"Good, everyone is here. Do not leave this locker room for any reason. If you do, you will run at practice all week and oversee washing all the mats in the gym after tumbling."

Coach puts her phone to her ear and talks to someone in a hushed tone. She looks at me and points to her office. I go sit down in one of the chairs across from her desk.

"Poppy, I'm not going to lie to you like the football coaches asked me to, but I think you have a right to know that it was your father looking for you." She pauses, looking at me, and waits so that information can sink in. "As you may be aware, the staff here is informed of your situation, so we know that it wouldn't be safe for you to be near him. He is gone now, but we don't know if he left the school grounds. The police are monitoring the stadium and looking for him."

I look down; I don't want her to see me cry. This is not only embarrassing, but everyone also knows what I've been through, and they know my father is crazy.

"You'll be safe on the field, and you will now be entering the field with the team."

"I'm not on the team."

"You're going on as a football assistant."

The girls do the pregame chant, lining up at the door before going into the hallway.

"Poppy, come up here with us," Coach Clarks bellows above the roar of the team and the chanting the girls are doing.

I walk past the team and give them all high fives and tell them to "KICK SOME ASS!"

I can see a look of pride on Jax's face, the closer I get to him. He is second in line because he's co-captain. I give him a hug and a high five.

I grab the face guard on Lewis's helmet and give a strong tug. He takes the hint and bends down. I lift his helmet and place a soft kiss on his cheek. Once I put his helmet back in place, I place a kiss on the side of his helmet, and I see the bright red of my lips left behind from my lipstick.

"Good luck! Kick some ass!"

"Did that leave lipstick there?" he asks in my ear.

"Yes, you also have it on your cheek. Stay still, and I'll wipe them off."

"Don't you fucking dare. I'm proud to have it there!" Lewis says in a growl.

The announcers introduce the other team, and I can hear faint cheering, but you can hear the very pronounced booing from our town. We are better than that; a frown takes over my smile.

Lewis straightens up, and I see him begin to bounce on the balls of his feet. He begins shaking his hands and doing this wiggling movement with his arms. I look around and see the team is pushing and slapping each other's helmets or shoulder pads. They are getting rougher with each other as their energy begins to surge stronger through their veins.

"WHO ARE WE?" Lewis yells.

The team replies in an unclear roar.

"I SAID WHO ARE WE?" Lewis whoops louder.

The team replies in a booming volume, so loud I cover my ears.

The announcer comes over the intercom, and we hear them call out for our cheer team. The girls plaster on smiles as they shake their poms and run toward the inflated tunnel exit chanting as loud as they can. Once they are in place on the field, the coaches are called, and then my name along with the title football assistant is called to come out on the field.

We walk to the center of the field and then they announce the players, one by one, leaving the co-captain and captain for last. The roar of excitement when they enter the field is deafening.

I'm surrounded by the team with their booming and chanting circling me, getting closer and closer. Then they close in on me in a huddle. Jax is on my right with his heavy arm over my shoulder, and Lewis is on my left, and he places a gloved hand on the small of my back. The coaches make a speech, and we all head over to the sideline for the game to begin.

I am so busy taking notes and stats, I don't realize that the first half of the game has come to an end, with music blaring from the speakers. They announce the homecoming court, and Lana has a shit-eating grin pointed in my direction as she stands up there with her arm linked with Lewis.

"The Homecoming King is LEWIS JACOBS!"

I am so proud of him. I clap and scream a long, "Woo!"

He walks and gets crowned, and the crowd goes absolutely nuts.

"The Homecoming Queen is…" the stands go silent as they are waiting for this year's royalty to be revealed.

Four seconds, five seconds, go by and you can almost hear crickets play their music.

"POPPY MONROE!"

Silence continues, but then the crowd chants my name. This must be a mistake. No one in this school would vote for me. I have no friends, and no one likes me.

Coach Leslie comes up to me and gives me a nudge. "Go on."

I walk to the center of the field next to Lewis. When the sash and crown are placed on me, the crowd go crazy again. We clear the field and then go into the locker room for a quick pep talk for the second half.

The energy in the second half is more infectious than the first. The crowd is more invested and cheers for our boys. Lewis gives me his crown and tells me to keep it safe for him. I press another kiss to his helmet. This mark is brighter than the first, because I reapplied before halftime was over.

When the game ends, I go and sit in the coach's office of the boy's locker room like I normally do.

I check my phone for the first time tonight and see a text from Roxi.

ROXI: Congrats, dear! You are stunning. :)

POPPY: Thank you,

Lewis opens the door. I stand up and smooth down my dress. I grab my small clutch and Lewis's homecoming crown. While Lewis leans down and kisses my check, then I place his crown on his head.

"Are you ready? The dance has started."

"Can we go get some ice cream first?" I want to have a moment alone with Lewis with less noise and people around.

"Yes, I am always down for more alone time with my girl." He holds his hand out to me, and when I take his, we walk to his Jeep.

I can't help but think about how I'm having too good of a time and that something is going to happen to make this night a nightmare.

We get ice cream, joke, and sing at the tops of our lungs on the short distance back to the dance.

"We don't have to stay very long. We are supposed to meet the team in an hour at the diner to celebrate the big win. It's a tradition we have adopted over the years."

"That sounds fun. I'm shocked I never heard about it."

We are almost to the gym doors when an eerie laugh comes from somewhere in the darkness. I tense up and try to pull away from Lewis so I can run away, but that is not possible, because Lewis's already firm grip gets tighter.

"Poppy, don't run. We have no clue where he is." Lewis pulls me flush to his body and wraps his arms around me like a defensive shield. I shiver, and I try again to escape.

"I know you're terrified, but if you run, you could go in his direction. Just try to wait. I will not let anything happen to you. I'll let you know when I think it's safe to run."

I'm crying now. "Where will I go?"

"Try to get to the gym or to an adult. If you can't, go to my Jeep and drive home as fast as you can. As soon as you can, call the police."

"What about you?" I'm sobbing, and I can feel a panic attack creeping into my chest.

"I'll be fine. I plan to distract him. He wants you, not me."

There is an ear-splitting bang, and the chilling laughter has stopped. Heavy footsteps get closer and closer until my father steps out of the shadows from our left under a light on the sidewalk.

"I told you I'd get you," Jack slurs.

Lewis changes his stance, and he pulls me until I'm behind him, so he is blocking me from my father. Lewis is trying not to show any fear, but I know he is scared because his hands are a little clammy, and they are shaking.

"I thought it would be fitting to make you Homecoming Queen. A spoiled princess needs a crown after all."

"What do you mean?" I yell at Jack from behind Lewis.

"It wasn't hard to pay the announcers to say your name. They were excited to get the money."

I tense. My mind is yelling at me to get the hell out of there, but I know I need to wait for the right time.

"I was really only here to get my daughter, but since I have no other choice, I'm going to have to take both of you with me." My father is oddly calm, but with the way his speech is faltering, he is also drunk.

"You're not going to get anywhere near her!" Lewis yells at my father between his teeth.

"So brave, but what about you?" My father is taunting Lewis now.

"Sorry, sir. I won't let you take her!" Lewis isn't entertaining his questions.

"You won't let me? I don't need your permission." Jack sways and takes a small step forward when he gains control over himself.

There is a stretch of silence. No one is talking, but I feel Lewis trying to take a step back. I move back, and he can move too.

"I wouldn't move if I were you," Jack slurs, stumbling again.

I think the alcohol or drugs are starting to flow through his blood now and take over his brain. He is swaying, slurring more, and his bloodshot eyes get a glassy look over them.

My father raises his left hand holding something up in the air pointing the dark object in his hand right at us. I can't tell what he has from where I am, but Lewis's back straightens, and he moves me behind him, silently telling me that something is wrong.

Jack gets angrier when he sees Lewis move me. "MOVE! I HAVE NO PROBLEM SHOOTING YOU TO GET TO HER!"

I look around, hoping to see someone that can help or at the very least go get help, but there is no one around. I feel my phone vibrate a few times in my purse before it stops, and a couple of seconds later, Lewis's vibrates in one of his pockets.

If I didn't want to delay going to the dance and asking for ice cream, we wouldn't be here right now. I could not stand it if Lewis got hurt because of me.

"Let's move," Jack demands. "We're going for a ride."

"Yes sir," Lewis says, holding his hands up and palms out like he is surrendering to Jack.

We walk in the direction Jack is ordering us to go. Lewis puts me in front of him. Again, he is shielding from my father. My whole body is shaking, and the more we walk, the harder it gets to convince my legs to keep walking when everything in me is telling me to run. We weave around several cars and then come up to the SUV Jack was driving when he ran into Roxi's car. I recognize the SUV from the large scrape on its side.

He begins to laugh and presses the unlock button on the key fob, "GET YOUR ASS IN THE CAR!"

I open the back door, climb up, and slide across the back seat, waiting for Lewis to get in.

Jack is yelling at Lewis, "GET IN THE DAMN CAR!"

"Lewis, get in," I whisper, getting angry at him for not listening and risking Jack hurting him.

"Run!" he mouths to me.

I shake my head. I don't want to leave him with Jack. I don't want him to hurt Lewis, and I know he will, so he can come after me. Lewis slams the door with me still in the car and turns at what looks like slow motion toward my father, who is halfway in the driver's seat.

Jack looks up and stumbles out of his seat, losing his footing. Jack almost falls, but he grabs a hold of the driver's door.

"What the hell are you doing? I told you to get in the fucking car!!" my father spits out giving up on trying to use the door to help him stand up.

Jack takes large steps in Lewis's direction, swinging an arm haphazardly. He misses Lewis and stumbles into his driver's door, causing it to close. He catches himself on the door again, but this time he can get his feet under him. Jack charges forward like he is going to tackle Lewis.

Lewis braces himself for the impact, knowing that Jack is going to ram into him. Lewis's stance is familiar, since I've seen him stand with his feet shoulder width apart and knees slightly bent, and his arms raised ready to push back.

Jack is so intoxicated that he drops the gun, and I take that moment to get out of the car. Jack punches at Lewis, but Lewis is just trying to hold Jack still.

I feel like I need to go find some help. I start to run, but my father yells, "If you run, I'll kill him now!"

I stop and turn around as my father gets loose of Lewis's hold and drops to the ground. I look in horror as my father reaches out with his long, and his slender fingers curl around the handle of the gun.

Jennifer Froh

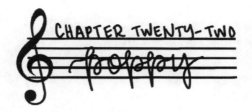

CHAPTER TWENTY-TWO
Poppy

My vision blurs at the horrific sight before me starts to spin. I hunch over by the rear tire, and I vomit all over the parking lot. Lewis backs up to me, and I stand up after my stomach is empty.

Jack stands on his feet, and I look over at Lewis, and I can see that he is momentarily locked in fear.

"Lewis, you need to get out of here," I yell in a whisper at him.

Something in my voice snaps Lewis out of the deer and headlights look, and he pulls me behind him, shielding me from my father again.

Jack is wobbly on his feet, and the arm he has raised begins to sag as if the gun weighs more than his drunken state can handle. Even though he has a gun in his hand, this may be the only time I have that I can stand up to Jack.

"LEAVE US ALONE!" I feel oddly good to yell at Jack.

Maybe I should have done this before now, and we wouldn't be in this predicament that we are in now, but I can't change that now.

Jack stumbles and looks for me with disbelief plastered on his face, but he can't see me, because Lewis is blocking me from his view.

"Lewis, this is between my father and me. You need to leave." I say, pressing my face into Lewis's back.

"Poppy, you can't be serious! He is going to take you somewhere and hurt you, if not, kill you."

"You heard her," Jack grumbles and stumbles a few times. "Get lost."

Lewis never takes his eyes off Jack, but I know he won't leave me. He promised to keep me safe, and that is what he will do.

"I'm not going anywhere without Poppy." Lewis balls his hands at his sides, and again, he changes his stance back to feet, shoulder width apart and his knees slightly bent.

"Well, isn't that a shame?" Jack laughs for a few seconds then breaks into a coughing fit.

I feel my phone vibrate again and maybe I can answer it. since Lewis is blocking me, and Jack can't see.

"Local football star dies trying to be a hero," Jack is trying to imitate a news reporter by using the gun as a microphone.

Jack sways and lowers the gun aiming it at the ground. As I get my phone out of my purse, Lewis shifts and moves like the football players do on the field getting ready for a play. He is now about a foot to my left, leaving me exposed. My father looks up and sees me without a human barrier. His grin of pleasure stretches from ear to ear.

I see a blur of movement close to my left and realize that Lewis is charging toward Jack while he is distracted.

I scream so loud that my father covers his ears. Lewis slams into Jack's thin frame, and they both fall to the ground with Lewis on top. Jack starts to spew out insults while swinging his arms trying to land punches on Lewis. I don't think my dad realizes he still has the gun clutched tightly in his hand, and I hope that he doesn't.

My dad's fists fly in Lewis's direction, and thankfully, Lewis does a good job missing the hits from the hand that is clutching the gun, but he gets punched by the other a few times. Lewis or I need to figure out how to get that gun out of Jack's hand and away from him.

I move to Jack's side and step down on his wrist with the point of my heel that has the gun. Jack's fingers straighten as he screams, and he lets go of his weapon.

I give the gun a little kick, and I watch as the sleek black object slide about a foot away from my father's outstretched arm.

"Poppy, RUN!" Lewis grunts, giving Jack a couple of good hits of his own never losing his hold on my dad.

My father starts to laugh, and he begins flailing his body and is now landing blows on Lewis. I almost feel like the beating he is giving Lewis is fueling his energy so he can escape.

Lewis makes the mistake of looking over his shoulder at me, and Jack sees his opportunity. My father's shoulder raises off the ground, and he punches Lewis square in the nose, causing a crunching sound and blood gushes from his face onto my father.

That pisses Lewis off, and he rams his shoulder into my father's chest, slamming him back into the asphalt. My father cusses and tries to gain control again, but Lewis rams his shoulder into him again. Jack cries out in pain, but Jack continues to wiggle around.

Lewis is trying with all his strength to keep my father pinned, but with Jack's squirming, I know he can't hold him there forever. I forget about the phone in my hand, and I call the last person on my recent call list.

I hear the faint sound of the ringing, before I hear Jax yell over the music at the dance.

"What the hell do you think you are doing, girl?" My father's voice comes out in a gurgling sound, almost like his mouth is full of liquid.

I look at my dad and see red liquid practically pouring out of his mouth.

I hear the bumping sound of music come through the speaker on my phone, "HELP! WE"RE IN THE PARKING LOT!" I shriek before I drop my phone, and it drops with a loud crunch, and the music disappears.

My father's face is now red from the rage cursing in his body. He is now hitting Lewis wherever he can, thrashing around and I can tell Lewis is losing his momentum.

Lewis pulls his fist back and lands a hard blow to my father's eye, but Jack is so enraged that whatever punches he gets is not bothering him. It is just feeding the flames that are blazing inside him. Lewis rears back even more, and then, with as much force as he can, he slams his shoulder into Jack harder than he has tackled anyone tonight.

This causes my father to lose his breath, and once he gains it back, he doesn't fight back. He lays there in defeat, looking like he has finally given up. Lewis relaxes a little but still doesn't stop pinning Jack to the ground.

Suddenly, there is a lot of other commotion in the parking lot. I hear Lewis's and my names being shouted as people are trying to find us. Jack's eyes widen, and I can see the panic and fear taking over him. Jack back hands Lewis in the face, and he can gain control. Jack looks to his left and sees the gun less than a foot away from where his hand was when I kicked it.

Jack reaches over, and his fingers brush the metal of the weapon he brought. He lifts his right shoulder and can get to his side long enough to reach out one more time, and he grabs the gun.

"POPPY!" I hear Jax call out from my left side.

I look over as Jax comes to a screeching halt about three parking spaces away. He looks to his left over at Lewis on top of my dad and Jack aiming the gun at me.

I hear a deafening pop almost like a firework being blasted off, but somehow worse. I feel something hit me so hard that I fall back onto the hard asphalt. My head bounces off the ground a few times, causing black spots in my eyes. The spots grow larger and larger, making the stars above me disappear. Warm water pools around me, warming me from the chill of the night.

"Jax," I cry out in pain as the black clouding my vision completely takes over the night sky above me.

CHAPTER TWENTY-THREE

Lewis

I remember everything from the night of the dance. Two months have passed and the distant shouting of our names echoing in the distance, the deafening pop of the gun going off, and Poppy as she cried out Jax's name before she blacked out. The smells from that night linger making my nose burn and my stomach burn. The way Jack reeked of whiskey and stale cigarettes, the gunpowder that burned in the air, and the faint smell of vomit from when Poppy got sick. Everything hasn't left me, and I think that night will haunt me for a very long time.

I feel like a walking zombie, like I'm dead on my feet. I just try to get through each day without the stabbing pain of grief and the hot rush of anger cursing through my veins, making the hole from that night in my chest feel larger. I've lashed out at practice and the last few games last season. The coaches told me that I need to get my head on straight for practice and the last few games, or they will have no other option than to bench me.

Playing those games should have been a piece of cake, but they were tough, and I couldn't get my head in the game, because I didn't have my co-captain and best friend with me. Those games felt long and hard, but mostly they felt empty without him by my side. Without Jax and his inappropriate trash talking football wasn't, any fun.

All I wanted to do was protect Poppy that night. She was the most important thing to me. I never once thought about myself or the fact that I could've been the one that was shot. Instead, it was my best friend that was the real hero and in a hospital bed. He has been unconscious for two months, because he jumped in front of a bullet for the girl. We both fell for her when we were little boys playing in youth league. We never talked about it, I had always thought that he moved on, and when he asked me if he could ask my sister out, I thought for sure that he was over her, and I got the girl we both protected that night, but it may cost him his life.

I've heard people say that senior year is supposed to be the best year of your life, but I'm not sure if that is true or not. I wanted to spend my time at parties, with girls, hanging out with Jax, and have a killer football season that would end with a football scholarship to a division one college. Instead, I had the chance to be with my dream girl and help her as much as I could through a very difficult situation that I don't regret, but I don't know if Poppy and I are still dating right now, because she has pulled away from me.

Saving Poppy, that is what we did, but at a cost we never thought we would be paying, and I'm trying to decide if it's a price I can pay

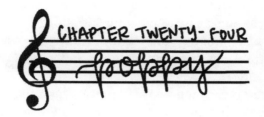

CHAPTER TWENTY-FOUR

I can't believe two and a half months has slowly crawled by since the night my father tried to take me at winter formal. He had somehow gotten his slimy hands on a gun. Lewis tried to protect me that night, and he had done just that by not letting my father take me in his SUV.

I sit in the hospital waiting room each day waiting for Jax to wake up. I will never forgive myself for calling him that night. I panicked and called the last person I talked to on the phone, instead of doing the smart thing by contacting the police.

"Poppy, how was school?" Roxi says, coming in the waiting room hugging me.

"It was all right," I shrug. School is not the same without Jax.

"There is progress today. They took him off the medicines last night that kept him in the coma, so now if he wants to wake up, he can," Shane says, and they both come and sit down next to us.

"You told us this last night. Is there anything else?" I whisper. Lewis comes into the room, too.

He sits next to me, and I grab his hand. We skipped science and talked about everything. We understand that each of us is hurting but pushing each other away is making us feel worse. We came to the agreement that we still want to be with each other, but for this to work, we need to let each other be there for each other whether that is just sitting together in silence.

"Yes, honey, that is all we know about Jax." Roxi sighs and I can see the quiver of her bottom lip. She is trying not to cry. "The detectives, your father's legal team is here. We also had our lawyers come in as well. They would like to talk to you." Roxi's soft voice is laced with concern.

"What's going on?"

The six people walk in in varying shades of black, blue or gray walk in and take a seat all staring at me with sad smiles.

"Poppy, this is about your father Jack. He was found early yesterday morning in a motel room." Detective Whitmen looks concerned.

My back straightens, and goose bumps cover my arms. That means they finally caught him and that he was arrested. I won't have to worry about seeing him again until they do the trial to convict him, and then after that, he'll be out of my life and can't hurt me again.

"He was arrested, right?"

Shane and Roxi exchange a wary glance and my father's lawyer Mrs. Lucas clears her throat.

"Not exactly. We're sorry to inform you that your father was found dead. It appears to be a drug overdose, as well as dangerously high alcohol levels." Mrs. Lucas frowns, and I can tell that she is uncomfortable telling me what has happened.

"So, what is going to happen to me?"

"That is why we are here." My lawyer's assistant Ms. Runes speaks for the first time.

She is the only one that doesn't look sad to be telling me about everything that is going on. I pace the room; I need to move, or I feel like I'm going to explode. I'm aware of the nine pairs of eyes watching me. Each of them has different emotions etched on their faces, but most of them seem more worried while the others look sad.

"As you know, you have no living family that can take you, but the Taylors are insistent about making sure that you stay at home with them. They would like to see if adoption is a possibility, if that is something you'd like." Mr. Steens opens his briefcase and pulls out some paper in a cream-colored folder and hands them to Shane.

"I would like that, but I understand that if you don't want me to. I'm the reason Jax is here and that you could lose him." Tears stream down my face as guilt claws at my heart.

"We love you, and none of this is your fault." Shane and Roxi give me a group hug, and I fully break down. "Our home wouldn't be home without you there," Roxi continues, rubbing my back.

We break apart and sit back down. My father's legal team looks slightly uncomfortable.

"We have your father's will. He has left you everything, and between his life insurance and the life insurance of your late mother, Ellenor Monroe, you'll be well off. They'll be going into a trust that you can't access until you're 21," Ms. Stilson, my father's lawyer assistant, says giving a file to Shane.

Shane puts that folder with the other and turns back to the group.

"I'll be in contact to set up a meeting about what needs to be done for the funeral and our next steps with moving forward for adoption," Shane says, reading a paper with a scowl on his face.

He is trying to dismiss everyone, and I'm more than grateful for that.

"Very well. I should let you know that adoption is time-consuming, and even though Poppy is in your care, and you have temporary guardianship over her, she could age out before you can adopt her." Ms. Stilson pushes up her glasses, shakes Shane's and Roxi's hand, without waiting for either of them to reply.

A few minutes after everyone leaves and we are talking about what just happened, an older nurse comes in asking for a moment with Roxi and Shane.

"You can finally live without having to be constantly afraid. You're safe," Lewis says, turning his attention to me.

"I should feel sad that he is dead, right? But, after all that he put me through, I feel relieved that I don't have to see him ever again. I should be happy that I'm safe, and I don't have to worry about what he is going to do to me next." I begin panting as anger surges through me. "More than anything I'm pissed at him, because he was a coward and took the easy way out. He'll never have to live with what he has done to me. Instead, he gets to be with my mother again!" I know I'm shouting, and I'm sure other people in the hospital can hear me, but I don't care.

I stomp around the waiting room and scare the few people that come in here enough that they leave to find somewhere else to sit. It's been 30 minutes of steam coming out of my ears when I flop in the chair next to Lewis and I start crying silently. My throat hurts and feels like I swallowed sandpaper.

"Poppy." I look up when I hear Shane, "Jax is awake, and he is asking for you. You can go see him in a few minutes. They are doing a checkup," Shane says, while Roxi is a blubbering mess.

I run to them, and we hug each other so tight that if we let go, we will all crumble. I can hear Roxi whisper, "my baby boy is okay," over and over, and my heart breaks for her.

I couldn't imagine what they must have felt and are still feeling through all of this.

When the nurse comes in and clears her throat, we break apart, and she is smiling at all of us.

"You may go see him now, but remember, only two at a time."

We walk down the hall, and the closer we get to his room, the more I shake from the nerves. What if he hates me? I think I could handle his anger or him yelling at me. How will I be able to forgive myself if he hates me? What if he can't forgive me for what I have done to him and his family? I'm selfish to stay with them after all they have been through because of me.

Shane, Roxi, and Lewis all go in, but I stay rooted where I am at in the hallway in front of the door. They all exchange a few words before I hear Jax.

"Where's Poppy?" Jax's usually smooth voice is raspy from the tube he has had down his throat for two months.

My heart pounds, and sweat beads at the nape of my neck. I tentatively step into the room. When I pass the curtain and see him sitting up in the bed, I can't control the blubbering hiccup that escapes me.

"Poppy, come here. I could use a good hug." He has his normal goofy smirk.

I go to him, nearly tripping over my own damn feet. I give Jax the biggest hug I've ever given in my life.

"I'm so sorry. I never meant for you to get hurt."

"What do you mean? I've never been better. This isn't your fault. Never blame yourself for what someone else chose to do."

"When did you get so wise?" I joke, and we both laugh.

We sit for a few minutes and catch Jax up with all that he has missed for the last couple of months. He asks question after question, and after a while, I can tell that he is exhausted. We all make lame excuses to leave so he can sleep. Roxi asked the nurse when Jax gets to move out of ICU, because she wants to spend the night here, so Jax is never alone. She did the same thing for me.

"I'm going to meet you guys at home. There is someone I need to go see first." I hug Shane and Roxi bye, and then I get in my car and drive.

This has been an extremely emotional day, but there is something I need to do before I go home.

I stop by the florist shop on my way to the cemetery for the first time since my mother passed away.

I tell her everything that has happened to me since she passed, and that for the longest time, I was so angry at her for leaving me with that monster. I tell her that I forgive her and that none of this was her fault. I don't know if I'll be able to forgive my father for all he has done, but I can forgive myself for being so mad at her for something that she had nothing to do with, because I know she would never have let my father treat me like that if she was still alive.

"Mom, maybe you were right about who I'm meant to be. I'm finally able to be at peace with myself, and I'm capable of love and being loved by others. I have so much growth left in me, but just like the flower I was named after, I will bend and move on from things trying to break me, like the stems do trying to find the warmth of the sun. I'm stronger than I ever was, because I had people come to my rescue, because they thought I was someone worth saving."

I put the bouquet of poppies I bought on my mom's grave and blew her a tearful kiss. I feel peace for the first time since my mom died.

"I love you, mom, and I'll make you proud, but I need to let go of my grief and anger, so I can start living."

I walk to my car and turn on some good music, so I can go home and start a new chapter in my life as another one closes.

Jennifer Froh

EPILOGUE

"Poppy Fae Monroe!" My name is called, and I walk across the stage to get my diploma.

I can hear my family cheer for me in the crowd. I switch my tassel to the other side and walk off the stage with the biggest smile I have ever had on my face.

I never thought I would get here by myself, let alone with a family and a boyfriend that loves me. I have fought a long and hard road to get here, but I made it. Each day I feel a little stronger and a little less scared.

I still have nightmares, and I sometimes catch myself looking over my shoulder for my father, but then I remember that he can't get me anymore. I didn't go to his funeral, which was a hard decision. Roxi and Shane didn't want me to regret that choice later, but I didn't want to face him even though he was alive, so why would I want to see him when he was dead? Every day that led up to his funeral, I would think about his death, or someone would ask me about it, and every time my father or his funeral was brought up, I felt like I was picking at an open wound. That hole was getting bigger, and bigger with no chance of healing.

Lewis and I could have lost our lives that night, but Jax was the one that almost paid the price. I was the one that called him. He found us that night, just like he was the one to find me at my father's house the day he delivered groceries. Jax saved me twice. He saw me and got me help without a second thought. I didn't know I needed him back then, but I know that I do now, and I never intend to let him go.

I constantly think about the night at the hospital when Jax woke up. I was terrified to see him, but he was so happy to see me, despite the fact he was hurting and weak. It didn't stop Jax from holding me tightly and whispering in my ear. "Everything we've been through all the pain and heart only made us stronger. This year has been hard, but I would do it all again, because nothing in this world feels better than saving Poppy."

Saving Poppy

Jennifer Froh

ACKNOWLEDGMENTS

This book would not be possible without so many people. I would like to say thank you to everyone that has read *Saving Poppy* and has given me feedback, this story would not be possible without you. My mom is a big reason I'm able to follow this crazy dream. She has never let me give up on following a path that will make me happy. To my dad, thank you for listening to me rattle on about my plans, hopes, and dreams about writing. You have always supported me and been proud of what I want to do in life. To my family that lets me do my own thing and be myself, helps make this journey easy and fun. Ariel, your help in reading, giving me suggestions, and your artistic eye has helped me shape *Saving Poppy* into the story it is today. You have been there since the beginning. Kenzie the barista turned friend, your eagerness to read *Saving Poppy* and give me feedback was the start of a friendship I didn't know I needed in my life. I met you when I frequented the coffee shop you worked at to write, and you were the first person outside of my inner circle that read my book. You have helped keep me on track by always being willing to listen to me and go to coffee shops to hang out while I write. Nevada, I love how eager you were when you read my book and your honest feedback helped me be more excited about the ending of *Saving Poppy.* Outside of my writing and book world, you have taught me so much about being a friend and what friendship really is. I have so many great memories with you throughout our friendship that formed when we were in second grade, but in the last few years of going to coffee shops to talk about our shared passion for writing is toward the top of my list. To Kim and Danny, thank you for always being there for me and being family to me. Your love and support mean the world to me. Rachel, thank you for the never-ending openness you have for listening to me rattle on about my projects. The safety I feel talking to you and giving you my books to read I get from you not judging me or the story but coming back with constructive criticism is a rare thing to find. To my teacher Andrea and my fellow classmates for teaching me so many new things. To the sweet Jeannette, you helped me feel more comfortable talking about my writing. To the readers that gave my book *Saving Poppy* a chance I hope that you can love her and her story as much as I do.

ABOUT THE AUTHOR

 Jennifer Froh's journey to becoming an author started with her love of reading. In 2016, she started going to book conventions and signings, meeting her favorite authors. She loved meeting like-minded readers and hearing the passion that those authors had for the books. This sparked a new dream that she wanted for herself, and she began her writing journey in the summer of 2021 at a coffee shop in Yukon, Oklahoma. From Mustang, Oklahoma, Froh finds peace and joy writing in local coffee shops as their atmospheres offer diversity, mannerisms, and conversation. Jennifer can be found playing board games with her family and friends. You can catch her listening to music or curled up with her dog Scout watching old movies and tv shows like *Meet Me in St. Louis, I Love Lucy*, or *Laverne and Shirley.*

Made in the USA
Columbia, SC
02 August 2024

39349147R00122